The Legend of Bijou Bay

Have you ever met someone for just a day or two and they changed your life's destiny?

A simple accident on her horse ranch stirs up the memory of the forgotten past for Victoria Rafael-Taylor; the Legend of Bijou Bay. In the darkness of the night, she finally shares the story of the past with her daughter. The search for answers leads to dark secrets, healing hearts, and more changed destinies.

I fought through the heaviness in my head to force my eyelids to rise. I don't know why. No one would expect me to wake for hours. But I fought off the haze and slowly opened my eyes. The house was dark, windows showing that it was night, and the only light in the house came from a soft glow in the kitchen.

I was lying on my comfortable sofa, encased leg propped up on pillows, and a soft green blanket carefully tucked in around me. I was comfortable, and my body had absolutely no inclination to move as I looked around the room.

Sawyer was sitting at the kitchen table reading a letter. Her brows were furrowed into a deep frown as she concentrated. On the floor next to her chair was my "important documents' box. I barely remembered her asking for my insurance policies. In the box were folders from many years back pertaining to the property and the insurance; both medical and business.

But her whole attention was on the letter. Even from a distance I could see the yellowing of the paper and the crispness of the edges; it was old, 50 years old to be exact. The last time I had read the letter, I had tucked it inside a leather wallet that rested on the table in front of her. The wallet had been securely stuffed under a few of the folders so it would not have been easy for her to find. But my daughter was a thorough person when it came to details. That is what made her a great insurance agent.

She set the letter down and picked up the well-worn aged envelope it had nestled in for the last fifty years. After a quick inspection of the addresses, she picked up the leather wallet and looked inside. I knew there was nothing left in there. After placing the wallet down, she lifted the letter again, her brows furrowing deeper causing wrinkles across her forehead. A hand came up and she rested her chin on it as she read.

My eyes closed and transported me back fifty years.

This book is fiction. The characters and dialogues are from the author's imagination and are not to be construed as fact.

Bijou Bay Ranch is based on the Northern Idaho ranch known as Blackrock Ranch. Thanks to everyone for allowing me to visit the ranch and ask a lot of questions.

Copyright © 2022 Gini Roberge

ISBN- 9781733952828

ACKNOWLEDGMENTS

A huge thanks to the following ladies for their support.

Tracy Hammond
Crystal Longfellow
Lori Smith
Gail Richardson
Dondi Hildebrand
Roni Coleman
Hanah Greene
The crew of Black Rock Ranch

More books by the author:

The Tagger Herd Series

Hoofbeats In The Wind

Coffee With Cowboys

The Legend of Bijou Bay

by

Gini Roberge

CHAPTER ONE

Falling back onto the cold, black asphalt, I swore to myself that no one would ever find out how I ended up lying in the middle of the long driveway at my ranch. Staring up at the fading stars, the early morning chill stung my lungs and bit my skin. It was a fierce contrast to the hot fire that coursed through my veins from the broken leg. I knew it was broken because I heard it and felt it.

For 50 years, I managed to ride horses without breaking a bone. There were dislocated shoulders, torn ACLs, and even a concussion, but not one broken bone. Sixty-one years old now, and I finally broke one, if not two, since the pain radiated from below the knee.

I lay on the path that led from my house to the main working buildings of the ranch and took deep breaths before I slid my hand into my pocket in search of my phone. There was no cold metal in the jacket and I sighed in dread. I was going to have to move to find it. Slowly, I rose onto my elbows. An overwhelming sense of relief swarmed through me when I turned slightly to see the phone just inches from my hip. I reached for it, not with the knowledge that I could call for help, but with the knowledge I *had* to call someone for help. As a very independent woman, asking for help did not come easily.

There was also no doubt my daughter would interrupt her life to be by my side. The fact that I had no intention of telling her how I broke my leg was going to irritate her. But there was no way I was going to tell her or anyone else.

I lay back onto the asphalt and adjusted my long braid, so it lay to my side instead of under me. I had almost left the long white and silver hair loose down my back but at the last moment captured it in the braid instead. That would be helpful in the next couple of days since I had no doubt that I was going to have to have surgery.

The phone screen let me know it was 6:02 in the morning. On the days we had appointments scheduled, I was always at the clinic by 6:15. So, I could lay and wait for them to come looking or I could swallow my pride and make the call. At this point, the pride was going to have to take a backseat to the fact it would just be stupid of me to lie and suffer in pain when I knew I was going to need help. With an irritated sigh, I pushed the speed dial for the ranch foreman, Bubb.

"Where you at?" He grumbled in an answer.

I loved Bubb, had from the moment we met, and I hired him to take care of the arenas, work with the younger horses, and the general ranch maintenance. He had a reputation of being a fair businessman, was known for a dry sense of humor, and was gentle with the horses. But, in the last few months, he had changed into a cantankerous old man. He was at least 71, so I had no issue calling him cantankerous to his face those times he upset a co-worker or me. I called him worse if his 'old man' attitude was shown to a client. In the last week, I had to 'check him' when he was dealing with a few mare owners. My breeding program business depended on my reputation as a person, rider, competitor, and the quality of my property and employees.   Being rude to a client was pushing the line on what I would tolerate.

"Good morning, Bubb," I exhaled. "Would you please bring the truck to me?"

"Ain't cha' at the house?"

"No, I'm lying on the ground about fifty yards up the driveway from the house with a broken leg."

"Well, what the hell did you do?" I could hear the roar of the truck engine over the phone.

"I fell."

"Off a horse?"

"No," I turned my head at the sound of the truck approaching over the hilltop. "I'm about twenty yards from the top of the hill."

"So, don't run you over," he huffed.

"I would appreciate it if you didn't."

I lowered the phone as he crested the hill and turned to look back at the brightening sky.

It was the end of June; breeding season was slowing down and show season was in full swing. Only two days prior, I had returned from a week-long show in Montana, but now I was going to miss the next eight weeks, if not longer. That was three horses I had been riding and fared well. The other horses had been ridden by my employees or hired riders. Now, after so much anticipation of the shows in Arizona and California, I was going to have to let someone else do it. Damn.

Bubb appeared above me.

He was in his 'uniform' of sorts; Wranglers, white button-up western shirt, boots, and straw cowboy hat. His hair was completely white under the hat and the mustache looked like someone had rolled a fluff of cotton into a cigar and placed it across his upper lip. It was unique, just like him. His icy blue eyes looked down at me with the crinkles of his face deepening.

"Alright, boss lady," He huffed with a smirk. "How do you want to do this?"

"Is the leg straight or did it angle?"

He knelt at the leg and barely touched the jean material, but I flinched at the anticipated pain and groaned at the pain that the flinching caused.

"It's straight from what I can tell."

I leaned up onto my elbows and looked up at him. "Get behind me and help me stand, then get me in the back seat. There is no reason for an ambulance if it's not a compound fracture."

"You have insurance."

"And how long will I have to lay here and wait for them to get here?" I growled. "You can have me at the hospital before they even arrive."

He shrugged his shoulder and stepped behind me, "You're probably right, but this is going to hurt, whereas they can give you painkillers before moving you. But, I know you well enough you've already made up your mind."

He tucked his hands under my arms as I braced the uninjured leg against the pavement, and he began to rise. Pain shot up my leg and made me fall against him as I stood.

"Give me a minute," I gasped as my mind swirled.

"If I was thirty years younger, I'd just pick you up and put your ass in the back of the truck and haul you there." His voice was right next to my ear; impatient and growling.

"Well," I exhaled as my mind cleared. "Your bedside manner needs work, so just get me to the damn truck."

He moved to my side and lifted my arm around his neck. With short steps and his leaning to lift me with each one, we made it to the truck.

"Let me get Lenny here so he can help get you up into the truck."

I said nothing and just leaned onto the seat through the open door. To brace the leg, the toe of my boot rested on the pavement. Within minutes, Lenny was in the six-wheeler ATV flying over the hilltop. He was a lean, but strong twenty-year-old, whom I had trained for three years before he came to work for me as the stock manager. He was responsible for saddling and warming up the horses I would be training and exercising the horses that I could not get to. He was an excellent rider with a big future ahead of him.

He parked the ATV in the grass and jogged to us, "An ambulance…"

"She said no," Bubb growled. "You go around and get in the back and pull her up onto the seat as I keep her leg braced."

I clenched my teeth to squelch the verbal assault, but I still groaned and cried out until I was finally lying across the seat.

When I looked down through the open door to Bubb, Anna, the office manager, was standing behind him. In her mid-thirties, she was married with five and seven-year-old boys. Her long dark hair was pulled into a chignon at the back of her neck, and dark brown eyes were narrowed in worry.

"I'm fine…" I assured her, but the words came out in a whisper.

"Pauline is in the middle of an insemination with Jeff helping," she grimaced.

"No need to bother them," I leaned back against the door. "Everybody just carry-on as normal while Bubb takes me to the doctor. I'll be home before you know it."

She nodded and began to close the door.

"Anna?" I moaned and the door widened. "Tell Jeff to prepare himself. He'll need to ride for me the next couple of months."

Her eyes widened, "I'll let him know…he'll be…"

"Mortified and elated," I finished for her.

With a slight smile, she closed the door. I had known Jeff and his sister, Ari, since they were children when both had started their horse careers by cleaning my stalls to earn riding lessons. Now, in his mid-twenties, single, and one of the best equestrians I knew, he could easily handle my schedule for the next couple months. His only issue was having the full confidence he needed in himself to excel like he should. This would give him an opportunity to prove himself…to himself.

On the ride to the hospital, I kept my mind busy by trying to remember which horse Pauline would be inseminating. I remained in control over the raising and training of my horses and gave her the breeding program to manage. We met when she was in high school, and I helped coach her with riding in western classes. She was a graduate of Cornell University where she earned 3 degrees; BSC, DVM, and Ph.D. She is a full clinician scientist and an equine theriogenologist. After her final graduation, we kept in contact for the next ten years as she worked at the leading equine fertility clinics across the country. Her success in equine fertility had been the reason I hired her the day after I purchased my ranch. Now in her late forties, she had raised two kids and divorced their father. Her full focus was horses and the challenge of the breeding program. We weren't just employer to employee; we were good friends.

Being side-lined and Jeff on the road, the running of the ranch would be down to Bubb, Anna, Pauline, and Lenny. With nearly all the ranch mares having foaled and most rebred, I had full confidence in them, especially since I knew my daughter would be at the ranch before I returned.

I sighed in relief when the truck came to a halt at the emergency doors of the hospital. Bubb opened the door, and I looked up at him in all seriousness, "There is no way I am letting them pull that boot off, so cut it down the seam so I can have it repaired."

"Right now?" He huffed as two nurses walked out the door toward us.

"Yes, before they get here."

He shook his head, withdrew his knife from his pocket, and flipped it open. Both nurses gasped and ran toward us.

CHAPTER TWO

The nurse waved the thermometer over my forehead and smiled, "What is your name?"

"Victoria Rafael-Taylor," I sighed through the haze and the comfort of the hospital bed. "And the woman behind you is my daughter, Sawyer Taylor."

"Sawyer Landers, Mom," Sawyer smiled. Her green eyes sparkled. "I still have my married name."

"Ah, because of my grandson," I nodded and looked at the nurse. "He is named after me…my maiden name, Rafael…he is Rafe." I don't know why I told her, because she didn't need to know and probably didn't care.

The nurse smiled politely as she slid the blood pressure wrap up my arm, "That is a handsome name; very romantic novel worthy."

I chuckled, "Exactly what I told her when she named him."

"How old is he?" The nurse asked.

"Ten…eleven now," I answered and glanced at Sawyer. She smiled and nodded. "Did you bring him?"

"Of course," she answered. "He's in the waiting room down the hall."

My mind began to drift again as I looked at my daughter. She was the light of my life but had been infuriated with me when I sold her childhood home after her father's death four years ago. After 38 years of marriage, I did not want to live in the home without him. I bought my own ranch; as Sawyer put it, in 'the middle of nowhere Idaho'. The picturesque ranch was located in Harrison, Idaho, just outside of Coeur d' Alene. Compared to where she had grown up in Arizona, and the ranch surrounded by thousands of acres of trees and Coeur d' Alene Lake, it would seem like the middle of nowhere to her. Since she still lived in Arizona, she had only been to the ranch once, right after I purchased it, but my grandson had never been there.

We video chatted nearly every day, and she always attended events when I traveled south so we were still close. Her brown hair hung just past her shoulders and was always tucked behind her ears. With a strong tom-boy side to her, she lived in jeans and boots; even at her job as an insurance agent specializing in the equine industry. It was a job she had done alongside her father. She took over the business after he died.

"Mom?"

The haze cleared. The nurse was gone, and Sawyer was at my side. "They are going to keep you here for the night, and if there are no issues, we can take you home tomorrow morning. Bubb and Lenny dropped off your SUV for me."

"What day is it?" I fought to keep from drifting to sleep again.

"It's Wednesday," she answered. "I talked to Pauline, and she said your calendar is clear until Monday so don't worry about anything." She gently swept the hair from my forehead. "You sleep and don't worry. You'll be home in less time than when you go to a competition down south."

I fell into a deep dreamless sleep.

Rafe's first appearance was at my hospital room door the next morning. He was carrying a McDonald's brown bag in one hand, and a bottle of milk in the other. Other than the straight dark brown hair that was cut just above his ears and bangs just covering his eyebrows, he looked like his mother. The dark hair was from his absent father.

Rafe stood in the doorway and watched as his mother moved the two side chairs next to each other. His eyes flickered to me then to her.

"Sit in one and use the other as a table," she told him.

With a glance at me, he followed her instructions. He took out the few items from the bag and set them on the chair then, trying to be quiet, he folded the bag and set it in the garbage can next to the bed. When he had everything set, he glanced back at me with a slight smile.

"Are you going to say hello?" I teased with a smile.

He looked at his mom then back to me, "Mom said I had to be quiet in the hospital and not to disturb you," he whispered.

"Well," I smiled. "When my eyes are open, you are not disturbing me. How was your flight yesterday?"

His eyes brightened, "That was fun. I've only got to fly a couple times."

As he chatted about the flight and the people in the airport, I realized how different it was to talk with someone in person compared to over a video chat. It was so much warmer and personable. The last few years, when I was in Arizona competing, he was with his father, so I didn't get to see him very often.

"Grandma?"

My mind jolted back to him, "What?"

"Mom says we get to go to your ranch now," He smiled in clear delight.

The broken leg was worth getting him…and Sawyer…to my home.

"You will have your own room," I smiled. "And you'll like all the people…"

"And the horses," He added quickly and sat up straight in the chair.

"Well, I have plenty of them to introduce you to."

"Can I ride too?" His eyes were wide and hopeful. "I haven't ridden much since we sold Brownie."

I gasped and my eyes darted to Sawyer, "You sold Brownie?"

Her face reddened, lips rolled into line, and eyebrows came together in a deep frown, "It's a long story…" She glanced at Rafe. "…but not for now."

Irritation bubbled in my stomach, but just as I opened my mouth to speak, the nurse walked in the door with a bright smile and pushing a wheelchair.

"You are officially released," She smiled. "But you have an appointment next Tuesday to check the surgery site and if everything looks good, they will replace the splinted wrap with a hard cast."

*****

It took an hour to drive from the hospital to my home. The silence between Sawyer and me was overshadowed by Rafe talking about the pine trees, lake, and his excitement over seeing the horses.

There were two roads into the ranch. The front entrance went through a stunning wrought iron and wood double-gate. In the center of each gate was the ranch logo: the jagged outline of a pine tree with the BBR inside. The road followed along the horse pastures to the buildings. But I directed her to the back entrance which climbed high up onto a mountain and wound through the trees. It peaked over a rise with a spectacular view of the property widening before us. Pine tree covered mountains stretched out as far as you could see and encircled the ranch. The dark blue water of the bay was visible in the distance on two sides. In the middle of the mass of trees, white vinyl fencing separated dozens of lush green pastures that were speckled with grazing horses. The buildings were to the left and just out of sight from this view.

"OH, MAN, look at that!" Rafe gasped.

I was stretched out in the back seat, so he was in the front gawking at the view.

Sawyer stopped the car so they could take it all in.

"It's just so beautiful," Sawyer exhaled. "Mom…so stunning."

"I love it," I couldn't see the view, but it was in my mind and heart. "The land itself hasn't changed since I purchased the property, but we did update and change some of the buildings; which included rebuilding the main house."

"With the water and trees…pastures…it must just be a winter wonderland when covered with snow," Sawyer sighed.

"It is," I nodded as if she could see me.

"Look at all those horses!" Rafe cried out. "Must be hundreds!"

"There are 63 in the open pastures and 23 in the stalls right now; all of various ages. The four stallions that are here have their own stable that is attached to the Trophy House." I smiled in anticipation of their reaction. "And there are 22 foals from four months to a week old."

"Oh!" They both gasped.

"We also have a dozen client's horses, a few boarded, and the brood mares the clinic is working with. We also have a dozen or so recipient mares."

"What are those?" Rafe asked.

Sawyer answered, "They take the egg from a show or working horse and put it in the recipient mare so she can carry the baby instead."

My back began to ache letting me know the pain killer was wearing off. I stretched and must have caught Sawyer's attention and she began driving forward.

"Oh, Grandma," Rafe exhaled as we passed by the white fencing and horses grazing in the lush green pastures. "It's so awesome."

My heart warmed at the wonder in his voice. After four years of living here, I still felt that way.

"Do you want to stop at the clinic?" Sawyer asked as she drove through the last set of opened double gates which led to the buildings.

"No, I don't want to get out until I'm home," I answered and closed my eyes to try and block out the back, neck, and leg ache.

"Look! An arena…what is that round building?" Rafe asked.

"A covered horse walker," Sawyer answered.

"What is that one?" Rafe continued.

"The clinic, and then the barn, and the stables…" Sawyer answered.

"And on this side?" Rafe asked.

"That is the…" Sawyer hesitated.

"The Trophy House with event space downstairs, a small apartment upstairs, and the stallion stalls are at the back," I answered.

"And that big building?" Rafe asked.

"Indoor arena with stalls inside…and that is a covered round pen," Sawyer said.

"What's behind those wood walls?" Rafe asked.

"There is a square pen then a large round pen we use for competition and practice," I answered. "There are cows in the next field and in the trees."

The SUV came to a stop.

"Can you get to your house from here?" Sawyer asked.

"Oh, no," I half chuckled behind closed eyes. "Turn on the road in front of the Trophy House and it will take you back."

She turned the SUV, then turned in front of the Trophy House, then turned again onto the drive that led to the house. With each turn, the ache in my leg grew.

"The garage is on the right as you approach the house," I said. "The door opener is above your head. Pull in there and I will have a straight clear trip from the garage into the living room. I'll go straight to the couch. It will be easier to brace the leg there."

"Oh, Grandma…" Rafe exhaled again. "Look at that horse, and that one, and that one looks like honey, and that one…look at the water, Grandma!"

Just behind the house, a small cliff led to a road and across from it was the wide bay of blue water.

When Sawyer stopped the SUV, I opened my eyes to see we were in the garage. As much as I wanted to show the pair the property, I wanted to be on that couch with pain killers in me.

As Sawyer helped me from the SUV and walked alongside me as I crutched my way into the house, Rafe inspected the house. It was all on one level and wasn't that big, so it didn't take him long.

"Where is my bedroom?" He asked. Excitement radiated from his voice.

"One of those down there," I said and pointed to the right as we made our way through the kitchen. "Your mother's will be the other one."

"Look at that," Rafe exhaled in disbelief.

He was standing at the large wall of windows that faced the water. With the rolling pine tree covered mountains and water of the bay reflecting the blue sky, it was a spectacular view.

"The sunsets must be spectacular," Sawyer sighed.

"I have a covered deck, and down the hill a bit is a hot tub," I lowered onto the sofa and my whole body relaxed causing even more pain.

"Well, you'll be finding me in that hot tub for sure," She helped me lean back and stuffed pillows under my leg for a brace.

I glanced at her as she lowered a blanket over the top of me, "How long can you stay?"

"If you are all right with it, I'd like to stay here while you recover and…maybe…for the summer…until Rafe goes back to school. I can set up an office in my room and work from here."

My heart soared, "I can't think of anything I want more."

"Maybe a painkiller?" She teased, but I could see the flush of embarrassment and nervousness.

"Yes, maybe that," We had time to discuss her request later, so I relaxed back into the pillows and into the warmth of the blanket. Within minutes of taking the pain killer, I was sound asleep.

*****

"Mom, you need to eat something," Sawyer's voice cut through the haze.

My eyes opened long enough to see the spoonful of yogurt she held in front of me. I knew she was right, so I let her feed me. She had moved a small table next to the couch. It was close enough I could reach an array of items including bottles of water, fruit, bottles of pain killers, a box of tissues and my small laptop. She was such a good caretaker. I smiled and my mind drifted again.

*****

"Mom, you need to drink…you don't want to dehydrate."

I sighed and drank as much water as I could before drifting away again. An hour later, she was helping me crutch to the restroom and back.

"Where is Rafe?" I whispered when I leaned back into the pillows.

"He's on the back patio drawing."

Another painkiller, a container of yogurt, and a glass of water later, I was drifting back to sleep and thinking I didn't have any toys for Rafe. In my dreams, I went shopping online.

****

"What time is it?" I could hear someone moving but kept my eyes closed.

"5:40," Sawyer answered.

"Thursday?"

"Friday night," She chuckled.

My eyes opened in surprise. She was walking a tray full of food to me, then nestling it in front of me, "You need a healthy meal. This sleep is great to help heal, but you need food to nourish and gain strength."

"Seems like I've heard that before," I teased and inhaled the smell of the scrambled eggs, hash browns, and toast.

"Yes, I can't tell you how many times my mother told me that as I grew up." She chuckled and stood to smile down at me. "…nor how many times I have said it to my own son."

"Where is he?"

"Well, he was asking me about the horses that are right behind the house, especially that gold stallion. Now he is outside on the back patio with my laptop watching your videos of riding it."

"It has a name," I took a bite of food and instantly felt better.

"Yes, but Rafe likes to call him 'the golden one' as if he was a king."

I raised a brow and huffed in amusement.

Her grin widened as she looked at the large portrait above the fireplace. "I told him that he was more of a prince since his father was the king. He thought it was pretty cool that the golden horse in the portrait was the stallion's sire."

"…and the sire of all the horses that have pictures in this house." I nodded. "Has he been to the Trophy House yet?"

"Oh, no," she chuckled. "He won't leave the house until you are better and can, personally, give him a tour of the place."

"That's sweet of him," I smiled.

"He is a very sweet and sensitive kid," she sighed. "Which, I should explain our situation."

I nodded.

"In the divorce…we had to sell everything and split 50/50 because Allen wouldn't come to an agreement."

"Even Rafe's horse? That I gave him?"

"Yes, sort of," She lowered to the edge of the sofa. "Brownie was in my name and even though Allen tried to get the horse off the list too, the judge had already ruled that everything, that wasn't a personal item, was to be sold."

"Why didn't you call me? I would have…"

"I sold him to a friend with the full knowledge that I was going to buy him back," Sawyer added quickly. "They are in complete agreement and understand the situation."

"How long before you can buy him back?"

Her shoulders lowered as a heavy sigh escaped, "Everything was split 50/50 including Allen's debt. So, it may take a year or two." Her eyes were wide and apologetic. "I have been trying so hard to keep Rafe unaffected by the divorce but Brownie just…"

"I can buy him."

"Mom," Tears welled in her eyes. "I didn't, and don't, want to come crawling to you for money."

Lowering the fork to the plate, I leaned back into the pillows. For the first time, she was lowering her guard and showing the hurt and desperation the last few years had caused.

"You are my daughter…he is my grandson…I want him to have that horse."

Her tears fell. "I'm a bit messed up right now," she admitted. "After finding out what Allen had been doing and how far he was into it…I just couldn't."

"Sawyer," I took her hand and squeezed. "You have never told me what happened, but that does not mean that I do not know. The horse industry can be very gossipy, but also concerned. I know Allen was addicted to pain killers and stealing from his company to pay for the pills. I know he was arrested and that your home was searched several times by the police."

The tears fell from anguished eyes, "It was broken into last week, and I used what savings I had to move our stuff to a storage unit. We've been staying at a friend's house to keep Rafe safe."

Anger bubbled through me; at her and her worthless ex-husband.

"And you didn't call me because?" I growled.

She shook her head and wiped away tears, "Embarrassment, the desire to recover on my own…"

"You have nothing to be embarrassed about," I squeezed her hand. "You did not cause the accident that hurt his back and caused the pain. You did not get him addicted to pain killers nor steal anything for him. You did nothing more than love him; more than he ever deserved."

The door opening had her frantically wiping away tears. She stood with a bright 'I'm all right' smile on her face as Rafe joined us.

He grinned when he saw me, "Grandma, I love this place. I love it, so much!"

"I am glad and am looking forward to showing you the rest of it and introducing you to the team. Your mother says you two can stay all summer."

His eyes widened and jaw dropped over-dramatically as he looked at her, "SERIOUS MOTHER?"

"If you want," She giggled.

"I do!" He shouted.

"Rafe?" I said and he turned to me with the widest, happiest grin. "Could you go get me one of the bottles of vitamin water in the kitchen?"

"Yep," He chirped and strutted to the kitchen.

I looked up at my daughter, "Call tomorrow and buy Brownie back. I'll pay for transport to get him up here for Rafe to ride for the next couple of months."

"Oh, Mom," The tears began to rise again.

As darkness took over the night, Rafe wandered to bed while Sawyer helped me settle in on the couch for the night.

"Where are your insurance papers?" She asked. "I can handle all that and anything else that needs to be done."

I closed my eyes and sighed, the drowsiness began to take over, "In the grey box in my office. It's labeled 'important documents'. I have not unpacked it since I moved here."

"Sleep well, Mom," She lowered to kiss me on the forehead. "I love you."

"And I love you." I whispered.

I fought through the heaviness in my head to force my eyelids to rise. I don't know why. No one would expect me to wake for hours. But I fought off the haze and slowly opened my eyes. The house was dark, windows showing that it was night, and the only light in the house came from a soft glow in the kitchen.

I was lying on my comfortable sofa, encased leg propped up on pillows and a soft green blanket carefully tucked in around me. I was comfortable, and my body had absolutely no inclination to move as I looked around the room.

Sawyer was sitting at the kitchen table reading a letter. Her brows were furrowed into a deep frown as she concentrated. On the floor next to her chair was my "important documents' box. I barely remembered her asking for my insurance policies. In the box were folders from many years back pertaining to the property and the insurance; both medical and business.

But her whole attention was on the letter. Even from a distance I could see the yellowing of the paper and the crispness of the edges; it was old, 50 years old to be exact. The last time I had read the letter, I had tucked it inside a leather wallet that rested on the table in front of her. The wallet had been securely stuffed under a few of the folders so it would not have been easy for her to find. But my daughter was a thorough person when it came to details. That is what made her a great insurance agent.

She set the letter down and picked up the well-worn aged envelope it had nestled in for the last fifty years. After a quick inspection of the addresses, she picked up the leather wallet and looked inside. I knew there was nothing left in there. After placing the wallet down, she lifted the letter again, her brows furrowing deeper causing wrinkles across her forehead. A hand came up and she rested her chin on it as she read.

My eyes closed and transported me back fifty years.

CHAPTER THREE

Fifty Years Before

A chill ran down my body and I reached for the blanket, but it wasn't there. Too tired to open my eyes and look for it, I rolled over and curled into a ball. It was a little warmer, but my sheets were rough, digging into my skin. As I wiggled to get comfortable, my mind went back to sleep.

Something was pulling at me, twisting me into the darkness. I moaned to complain, but warmth suddenly encased me. I sighed as the pressure pulled me up into an even warmer hard source. I wigged into it, and then slowly opened my eyes to see blue sky, tops of pine trees, and a man holding me. A blue cap covered dark hair and there was a silver badge on the front showing he was a policeman.

As his hand tucked a blue blanket around me, his head was turned looking back behind him. He began to rock back and forth causing me to lean further into him. Sweat beaded across his wide tan forehead. His eyes were pleading, jaw clenched; he took a deep breath then exhaled. I could feel his chest lower and a grumble of dread…disappointment…agony escaped him.

His head turned and he looked down into my eyes.

"Hello, Honey," He whispered with a forced smile on his lips and his eyes glistened with tears. "I'm glad we found you. You are going to be just fine. You're safe now."

I didn't say anything because the warmth of the blanket and the comfort in his eyes began to ease my mind. My body slumped and his arms tightened. Darkness descended.

When I woke, I was lying on comfortable sheets but looking up into the blue sky.

"She's awake," A man's voice whispered.

I turned to see the policeman that had cradled me, he leaned closer, "I'm Officer Lucas, what is your name?"

No words formed and my brain seemed fuzzy. I was too tired to talk.

"Honey, you're going to be okay," His smile made me feel safe and protected. "The medics looked you over and you're okay."

I just stared at him.

He took a step away and a woman appeared with a warm comforting smile and relieved blue eyes that made me feel comfortable. Dark blonde hair was pulled back into a ponytail and a red knit cap covered her head. One hand gripped the front of her grey jacket to hold it closer to her chest and one hand touched my forehead.

"Hi, Honey," She whispered and picked a leaf from my long black hair. "Officer Lucas is going to drive us to my office. I'll ride in the back of his car with you. OK?" Her gentle fingers tucked my hair behind my ears.

Still no words formed as I just looked at her, then over to the police officer.

"It's okay, Honey," He nodded. "This is Betty Sanders, and she is going to make sure you're taken care of."

My eyes darted between the two of them, but I just lay still; warm and waiting.

"You're on the ambulance gurney now and we're going to help you into Officer Lucas' car," Betty said.

The two of them helped me sit up and I looked around. His black and white patrol car was on a dirt road and surrounded by pine trees. The sun was just rising over the tops. Two more police cars were on the road behind his and a dozen people were standing at the back of one of the cars. They were looking into the trees.

I leaned to see what they were looking at.

"Don't you worry about them," Betty tightened the blue blanket around me and gently pushed me toward the patrol car. "We'll get you to my office for now, and then see what we can do."

About what? I wanted to ask, but no words formed, so I just stared at her instead.

It was quiet as we drove down the dirt road and away from all the cars. Betty's arm was around me and I leaned into her side. She was comfortable and the warmth of the blanket and her trying to comb my long hair with her fingers made my eyes close again.

*****

I sat in a chair with the officer's blue blanket wrapped around me and Betty in front of me sitting at an old wood desk.

It was covered in papers strewn over the top. There was just a small spot in front of her that was clear as she wrote on a pad. I looked around the room as I waited. The walls were full of framed flower pictures. They brightened the room and made me feel even more comfortable. Pulling the blanket even tighter and leaning back in the chair, my feet began swinging in the air inches from the ground. The blue dress I was wearing was barely visible under the blanket, but I could see my white socks. They were dirty with pine needles stuck in the lacy tops. The blue and white shoes no longer shined.

"OK, Honey," She smiled up at me. "We're going to take you over to the Campbell's home and they will take care of you until tomorrow." She hesitated, then crossed her arms on the desk and leaned toward me. Her blue eyes were full of concern, "Do you understand?"

There was still a haze in my head and numbness in my body, so no words came out, but I did manage a nod.

"OK, Honey," She repeated. "You'll only be there for a day or so until we find your family."

Betty stood and smoothed the wrinkles from the grey skirt she wore. Her heavy-heeled shoes thumped on the floor as she led me down a long hall, then out a door where a white car was waiting. I didn't remember walking into the building, so I looked around. There was a Safeway store with dozens of cars parked in front of it. I turned and looked at the building we had walked out of; the door was glass, but the building was white brick with red lettering on the side. We moved too fast for me to read what it said.

Betty sat me on the back seat and smiled encouragingly as she buckled my seat belt.

"You're going to be okay, Honey." She patted my arm as her eyes began to glisten. It seemed to startle her, and she quickly turned away.

I watched the top of pine trees pass as we drove down the highway. My eyes were drooping when she finally stopped the car in front of a white house. A short grass yard led to cement steps and up to a blue door. To the right and left of the door were tall bushes that nearly covered the few windows. There were no other houses in sight, but a tall red barn set behind the house. Behind the barn was a wide river. It was a pretty scene and reminded me of a book I had read at school.

Betty opened my door and stretched out her hand, "It's only for a day or two."

I unhooked the seat belt and took her hand. My other hand gripped the blanket the police officer had wrapped me in. It gave me a bit of comfort. As we walked toward the house, the door opened with a large man and tall heavy-set woman appearing. They both smiled a welcome, but there was something inside me that made me lean into Betty.

She stopped at the base of the steps and smiled in return.

They look huge, I thought as my head tipped back to look up at the man. He dressed just like my dad; light tan pants and a white shirt. Except, this man had a stain on the left side of the shirt. My dad's shirt never had a stain. If he spilled something on it, he always had one in the car or in his office desk drawer to replace it.

"Honey," Betty was saying, "This is Mr. and Mrs. Campbell."

My eyes darted between the pair.

"Is that your name?" Mrs. Campbell asked with eyebrows high, and she seemed to lean forward as if encouraging me to speak.

I just stared at the big woman with white hair piled on top her head and black dress flowing around her. Big black shoes were too tight and made her ankles look pudgy.

"She's still in a bit of shock," Betty said hurriedly. "She hasn't spoken a word since they found her."

"Of course," Mrs. Campbell nodded. "Let's get her inside and settled."

"You still have the clothes I dropped off the other day?" Betty asked as she held my arm going up the stairs. "I'm afraid she has nothing more than the clothes on her back and that blanket."

"Of course," Mr. Campbell answered as we stepped into the house.

My stomach felt sick. There was something about his voice that made me step behind Betty. She didn't seem to notice.

"She'll take a hot bath and we'll get her into clean clothes," Mrs. Campbell gushed. "Once we get some food into her, she will feel better. We will get you taken care of...Honey."

She did not seem to like that name.

We walked into a small living room that held an orange paisley sofa that had a green and orange knitted blanket lying over the back. Two rocking chairs were across from us, and all were angled toward the large television cabinet. A door was right behind the chairs. A hallway in front of us led to two more doors on the left and one on the right. At the end of the hallway was a door with a window and I could see the top of the barn. To the right of the living room was a kitchen; pink cabinets, turquoise sink, white refrigerator, and a long wood table that was surrounded by 6 chairs.

"Where are the kids?" Betty asked as she walked into the kitchen.

The Campbell's glanced at each other then followed her.

"Out fishing at the river," Mr. Campbell answered.

I slowly lowered onto the sofa and pulled the blue blanket tight around me. I could see down the hallway and into the kitchen as their voices lowered so I could not hear them.

I could see the backs of Mrs. Campbell and Betty. Mr. Campbell was facing me, and his eyes moved from the women and looked right at me. He stared at me...eyes narrowing, and his lip slowly lifted on one side. My fingers gripped the blanket tighter and I turned away to see a door opening down the hallway. Much to my surprise, a head leaned out. A boy just a few years older than me stepped into the hallway. He was in blue jeans, a white t-shirt, and black and white sneakers. Shoulder-length blonde hair fell across his face, and he brushed it away. His eyes connected with mine and he smiled then lifted a finger over his lips.

He slowly tip-toed down the hallway; stopping just before the door where the adults were gathered. His eyes carried a mischievous glint as he leaned to the wall to listen.

I watched the adults talk but avoided looking at Mr. Campbell's face. Minutes passed before the boy suddenly turned and quickly ran down the hallway and disappeared into the room. I didn't hear his footsteps or his door close.

"Honey," Betty was walking to me.

I rose and leaned into her. My heart pounded in my chest in fear of her leaving me with the older couple, but I also wanted to know more about the boy.

"There are kids staying here so you'll have someone to play with," Betty smiled. I desperately wanted to go with her and the look in my eyes must have told her. "It's only a day…maybe two." She whispered and gave me a quick hug then turned to the Campbell's. "You have my business card?"

"Oh, somewhere, of course," Mrs. Campbell nodded.

"Well," Betty lowered her purse and opened the clasp then slid a hand in to lift a small white card. "Here is another just in case," She handed the card to Mrs. Campbell then turned back to me. "If you want to talk to me, just call."

No words formed and the haze in my head increased; I just stared at her. Within moments, the woman was gone, and I was standing and looking at the Campbell's.

"What is your name?" The woman demanded with hands on hips and the sweet smile was replaced with a scowl. "Girl, what the hell is your name? I am not going to be calling you, *Honey*." The name was spewed out.

My heart clenched, eyes widened, and throat constricted. No words would have come out even if I had tried. She glared at me, then flipped a hand as if dismissing me and turned to her husband, "You get your ass to work."

With a snarling smile, he slowly walked past with his eyes watching me until the door was completely closed.

Mrs. Campbell stomped to the door behind the two chairs. My heart was pounding and eyes rolling around the room looking for an escape.

"This is your room," She shoved open the door then just as quickly shut it again. "Kids are not allowed in the house during the day, so you'll go outside, and I'll call you in for your meals."

I had no idea what to do, so I just stared at her as my fingers curled into the blanket in front of me.

"Down the hallway and out the damn door," She turned on the television, adjusted the nobs, then flopped down on the sofa and pushed off her shoes with her toes.

After a moment, her hand rose, and she pointed down the hallway.

With blanket held tightly, I walked down the hallway and hesitated by the door the boy had disappeared through, then I walked down to the windowed door.

Much to my surprise, the boy was standing at the far end of a large yard and in front of the barn. He waved a hand to me to join him. One last glance back at the woman sitting as a statue watching the television, I opened the door and stepped outside.

"Come on," He waved an arm. "We'll be out here until the old guy comes home from work."

The further I was away from the house and woman, the wider my strides became. The air was warm and smelled of pine trees and water. The sound of the river calmed my nerves.

To the left of the barn door was a stack of chopped wood. Just in front of it were full round pieces that had not been chopped yet. The boy stepped up onto the first one then jumped to the second with a flourishing twist at the end, his long hair swirled around him.

"Come, have a seat in the queen's chair," His arm dramatically swung out and stopped at the large cut log next to him.

Queen's chair? I looked at the log, then back to him.

"Imagination," He chuckled and jumped in the air and landed with both feet on the ground. He dramatically flopped onto the log next to the 'queen's chair'.

His smile was inviting, so I walked to the log and sat down with the blanket firmly wrapped around me. My fingers gripped it tightly.

"I'm Jesse," He smiled. "Well…this time anyway."

I frowned at him.

He laughed, "I have been to one orphanage, and this is my second foster home. Each time I give them a new name."

That was confusing.

"What's your name?" He asked.

"Victoria Moreau," The words flowed off my lips at a whisper.

"That's a beautiful name and fitting for a queen," He grinned. "But, do you have an accent?"

"I was born in France," I nodded. "We just moved here last year."

"Cool, accent," He grinned. "I was born in New Zealand. My dad brought me here two years ago."

"Where is he?"

He shrugged in disinterest, "Don't know."

"Jesse?"

"Yeah?"

I looked him straight in the eyes, took a deep breath and asked, "Are my parents dead?"

CHAPTER FOUR

His smile dissolved, and eyebrows came together in a confused frown, "Didn't they tell you?"

"No," My stomach tightened, and tears began to rise. "We were driving down the road, they were laughing at something, and then I woke up with Officer Lucas holding me." My chin quivered. "Betty is searching for my family which means…my parents…"

He sighed, "I'm sorry, Victoria. I heard Betty tell the old people that they were killed in the car accident and found you 20 yards away, unconscious but unharmed."

I buried my face in the blanket and cried.

*****

When the tears stopped, I looked at Jesse. He was staring at the back of the house. He turned back to me with a determination in his eyes that I didn't understand.

"Let's go over by the river," He stood and swept the long blonde hair back. "The sound of the river always makes me feel better. It makes me dream and fills my imagination."

After a deep breath, I stood and with dragging feet, I followed him behind the barn to a small beach next to the swiftly flowing river. The closer I walked to the river and the rumble of its water, the more the haze in my head eased.

"Are you hungry?" Jesse asked at the water's edge. He held a fishing pole.

"No…yes…I guess," I muttered.

"Did they feed you anything this morning after they found you?"

I shook my head.

He dramatically huffed, "What the hell?"

My eyes widened at his swear word. No kids in my world ever cussed.

He threw the fishing pole on the ground and walked into the trees behind us. Was I supposed to follow him? After a hesitation, I took a step forward then stopped when he returned carrying a bag. It was a light green pillowcase with something inside.

"Take a seat, Queen Victoria," He swung his arm toward a log.

No one had ever called me that before and I thought it was a bit funny, so I did as he asked.

He withdrew an apple from the bag and handed it to me, "You like apples?"

The words were barely out of his mouth when the first bite was taken.

"Good," He smiled. "There is a tree upriver that we can eat from. The old lady doesn't feed us during the day. She eats all the food herself except when the old man is around in the mornings or at night."

Two more bites from the apple and he handed me a biscuit wrapped in a napkin.

"I smuggle things out here sometimes," He shrugged. "I wasn't going to be around much longer but I'll stay until your family comes to get you." His eyes narrowed as he watched me take another bite. "I'm going to make sure you're alright, then I'll head out west."

"You're going to run away?" I gasped.

"Of course," He chuckled and stood with a flourish and jump back. "Jesse's adventure is about over and it's time to become someone else; maybe a pirate."

"A pirate?" I smiled at the vision.

"Sure," He knelt to the pillowcase again and withdrew a book. Its pages were wrinkled, and the cover nearly torn off. "Like in my book here," He held it up to the air as if it was a trophy. "The boys escape down river on a raft and land on a deserted island. They become pirates and live off the land with dreams of stealing riches from the wealthy."

"It sounds very adventurous," I finished the apple and looked at the core. "What shall I do with this?"

Jesse chuckled, took the remains of the apple, and threw it as far into the river as he could. His long blonde hair swished around him. With a hand pushing it back, he turned to me. "The fish will eat the rest and then we'll eat them." He laughed and picked up the fishing pole.

The line went flying in the air with a white and red bobber on the end. We watched it bounce in the water as I ate the biscuit.

"Tell me more about your book," I said and pulled the blanket around me tighter.

"I stole it from the store."

"What?" He was a thief too?

"I was hitchhiking, and it started to rain so I ran into a store," He shrugged. "I was looking at magazines and saw this book, so I started reading it." He turned and looked at me with a smile. "I hid in a backroom when they closed the store and read the book and slept all night; all warm and cozy."

I looked at him with wide eyes. I'd never heard of such a thing.

"When they opened," he continued. "I stuffed the book in my back pocket and snuck out when no one was looking."

"That sounds dangerous…but adventurous," I admitted. "Isn't hitchhiking dangerous, too?"

He shrugged and sat on the log next to me, "Not something I would suggest YOU do, but I usually try to flag down trucks so I can just sit in the back. That way they can't talk to me."

"How did you end up here?"

"I stole some milk from the store, and they called the cops," He huffed. "I told them I was eighteen, but they didn't believe me so that Betty lady was called, and she brought me here."

"How old are you?"

"Thirteen, how old are you?"

"Eleven," I sighed. "I had a birthday party last week and now…" The tears began to rise again and we remained silent and just listened to the river.

"Since the fishing isn't good today, I'll read the pirate part of the book to you."

The day went by with him reading and fishing and me listening and every once in a while crying. We were standing at the river's edge when the sun started going down over the horizon.

"Vickie!"

I looked at Jesse, "My name is Victoria."

He smiled and looked over his shoulder, "I know that, but it's the old lady calling you."

"But, I didn't tell her my name."

"Someone did," He whispered and picked up the pillowcase of apples, slid the book into it, then tossed it into the bushes.

"Vickie!"

I did not want to let her know I could hear her. I did not want to talk to her or her husband until Betty returned. My heart raced and throat constricted at the thought of being near either of the Campbell's.

"She'll come stomping out here," Jesse whispered and slowly turned.

With a sigh, I turned to look at the house. She was standing on the top step, hands on hips, and even across the wide yard I could see she was glaring.

"Get up here!" The woman yelled.

I had set the blanket on top of the log and picked it up to wrap around me again. It made me think of Officer Lucas; *you're going to be okay.* His words surrounded me as I pulled the blanket in tight.

Jesse walked with me to the house.

"Betty called and told me your name, Vickie," The woman huffed as we drew close.

My name is Victoria, I whispered in my head, but the woman made the words freeze in my lungs. I just stared at her. Not once did she even acknowledge that Jesse was standing next to me before she turned and walked into the house. With lead feet, I walked up the steps and followed her. She was in the kitchen standing in front of the stove with a long wooden spoon in hand. It was shoved into a large pan and stirred dramatically before she turned to me. The look was so mean I took a step back and bumped into Jesse.

"Say something now or you can go to your room for the rest of the night," the woman growled.

More than anything, I wanted to hide in the room until Betty came back. I said nothing.

The wooden spoon flying out of the pan and tapping angrily on the side of the pot had me turning and nearly running over Jesse in my fear and desperation to get away. I ran right into the room and shut the door behind me. Leaning my back on the door, my body trembled. I held the doorknob tightly so I would have a warning if she tried to enter. My breaths were coming strong and fierce…the tears slid from my clenched eyes and down my cheeks.

How could this happen? One day I'm happy with my loving, doting parents, then the next I'm running in fear into a room I had never been in and hiding from an old woman who obviously hated children.

In between deep breaths, I heard it; a light tapping. I knew it was Jesse trying to get my attention and my eyes flew open. A low window that set barely a foot above the floor, was to my left and I tried to run to it, but my leg hit the edge of the bed with such force I tumbled to the ground. The blanket around me made it hard to stand, my breaths were coming faster, and I had to hold back the sobs of panic. I finally scrambled to the window and could barely see him peeking through. The sky had darkened so fast.

With trembling fingers, I unlocked the window and slid it up. I nearly jumped out, but Jesse pushed me back and I fell to my knees with my arms stretched out to him.

"I want to go home," I sobbed with tears streaming down my face. "I want my mum and pop; I want to go home."

His hands took mine as he whispered, "It will be all right Victoria. You are strong. You're going to be okay. I won't let anything happen to you."

"I want Officer Lucas," I cried. "I want Betty. I want to call her, but I don't know where that card went."

Jesse tightened his grip on my hands, "The old lady wouldn't let you call anyway."

"I want to go home, Jesse," I pleaded in desperation with the tears tumbling.

"Just one night," he whispered. "I'll be right here. I promise, I will not move."

"What if they come in?"

"I'll pull you through the window, and we'll hide in the barn for the night."

There was so much conviction in his voice and in his hands as they squeezed mine that my trembling began to ease.

"Pull your blanket back up and just sit here with me," he whispered. "I'll tell you more about the pirates. You can use your imagination and pretend you are on the island with them."

"Okay," My voice quivered as I reluctantly let go of his hands just long enough to pull the blanket tight.

When I heard the car pull into the driveway, in my mind, I was on the beach with the pirates. We were dancing around a fire waving sticks as our swords, but the beach disappeared as my fingers tightened again around his. I leaned toward the window as if to jump.

"You're okay, Victoria," He whispered. "They'll just have dinner, watch television, and then go to bed."

We were frozen in time; my head down as if in prayer as we silently listened to Mr. Campbell walking up the steps and the door to the house open and close. Voices…they started low and escalated until they were so loud, we could almost make out what they were saying. The words were angry and footsteps walking to the door had me rising and my body leaning out the window. Jesse's hands tightened as if prepared to pull me through. A thump startled me so bad my head whipped around and looked at the door expecting that awful man and mean woman to come through at any moment. I was halfway out the window and ready to fall into Jesse's arms.

CHAPTER FIVE

More words were yelled, and then their voices slowly faded away.

Jesse and I froze again as we waited. Minutes ticked by before my body began to relax and I slid back into the room. Our hands remained tightly bound.

The room was dark with only the light under the doorway showing. I watched that crack of light until it disappeared. Their footsteps passed along the wall, then the house became silent.

"Okay, Vic," Jesse whispered.

"Vic?" My voice shook in fear and amusement.

"Yeah," His voice was light as if trying to entertain me. "Sometimes, Victoria is just too long to say and now we both hate the name 'Vickie' so you get to be Vic every once in a while."

"I like that."

"It sounds strong, and you know…victorious."

We both chuckled with nerves tingling and bodies beginning to relax.

"Now what?" I pulled the blanket around me again.

"We just wait until morning then, hopefully, Betty will call or we can figure out a way to call her to come get you."

"What about you?"

"Once you're safe, I'm down the road, and on to the next adventure."

We were quiet, just listening to the night when the long stressful day began to make my eyelids drop. I was too terrified to go to sleep in the room and even more terrified that I could not stop myself from falling asleep.

"Jesse?"

"Yeah?"

"Can we just go sleep in the barn and sneak back in the morning before they wake up?"

"That's a good idea," He whispered, and his hands let go of mine.

I handed him the blue blanket so it wouldn't get torn as he helped me through the window. Once out, we ran across the yard and into the barn. It was so dark, I could not see anything.

"I have a hiding spot out here," Jesse whispered. "In the corner over here under a tarp." He took my hand and we walked along the wall of the barn. "Even if they knew we were gone, and were going to come lookin', they wouldn't find us. We'll just have to lay on the ground with the tarp over us."

"Ok," I whispered. "It's better than in that house."

He chuckled as he helped me lower onto the ground, "It's not too cold out here. Your blanket will help keep you warm."

"What about you? I can share."

"Nah, once we're under the tarp, our body heat and breath will warm it up."

I curled onto the ground and wrapped the blanket around me as he lowered the tarp over us. Within minutes, the warmth of the air, rumble of the river, and the knowledge we were out of the house, made my eyelids fall again.

"Thank you, Jesse," I whispered.

"He won't hurt you."

My mind went dark.

I woke to my hand being shaken.

"Just a couple more minutes, Mum," I whispered into the haze.

"It's Jesse, Vic."

My eyes flew open, and I sat straight up. Everything from the day before flooded my mind from Officer Lucas, Betty, my parent's death, the Campbell's, fishing, pirate stories, and the terrifying moments at the window. Any haze remaining disappeared when I remembered we were hiding under the tarp in the barn.

"We have to get back to the house," Jesse stood and lifted the tarp away.

Light was just beginning to fill the barn. Weird shapes appeared in the shadows.

"What's in here?" I asked and shook the dirt from the blanket.

"Old tractors," He answered. "They are pretty cool. We can look at them later."

"Okay…"

He peeked out the door; nothing was moving and the only thing we could hear was the sound of the river. We ran across the yard and back to the bedroom window.

"Damn," Jesse muttered as he came to a halt. "This ain't good."

I followed his gaze…the bedroom window was closed. We had left it open for the return trip. With hands cupped around our eyes and pushed against the glass we looked into the room. The door into the living room was open and the bed was tipped onto its side with the mattress leaning against the wall.

"Why would they be in there already?" I whispered.

"He was…" Jesse shook his head. "You need to be with Betty."

"I agree, but what do we do until then?"

"Let's go down to the river and just pretend we went fishing early and like nothing happened."

I sat on the log and ate an apple from his pillowcase as the sun finally rose. My legs were dirt. Not even dirty…they were dirt. My white socks were no longer white, and the dress was covered in a fine layer of dirt. The blanket had dirt, leaves, and pine needles stuck to it. I couldn't even imagine what my hair looked like. I walked to the river's edge and lowered to the water.

"What are you doing?" Jesse asked and was quickly by my side.

"Just washing up a bit," I smiled. "One night in the woods and another on a dirt floor in the barn and I'm a bit dirty." I took off my shoes and socks to wash them. "I don't think I have ever been this filthy."

I washed my feet, legs, arms, and face as much as possible then brushed off the dirt from the dress. The sleeves were short and, I don't know how it happened, but there were tears in both. It was going to need to be sewn. My mother's vision flashed in my eyes. She was laughing at the thought of her sewing something. We always took our clothes to a seamstress.

Tears welled in my eyes as I sat back on the log. Jesse was quiet as I cried. Once the tears dried, I watched him fish as I picked leaves and pine needles out of my long black hair, then began running my fingers through it to release the tangles.

"Got one!" Jesse called out and reeled in a wiggly fish. He was grinning when he turned to show me, but his eyes rose above me, and the smile faded.

With lungs suddenly tightening, I twisted on the log while lifting the blue blanket and holding it tightly in front of me and looked behind me. Both the Campbell's were walking across the yard, and both looked angry.

"Jesse," I whispered as my body trembled.

"You'll be okay," His voice was low and soothing, then rose in energy, "Look what we caught this morning!"

The frowns on the couple disappeared as both looked confused.

"Vickie! Why aren't you in your room?" Mrs. Campbell growled.

No words would escape, and I shrunk away from her as my eyes widened in obvious fear. I was deathly afraid the apple was going to come back up.

"You damn child," She stepped forward.

"We just came fishing," Jesse hurried to my side with the fish dangling from the end of the line. He was so close to me, it nearly hit me in the head. "Before sunrise is always a good time to fish."

"It was…" Mr. Campbell started gruffly then stopped. He glowered at Jesse.

"I have never seen a child more addicted to fishing than you," Mrs. Campbell grumbled at Jesse and took the pole and fish from him. "Get it on up to the house and we'll have it for dinner tonight."

She turned and stomped across the yard. Jesse waited until I rose and walked between me and Mr. Campbell. He chatted about fishing all the way to the door.

I followed Mrs. Campbell down the hallway and to the kitchen. Just as I turned into the room, I heard a thump and walked back to look down the hall. Neither Jesse nor Mr. Campbell were there.   I froze. Where was he?

"Sit down," Mrs. Campbell ordered as she unhooked the fish. She tossed it into the sink then set the pole in the corner.

I slowly turned to look at her, then to the table where there were two bowls set at each end of the table.

"Jesse likes the chair by the window, so you sit there," She washed her hands then gruffly dried them with a towel.

I slowly walked to the chair and lowered to just the edge so I could get up and run if needed.

A large spoonful of what I guessed to be oatmeal was plopped into the bowl in front of me. I looked at it in horror, then quickly caught myself and forced a smile as she turned to look at me with another spoonful that was dropped into the bowl.

I just kept the smile frozen on my face, until she turned away to put three plops of the oatmeal in Jesse's bowl.

Where was he?

I looked back to the hallway as heavy footsteps echoed. They were too heavy for Jesse, and I nearly cried when Mr. Campbell walked around the corner. His wife was at the stove with her back to us when he gripped my shoulder tightly then lowered his face to mine. He kissed my forehead with his breath oozing across my skin. My eyes scrunched together, body tightened in horror, and the scream froze in my lungs.

When Mrs. Campbell began to turn, he rose quickly and hurried to her side.

"I'm off to work," He patted her butt, then kissed her cheek and turned back to me. The outright fear kept my eyes on him when his lips puckered into a kiss toward me.

My stomach soured and my eyes went to the grey oatmeal in the bowl. Where was Jesse?

"You'll eat every bit of breakfast, then wash your own dish and put it in the strainer here," Mrs. Campbell ordered. She didn't look at me as she walked past me to plop on the sofa again. "When you're done, go outside."

I looked at the bowl of grey oatmeal and then over to Jesse's bowl. The window in the room was behind his chair but I couldn't see anything but pine trees. Behind me was the sofa and woman and there was no sound in the house besides the television. If I was going to find Jesse, I had to eat the oatmeal. I grimaced. In the middle of the table was a small covered bowl so I slowly leaned forward to see what was in it. Sugar! I pulled the container to me and dumped half of the it on top of the oatmeal. The white sugar made it look even greyer. I stirred it all together then took the first bite. It tasted like sugar, but it stuck to my cheeks, teeth, and tongue; my mouth worked as if trying to chew a really big piece of bubble gum. There was no water or milk in sight to help wash it down.

With no choice, I concentrated on the flavor of the sugar and took another bite, then another, then another, until it was almost gone. I walked to the sink to wash the last part of the oatmeal away. As my mother had taught me, I inspected every inch of the bowl to make sure it was clean then carefully set it in the strainer right next to the other dishes. I washed out the sink to make sure there was no evidence of the oatmeal I did not eat.

I turned and looked at Mrs. Campbell sitting on the sofa watching television then slowly looked around the room. The refrigerator was covered in little decorative magnets and under one of them was the card Betty had handed the Campbell's. I watched the woman closely as I inched to the card and quickly removed it, and stuck it in the pocket of the dress. I looked for the phone, but the hopes of calling Betty escaped because the phone was on the table next to the sofa and right next to the old woman.

Without a word, and blanket firmly wrapped in my arms, I walked out of the kitchen and down the hall. I tried hard to hear anything as I walked by Jesse's door but there was no sound. I opened the outside door and slowly shut it behind me. Once the door clicked, I ran down the steps and across the yard.

"Jesse?" I whispered as I neared the barn.

He was not by the river nor was he in the barn. I looked back at the house and realized he had to be in his room. I ran across the yard again and to the window I guessed was his. Looking around me, I saw no one so I rose on my tip-toes and peeked in the window. The first thing I noticed were nails pounded into the bottom of the window to hold it shut. The fresh paint flecks were proof they had just been put there. My stomach quivered as I looked into the room. There was a bed, a dresser, and lying on his back on the floor in front of the door was Jesse. He wasn't moving.

CHAPTER SIX

I tapped on the window…nothing. I tapped louder…still no movement. If Mrs. Campbell was still at the front of the house watching the television the noise would cover my voice.

"Jesse?" I tapped again. His foot moved and my heart jumped. I tapped louder, "Jesse!" His hand rose to his head. "Jesse!" He started to rise then fell back on the floor. I started to bang the window when…

"Vickie! Where the hell are you?" Her voice came from the back door and my hand stopped within an inch of the window.

One more desperate look into Jesse's room, I wanted to scream but turned away. Not wanting her to know I was at the window, I ran to the front of the house and quickly stepped in the front door. The back door was closed now, and I just caught a glimpse of the back of her head as she descended the steps to the yard.

I ran for Jesse's door and grabbed the handle. It was locked and a cry of frustration escaped. How could he be lying on the floor and the door be locked? "Jesse!" I tapped frantically and shook the door handle, and then I noticed the lock was on the outside.

"Vickie!" Her voice was just outside the back door, and I could see the top of the white bun on her head as she climbed the few steps.

I barely had time to unlock the door, then run back down the hall to the living room. I turned when I heard the back door open and stood frozen in the middle of the room as she walked down the hall. She looked up in surprise.

"Where in the hell were you?"

The woman scared every nerve in my throat, and I just clenched my teeth together and stared at her.

She stomped down the hall toward me, "Ms. Sanders called and said they found your aunt, but she wouldn't be here until tomorrow morning to pick you up."

A wash of dread flooded over me and tears rose. Fear gurgled in my stomach.

"Get in the kitchen," She continued and walked to a box that was sitting on the floor by the table. "Might as well find you another dress; wouldn't look too good if you were in the same clothes as yesterday."

She began pulling clothes out of the box as I just stood frozen and stared. My fingers slowly curled around the blanket.

"Get over here," she demanded.

I had to force myself to take a step, then another. I looked at the pile of dresses and wondered who they belonged to.

Her head turned with a jolt and my body jumped back away from her. Dark, angry eyes wandered over my hair.

"Let's take care of that mess first," She stood away from the box and walked to the cupboard. "Do I have to tell you everything? Get your ass in here!"

Five more forced steps, my fingers curled into the blanket so hard my knuckles hurt and I held my breath until I stood next to her.

She had yanked open a drawer and was ruffling around then suddenly twirled and slapped a brush onto the table. My whole body shook as I jumped back. My foot caught the bottom of the blanket and the tension pulled it from my fingers. She turned again and looked at my hair as if assessing what she was going to do. There were scissors in her hand.

"Might as well cut off the worse part."

My lungs filled with air as I gasped. My hair? But my mother loved my hair! She would spend hours curling it and brushing it and we loved that time together.

Before I could move, Mrs. Campbell grabbed a handful of hair and the scissors were closing.

She was cutting my mother away from me! Every bit of air came out of my lungs in a high-pitched scream. The scissors clipped off a long strand as she jumped back. More air in and I screamed again. She threw the scissors on the table, raised her arm across her chest, and swung at me with the back of her hand. I ducked and it brushed the top of my head. I sucked in more air and screamed again.

"Stop that damn screaming!" She grabbed my arm with one hand and the other rose over her head. I screamed and closed my eyes to the impending blow.

I was jerked to the side and her hand slipped from my arm. I sucked in more air and filled the air again with a scream that vibrated from the walls.

My arm was grabbed again and I pulled away.

"Vic, it's me," Jesse's voice filtered through the end of the scream and my eyes flew open.

"You damn…" Mrs. Campbell yelled from the floor as she scrambled to stand.

Jesse pulled me out of the kitchen, down the hall, and we burst out the back door. We were halfway to the barn when we heard her.

"Wait until Mr. Campbell gets home, you little son-of-a-bitch!"

Terror shook through me making my strides wide. When we stopped behind the barn, we were both breathing hard. My hand went to my hair and his went to his side with his eyes scrunched in pain as he stared at the house.

"She won't come out here," he groaned.

"Jesse? Are you hurt? What's wrong? What happened?"

"I'm okay," he grimaced and turned toward the river. "He got me before I realized what was happening."

"What do you mean?" Desperation and fear dripped from my voice.

"He just got a couple blows in before I could get away then, I guess, I hit my head," His hand went to the back of his head. "It hurts like hell."

"I saw you through the window. You were lying on the floor. He must have knocked you out."

We stood silently for a moment as he rubbed his head with one hand; the other was wrapped around his side.

"Are you sure you're okay?" I whispered.

"Yeah, I will be," He huffed. "I've been hit harder, but I've never been knocked out before."

"Oh, Jesse," Tears filled my eyes as my hands went for the blanket…that wasn't there. The tears fell as I looked back at the house. The blanket was in there. The security of Officer Lucas and Betty were in with that woman. She was probably destroying it. The thought made more tears fall.

"It's been a long morning, Vic," Jesse whispered and put a hand on my shoulder.

The image of Mr. Campbell's face next to mine and the memory of him grabbing and squeezing my shoulder made me flinch.

"Sorry, Vic, I didn't mean anything." His arm fell to his side.

"No," I cried. "Mr. Campbell…he…he…"

"Did he hurt you? Touch you?" Jesse growled.

My face flamed red, "He grabbed my shoulder and he…kissed my head…" My whole body trembled. "It was awful."

"Oh, damn, Vic, Betty better show up today." He shook his head then moaned with a hand going to the back.

More tears fell as I looked at him in desperation, "She called…they aren't coming until tomorrow."

His body slumped and eyes widened, then he turned and looked out at the river. He stared for the longest time then slowly turned to look at the house.

"Maybe we should try and call," I whispered and pulled the card from my pocket. "I found this but the phone is right next to Mrs. Campbell."

"Well," Jesse huffed. "Then we head upriver until we find a place we can make a call or find Betty's office."

"Okay," I nodded in desperation to leave. "Let's go."

"Nah, can't in the daylight. One thing I've learned, if adults see kids walking by themselves they'll call the cops on ya. That's how I got caught and thrown into the first foster home."

"So, what do we do now?"

"Did ya get something to eat?"

"Gray oatmeal with lots of sugar on it," I grimaced.

He chuckled and turned toward the river, "That stuff will stick to your ribs. I think they could use it to build a brick house."

With a grimace and a nod of agreement, I glanced over my shoulder to the house. I was relieved to get away, but sad that the blanket was going to be left behind. We walked to the apple tree, picked a dozen apples, and stored them in his pillowcase. He ate three, the last biscuit from the bag, and then he caught a fish and ate it raw.

"Ewww," I cringed as he grinned at me.

"Sometimes, you got to do what ya got to do," he chuckled. "I don't know how far away the town is, so it may be a long walk and we need energy."

"I guess it's a good thing I ate the grey oatmeal then."

We both chuckled.

The day was spent at the river with him reading the book aloud to keep my mind busy. We even pretended to have a sword fight with long sticks. As he read about the kids on the raft again, I imagined us building one from the wood from the barn and floating down the river. It would be peaceful…unless we ran into rough water or, even worse, a waterfall. I could not swim, so the thought was just going to remain a dream.

When the sun began to lower, Jesse stuffed the book back in the bag and looked at the house.

"In the kitchen, she has a drawer called the 'junk drawer'," He glared at the house. "I looked in it one time and saw a map of the area and some matches."

I gasped, "You can't be thinking of going in there!"

He looked at me with determination as he nodded, "Yep, we need that map. I don't know the area and we could really get lost or go a lot farther than we need to."

"Jesse," I whined and looked at the house as if it was haunted with monsters inside. "Please don't go."

"I gotta, Vic," he sighed. "We need that map and the matches could be helpful, too." He looked at me with resignation. "The old man gets home right after dark, so I gotta go now."

"What if she catches you? She can see the whole house from where she watches television."

"I'm faster, so I can get away from her…I can't from him, so I gotta go."

"Jesse…" My voice trembled.

"You stand right here behind the barn and in the brush," He walked me to the spot. "Keep the bag in your hands because I might come a running and we want to move fast."

"What if…" My voice trailed off at even the thought of him not coming back.

"No matter what happens," Jesse glared at me. "Don't you go to that house again. You find somewhere out here to hide so you can see the road when Betty arrives. Don't come out until you see her."

"Okay," The whisper trembled.

"Stay here, it might take a while so don't go to the house no matter what."

"I won't, please be careful."

He swept the blonde hair back and slowly walked toward the house. I stood at the edge of the barn and peeked around the corner to watch him walk to the back door and slowly climb the steps. He squatted as he peeked through the window…he quickly lowered and backed down to the yard. My stomach clenched when he disappeared along the side.

Minutes passed as I stared at the door.

"Hurry, Jesse," I whispered with eyes beginning to burn.

Lights appeared down the driveway and my heart sunk. Mr. Campbell was home early.

I began praying and watching for any movement from the house. I could do nothing more than hope Jesse heard him arrive as the old man disappeared to the front of the house. Minutes passed as the sky grew darker, then a muffled sound came from the house, then another, then a loud bang echoed into the night. A gunshot!

The back door opened, but it wasn't Jesse, "You son-of-a-bitch!" Mr. Campbell ran down the steps and sprinted across the yard toward the barn with gun in hand. He was coming right at me.

CHAPTER SEVEN

I rolled back, fell to the ground under the bush, and curled around the pillowcase filled with apples. Both hands covered my mouth to stop the cry of fear as the man appeared huffing with exertion. The long gun was held to his shoulder as he looked toward the river and into the trees. My heart pounded, tears stung my eyes, and body trembled. He was so close I could reach out and touch him. I tried not to breathe.

"I'm gonna kill you, you son-of-a-bitch!" The man called out over the rumble of the river. It echoed into the trees.

"You see him?" Mrs. Campbell appeared at his side.

I stared at them with body frozen in fear, but heart pounding so loud I thought they would hear it over the rumble of the river.

"Nah, he's quick like a rabbit and probably has the girl stashed out there somewhere."

"Well, we won't see them again," Mrs. Campbell huffed. "When Betty shows up tomorrow, we'll just tell her Jesse took 'em and run off."

"We'll blame him alright…all the cops will be looking for him."

"Good riddance to that little smart ass. You best get that room set back up," Mrs. Campbell turned and disappeared.

Mr. Campbell stared out into the increasing darkness. He took a deep breath and released it with a curse before turning to disappear behind the barn toward the house.

I did not move…not one inch. I took in a breath to fill my lungs and calm the haze in my head. Another breath but still I did not move. As far as I knew, he was still standing at the side of the barn.

The night became pitch black with just the moonlight dancing on the river. Over the rumble of the water, I thought I heard a movement and took the chance to look down but I could not see anything.

"Vic," Was whispered from the trees behind me.

I froze, what if it was the Campbell's trying to trick me?

"Vic the victorious, it's me."

My body melted to the ground then instantly shot up.

"Where?" I whispered.

"Edge along the back of the barn. Don't go into the open in case they are watching."

I crawled on my belly and drug the pillowcase of apples alongside of me. I could feel the brush scratching the skin of my arms and legs and getting caught in my hair and pulling.

"I see you," he whispered. "Hold out your hand."

When my hand slid into his, I nearly fainted in relief. Our fingers tightened together as he pulled me up. It was so dark I couldn't see him.

"Keep hold of my hand. We'll get upriver a ways before we stop."

He turned and pulled me behind him. We stumbled over fallen trees and were scratched by unseen brush, but the sound of the river helped keep me calm. We must have walked an hour before he finally stopped to look around.

"I found a flashlight so we can read the map," He said aloud and I jumped from the sound.

I looked around but there were no lights anywhere until a beam of light appeared and shown onto the ground.

"It seems pretty bright," He chuckled then groaned.

"Are you okay?"

"I'll be alright," His voice was low and strained.

He knelt and aimed the light to another pillowcase, "We're close enough to the river that anyone seeing the light will just think it's a reflection off of the water."

I sat on the ground and pulled an apple from the bag, "You want one?"

"No…I couldn't…no," He exhaled and pulled a map from his bag. Then his hand went in again. "I found this…" He pulled out the blue blanket.

I jumped in excitement, "Officer Lucas's blanket! Oh, thank you, Jesse. I thought she was going to destroy it."

"Well, I did pull it out of the trash can so it will stink."

I wrapped the blanket in my arms and the words, *you're okay, Honey,* filled my heart.

"We're going to be okay, Jesse," I declared and stuffed the blanket into the pillowcase with the apples to keep it safe.

"Well, I thought so too until this," He pointed to the map, and I leaned down to see a puzzle of lines. "To get to town by morning, we have to cross the river."

"Is there a shallow spot?"

"Don't know, I can't tell on this map. We'll just stay along the river and hope for the best. Worse case, it takes us until late morning to get there."

"But Jesse, they are going to blame you for my running away. They are going to tell Betty in the morning and have the police looking for you."

He exhaled heavily, "Then we got to get moving fast, Vic. Just in case we don't find a way to cross the river and have to go all the way to the bridge, we need to go fast."

"*Le rivière* will not stop us, Jesse," I declared. "Let's continue with our adventure."

It was too dark to see his face, only an outline of his shadow let me know where he was, and that he had turned.

"What did you say?"

"We continue with our adventure, like the pirates on a quest."

"No, the first thing…lay riveera?"

I chuckled, "*Le rivière*…it means *the river* in French."

"Well, I really do like to hear your accent, but you haven't spoken much French."

"My parents and I have tried to be better at English so Pop…" I envisioned my father smiling at my attempts to say English words and my heart hurt and the tears rose.

"Let's get moving," Jesse said, and I felt his hand hit my arm in search of my hand. When they came together, I gripped his tightly.

"I've spent the time reading you the pirate adventures, so this time, while we walk, you can teach me French words."

"I can do that."

We each picked up a pillowcase full of supplies, and holding hands tightly, walked along the river's edge. Listening to him try to pronounce the words was entertaining and made the falls, scratches from the bushes, and hitting our heads on unseen branches go by faster.

When we stopped to rest, he chuckled, "After all them words, I like rivière the best. It's fun to say."

"The English for ânesse made me laugh."

"What's it mean?"

"Donkey."

We both laughed and started walking again. We came along a beach and began to jog across the sand. When the trees appeared again, we slowed to a walk.

"What's your favorite word in French?" He asked breathlessly.

"Bijou."

"Be jew?"

I giggled, "No…it is like your bumble bee…bee and then like shoe but with a zhoo sound."

"Be zhoo, that right? How do you spell it?"

"B…i…j…o…u."

"Be zhoo," He huffed.

"Faster, roll them together."

"Bijou," He said quickly then repeated it several times. "What's it mean?"

"Jewel," I whispered with my heart pounding from the walking and aching from the memory. "It is what my father called my mother; *son bijou*…his jewel."

"That's beautiful," He sighed "Was that her name?"

"No…it was Juliette."

Was…my mother's name *was*…she would, forever, be a *was*… My breath shook as I tried to hold in the tears. We walked out of the trees and onto another beach.

"You okay to run again?" He asked.

"Yes…yes…" The tears started to fall, and I squeezed his hand and ran as fast as I could. The moon lit the sand enough I could run while holding his hand and the pillowcase swinging wildly at my side.

I ran away from the 'was' of my mother and father. When my lungs could not take another breath, I fell to the ground as sobs shook my body. Jesse knelt next to me and took both my hands and squeezed tightly. He just held them, until the tears stopped.

"Let's go," I whispered and stood to wipe away the tears and begin to walk.

We were quiet until we rounded a bend in the river.

"Look, Vic!" He pointed over the water where the moonlight revealed an island in the middle of the river. "The river splits on each side of it so it will be shallower there."

"Then we cross le rivière here."

We stopped and accessed our path. The water would rise to his knees, but over mine and the flow was strong over uneven rocks. We could see the island, so it wasn't far away.

"We can make that," Jesse nodded. "But, it might be worse on the other side."

"Well, we won't know until we get there," I walked to the edge of the river and hesitated. "Should we take off our shoes?"

"No, it won't be sand out there and the shoes will protect our feet from the rocks."

I took the first step into the water and hesitated again, "It's a bit cold."

"We have to just go for it."

Five giant steps in and I tripped on a rock and began to fall. The pillowcase fell from my hands as I fell forward into the water.

"Ahhh!" I cried out. "The blanket…"

"I got it," Jesse said quickly. "I'll carry it, so you have both hands to balance. That dress will make it harder for you."

I took another step with one hand gripped tightly in his and the other held out to my side. The dress swirled around me with its wet weight trying to pull me down river.

"Don't go too fast this time," Jesse ordered.

One step at a time, with eyes focused on the island, we made our way through the flowing water. Relief bubbled out of us in cautious laughter as we reached the island.

"One more adventure down," I huffed and started walking again.

It was easier to see the rocks since the moonlight wasn't blocked by trees. The rumble of the river grew stronger as we crossed over a mixture of sand, low brush, and rock.

"Deep, rough water makes it loud," Jesse called out.

He was proven right when we came to a rise on the island and the river before us narrowed with fast water crashing against rocks that rose from its depth. There was no way either of us could walk through it.

CHAPTER EIGHT

"Dang," I huffed.

"Well, hell."

I was not going to give up, "We have to keep going, Jesse. We have to get to Betty first."

"Right," he sighed. "Let's follow the island up farther and see what happens."

I took back the pillowcase and withdrew an apple for both of us.

"Nah," He whispered.

"You have to keep your energy up, Jesse. You told me that." I tried to look at him, but it was dark and his hair covered his face.

He didn't answer, he just took my hand and we started walking as I chomped on the apple. When I was finished, I pulled him to a stop then threw the apple core into the water. We both chuckled and continued up the island.

"*Nous sommes des pirates sur notre île,*" I walked faster.

"What's that mean?"

"We are pirates on our island," I chuckled.

We both laughed and our pace increased. Another rise in the island had us puffing for air when we crested the top.

"Oh, Victoria, Queen of the Pirates, look what lays ahead," Jesse exhaled.

My heart soared. The river was twice as wide as the first portion we had crossed, and it was shallow. It would not even come up to my knees. But more importantly, in the distance, we could see a cluster of lights.

"That has to be the town," I cried out. "Let's go!"

We quickly made our way to the river's edge and without hesitation stepped into the water. In our hurry, we both fell into the water at least a dozen times and were soaked from tip of the head to our toes.

"We'll have to keep moving to get warmed back up," Jesse said as we stumbled out of the water.

"Yeah," I huffed. My legs and arms were exhausted. There were dozens of cuts from the rocks and my legs were streaked with blood from the scratches as we walked into the trees.

We were silent as we tried to catch our breath and keep from falling. When we walked out of the trees and into a clearing, the sky had begun to lighten.

"I wish I had a watch," I moaned and increased the pace since we could finally see the ground.

"We need to find a road," He said softly. "I can find where we are on the map if we find a road."

I took a deep breath and started to jog but he held me back.

"Jesse, we have to…" I turned and looked at him. My words stopped.

The light from the rising sun allowed me the first look at him since he had gone back into the Campbell's house. The left side of his face was swollen twice the size as it should have been. Both eyes were swollen and darkening from bruising. His jawline was scraped and bloody.

"Jesse!" I gasped with wide eyes. "What…?"

"Let's just keep moving," He whispered.

I stood frozen in shock. How could he have walked that far with all the falls and slaps from the trees? And the beating he'd taken when the old man had knocked him out! "You need to rest."

"Not until we get closer to town."

Tears filled my eyes again as we started walking. I let him decide our pace.

"You hear that?" Jesse stopped.

We were both quiet; our heads tipped to listen.

There was the distinct sound of a car driving on pavement. Without a word, we started running. Our hands held tightly and the pillowcases swung at our sides. We saw car lights through the trees and slowed to a walk, careful we didn't let them know we were there.

"Do you think they are driving toward town or away from it?" I asked.

"We just need to find a sign," He answered and stepped out onto the road to look both ways. Just to our right, we could see a crossroad that disappeared on the other side. "There…" He pointed and we walked into the cover of the trees and jogged down to the sign.

We waited in the trees as another car passed then walked up to the sign.

"River Bend Road and Route 412," Jesse whispered.

Hidden back in the trees, he opened the wet map and used the flashlight to find the roads.

"They are going into town," Jesse nodded. "It's not very far away."

"Okay, we can do this Jesse," I looked into his swollen, bruised, and scraped face and grimaced. "I can't believe you didn't tell me."

"No reason to," He said and stuffed the map in the pillowcase. "Let's stay up on the road so we can go faster. But, we'll just have to watch for cars and hide so they don't see us."

We jogged until our lungs hurt, then slowed to a walk. Two cars passed after we had hidden in brush. The light of town grew brighter and the traffic thicker.

"It's not a very big town but I don't remember where her office is located," Jesse huffed as we neared the first building.

"It's across from the Safeway store," I said. "And it's a white brick building with red letters."

We walked along the edge of the building and peered out onto the streets.

"You see it?" I whispered.

"Nah, do you remember anything else?"

"No, and I'm not really sure why I remember that. Everything was so hazy that day."

He leaned his back against the wall and took a deep breath, "Funny, isn't it?"

"What?"

"That was only two days ago."

I fell against the wall and leaned my head on his shoulder, "You're not hurt there, are you?"

"Nah…just my face…and head…back…and ribs."

"You need to go to the hospital."

There was silence as more cars passed.

"Let's walk down farther, and see if we can find the store." He groaned as he moved from the wall.

Slow and quiet we walked behind the building until we passed four cross-roads then peered back onto the main road.

"There it is," Jesse exhaled in relief and swept the blonde hair back. "Right across the street."

"So, we're right behind her office," I turned and smiled at him. "We did it, Jesse."

"Yeah, we did, and Queen Victoria was strong and brave on the journey."

"Only because the mighty pirate led the way."

We both chuckled, but the energy was draining.

"Now what?" I asked as the pillowcase dropped from my hand.

"We wait until she gets here, then you can go with her."

I turned and looked at him in disbelief, "Jesse? You're not coming with me?"

"I'm on to my next adventure out west as soon as you're safe with Betty."

"But…" The tears instantly slid down my cheeks. "I don't want you to leave."

He smiled with a sigh, "You have a family waiting for you, and I have an adventure waiting for me."

He leaned against the wall, then slowly slid down to stretch his legs out across the ground in front of him. His eyes were closed.

"You sleep," I whispered. "I'll wake you when she gets here. I remember she drives a white car."

"I'm leaving as soon as she gets here so she can't put me in another foster home," He whispered as his head slowly lowered.

I didn't say anything, but I watched as his chin came to rest on his chest with his hair falling forward, arms lay out to the sides, and his breaths deepened. Officer Lucas's blanket was removed from the pillowcase and shaken before I lowered it over him. It was a little damp, but his body sighed into the warmth.

"You'll be okay, Honey." The officer's words warmed me.

The swelling on his face was bright red and glistened from sweat. Both eyes were puffy and a mixture of dark blue and black. The scrapes along his jaw were raw with tiny blood droplets dried a deep red. The skin on his arms and neck were just as scratched and dirty as my legs and arms.

I pulled his book from the pillowcase and set it on his lap. The edges were crinkled from the water but, hopefully, it would dry so he could still read it.

I turned away as a car passed by, then hid in the bushes so I could see the parking lot clearly. I waited as the sun rose higher, traffic grew noisier, and the town came alive. It must have been two hours after Jesse fell asleep before I saw her car approaching the building.   I hurried to his side.

"Jesse, Betty is here," I whispered and took his hand.

His eyes slowly opened, and he began to sit up. A deep painful moan escaped, and I grimaced for him. I took the blanket and folded it carefully and stuffed it back in the pillowcase then helped him rise.

He tucked the book into his back pocket, then I helped him walk to the corner of the building and we peered around the corner. Betty was just walking into the building, but her car door was still open.

"She's coming back out for something," Jesse whispered then turned to me. "Queen Victoria?"

My breath caught as our eyes connected, "Yes, Pirate King?"

"You be strong and have a good life," He whispered and brushed the hair away from his injured face. His left eye was nearly swollen shut and the white in the right eye was now a deep red. "Promise me you'll have the life your parents would want for you. A happy life."

"I promise…will I ever see you again? How will I know you're okay?" My voice quivered as the tears rose.

"I have Betty's card. I'll send her a letter to send to you and let you know where my adventure led me and that I'm okay."

I nodded as the tears fell, "So…this is the end of Jesse's adventure. Who will you be tomorrow?"

"No matter what name I am called in the future, I will be your Jesse."

Betty appeared out the door and walked toward her car.

"She needs to at least see what that horrible man did to you."

"Yeah, okay," He sighed. "I'm going to make sure it never happens again."

We walked away from the building and toward Betty.

She glanced up with a startled smile, then stopped. The keys in her hands fell to the ground as her eyes widened and jaw dropped.

"Victoria? Jesse?" She took a step and stopped as if we were an illusion.

"I brought Vic to you so she was safe," Jesse pushed me toward her.

"What? What happened…?" Her voice shook and legs trembled as she slowly walked toward us.

"He beat Jesse," I said.

"He was going to hurt, Victoria," Jesse added.

"We left last night and walked here so they couldn't say Jesse made me run away with him." I stood straighter, which made my muscles and back ache.

"Mr. Campbell did this?" She cried and cupped Jesse's cheek gently as her face paled.

"Yeah, and this," He carefully untucked his shirt and lifted it high to show the red, black, and blue ribs. The bruising nearly wrapped around his whole body.

"Ahhh," Betty gasped as the first sob escaped her. Tears slid from her horror filled eyes. "The manager said they were good people…good foster…I would never have…if I had known…" She sobbed again and turned to me. Her hand stroked my tangled mass of hair. "How could anyone do this?"

"They didn't really like us," I said truthfully.

"Your aunt and uncle will be here soon," Her eyes pled for forgiveness as she wiped away the falling tears. "You'll be safe, but Jesse…"

When we turned, he was gone.

"Jesse?" She called out and ran to the corner of the building. "He left?"

"He didn't want to be put in another foster home."

Her hand flew to her mouth as if to stop the gagging sob that escaped her.

My body was tired, and a sad sigh escaped. Slowly, I picked up the two pillowcases from the ground.

"Victoria?" Betty's voice shook. "Where is Kathy?"

I turned and looked at her, "Who is Kathy?"

CHAPTER NINE

My eyes slowly opened to see Sawyer still at the table, but her laptop was now sitting in front of her. With a hand covering her mouth, tears fell from her stricken eyes as they stared at the screen. I had no doubt she was reading the same article I had found concerning the foster parents. My aunt and uncle had shielded me from the fallout of our escape by adopting me quickly and changing my last name so reporters could not find me. It was not until the internet became a collection of history that I finally read what happened. I was twenty-one…ten years after Jesse saved me.

Sawyer's head turned and her glistening eyes met mine.

"You were there?" She whispered.

"For two days," My voice was hoarse and low.

"Did they…?"

"I escaped unhurt because of a young boy that is not named in any article," I answered truthfully. I'm not sure that I would have even told her that much if I didn't have the drugs in my system or was so exhausted.

"You were one of the two that ran away and went to Betty for help?"

"Yes."

"It says she went out to their house to confront them and that…that…"

My eyes closed to the memory. My aunt and uncle had been shocked, angry, and aghast at my condition when they arrived only minutes after Jesse had disappeared. Betty had been so shaken she hadn't even tried to comb my hair. She left when my aunt and uncle arrived.

I opened my eyes to find Sawyer reading the letter again. She looked up at me then back to the letter.

"This is a letter from a Jesse…this is the boy that helped you escape that…place?

"Yes."

"Where is he?"

"I don't know."

"Did you look for him?"

I sighed with a nod, "For a while…I didn't really know where to look. So, I did the only thing I could."

"What?"

"*If you can't be a pirate, then a cowboy is the next best thing,*" I quoted Jesse's letter.

"He…" She stopped with eyes flickering in confusion, then they looked around the house.

"The day after I received that letter, I asked my aunt and uncle for a horse."

"All of this? What you have accomplished in your career started because you were searching for Jesse?"

"My eleven-year-old self had no idea how big the cowboy industry was or how many disciplines there were. Just because I had a horse, did not mean I was going to run into that one cowboy in a million."

My back began to ache, so I leaned up on my elbows. She dropped the letter and rushed to my side.

"Just add another pillow," I sighed.

She tucked it behind me, and I wiggled back into a comfortable position.

"Do you need a pain killer?"

I looked up into her warm green eyes that still glistened from the tears. Maybe it was past the time to tell her. "They make me sleep. Do you want the story or to watch me sleep?"

"Mother," She exhaled. "I want the story, but not you in pain."

"My heart and mind are ready to tell the story now, it may not happen again."

She lowered onto the sofa next to my hip and rest her elbows on her knees with fingers laced under her chin, "Tell me."

"First, go get the green flowered box at the top of my closet."

She gasped, "You have never shown me what was in there." She rose and nearly ran to the room.

When she returned, the box was wrapped protectively in her arms. She lowered onto the sofa next to me and placed it on her knees with a hand on the top.

"No one knows what caused the accident that killed my parents, but I had been thrown from the car. They found me the next morning curled on the ground, unconscious but unharmed. I woke to Officer Lucas holding me in his arms, cradling me, and telling me I was going to be okay. He was tucking a blue blanket around me." I nodded to the box, and she carefully lifted the lid to reveal the blanket. "It is 50 years old, a treasure I have kept all these years."

Her finger caressed the old material, "It's…dirty." Her eyes twinkled at the admission.

"That blanket went through this adventure with me and I would not let Aunt Trish wash it. She understood and found the decorative box to keep it in."

As Sawyer lifted the blanket from the box and set it on her lap, I leaned back into the pillows and began the story. The only detail I left out was the horrible kiss from Mr. Campbell. Fifty years later and it still made my stomach sour.

I finished with our hands clasped together and resting on top of the old blue blanket.

"You were so strong and brave," She whispered.

"I was a healthy eleven-year-old naïve, scared child on an adventure. Jesse had endured two beatings to help me escape those awful people, and the fate he knew lay ahead of me if I had stayed."

"So brave…a true young hero," Tears filled her eyes as she lifted them to the letter that lay on the table. "He kept his promise and wrote you. Did you ever get another letter?"

"No, just the one, and I didn't understand why until I learned of Betty's fate when I was twenty-one. I read the same internet article you just did."

"I now understand his pirate and cowboy comment," She smiled. "I wish…"

"There are a million cowboys in the country and there is no way to know what he called himself after he left Jesse's adventure."

She nodded with a sigh then her gaze rose, and she took in the portraits and awards I had throughout the room. "So, for the first ten years you owned horses, you were looking for Jesse?"

"Yes, I promised him I would have the life that my parents wanted for me…that I would have a good life. I tried very hard to make him proud and not regret what he endured to help me, even though he would never know."

"But you would know," She whispered.

"Yes…"

She wiped away tears as her loving eyes met mine, "I now understand your drive for perfection when it came to the horses and being a success."

"After reading his letter and asking for the horse, my world became the horses. It was only a month after my parents had died and my world had so drastically changed. They insisted on an older horse that knew what he was doing and could help teach me. His name was Henry and I fell in love with him the moment I touched him. His love and understanding…my dedication to taking care of him and loving him…he healed those broken pieces inside of me. Horses heal…"

"You've said it a thousand times and now I understand just how heartfelt you meant it," she sniffed.

"When times were hard and I struggled, I always thought of Officer Lucas and the first thing he said to me, 'Hello, Honey' then he told me I was going to be okay."

She gasped and looked up at the portrait of the honey-colored stallion above the fireplace, "That's how Honey got his name?"

"Yes, your father never understood the odd name, but he didn't question it."

Her head jolted back to me, "Did Dad know all this?"

"No," I sighed and stretched my back causing a shot of pain down my leg. "You are the only one I have told of those days." I groaned.

"Let me get your pain killer," Sawyer stood. "It's nearly 1:00 in the morning, so we can talk more after you rest."

The river's roar was deafening as I stood at the edge of the water on the pirate island. The rumble made my heart race. I turned and looked over the rocks and clusters of brush, but Jesse was nowhere to be seen. I yelled, but barely heard the words over the river. A movement to the left drew my attention; it was Mr. Campbell walking right at me. His eyes bore into mine and his lip curled into an ominous smirk. The fear racing through me froze the scream in my throat. The memory of his breath oozing over my face sent a chill down my body. I turned to run but fell to the ground and frantically searched for a rock to throw. My fingers gripped the rock, but when I turned Mr. Campbell was gone and I was in a library.

My wet hair was matted to my skin and water dripped from the blue dress and onto the library floor. I sat in a chair in front of the computer monitor in Gatlinburg and read the headline of the article: HORROR UNCOVERED AT

FOSTER HOME. The article revealed the investigation began after a boy and girl had escaped the house and appeared at the Children's Bureau office. Twenty-two former foster children, that had spent time in the Campbell home, had been interviewed. There were tales of beatings, starvation, mental torture, and rape.

The bodies of three boys had been found buried in the trees. The coroner's office reported that each body had multiple broken bones and skull fractures. The Campbell's had reported that all three had run away from the foster home. Human bones were found downriver from the Campbell's house. The investigation was ongoing as authorities tried to determine if they were from the missing children and the search for more victims continued. The article continued with detailed accusations from the children.   It was horrifying.

The library began to shake and the sound of the rushing river had me placing my hands over my ears. The chair fell as I jumped up and turned to the room…but it wasn't the room. I was back on the pirate island, standing next to the river with Mr. Campbell running toward me.

My body was frozen, the scream silent.

CHAPTER TEN

"MOM!"

My eyes flew open to Sawyer leaning over me. Her hands were at my shoulders as she shook me, but fell when I gasped.

"What are you doing?" I exhaled.

"You were moaning and crying," Sawyer lowered onto the sofa next to me. "It looked like you were having a nightmare."

I didn't want to talk about the horrible vision, so I just let out an exasperated sigh, "What time is it?"

"Almost six in the morning. You've only slept for five hours."

"And days before that," I huffed. "...and I'm tired of laying here. I need a shower and fresh air."

She hesitated then nodded, "Alright, I'll get a plastic garbage bag so we can cover your cast then we'll get you into the shower." She stood, then turned and looked back down. "Are you sure you're okay, Mom?"

"I'm fine, Hon. Talking about Jesse just brought back memories and they will have to work themselves out."

"Let me know…"

"I will."

There was a heavy silence over us as she helped me shower. I chose a mid-calf sundress to wear so the braced leg was covered. As I crutched back to the living room, I glanced outside. "I need some fresh air. Let's sit out on the patio."

"I'll do your hair out there and Rafe would love to have breakfast with you by the fire."

She helped me settle into the corner of the oversized u-shaped outdoor couch that had a brick fire pit in the middle. A simple flip of a switch lit the flames.

The long sundress covered the cast and a pile of pillows braced underneath it. When Sawyer stepped back in the house for my small table of supplies, I looked out at the bay and mountains. Deep breaths filled my lungs with the scent of pine trees and water.

"I almost feel back to normal," I smiled at my daughter as she flipped a blanket over the top of me. "That shower and the fresh air…hmmm."

"How would you like me to do your hair?"

"We'll keep it down and let it breathe," I chuckled. It was an expression she used to say when she was young.

She giggled and began to brush the length of the white hair that turned to different shades of silver toward the end. It flowed down my back to the point it just touched the back of my elbows. My daughter brushing my hair brought back visions of my mother doing the same thing when I was Rafe's age and before the fateful accident.

"Where is my grandson?"

"Sleeping."

"Did I wake you?"

"No, I had just ended the call with Ray and Nora Nuxoll."

"They bought Brownie?"

"Yes," Tears glistened in her eyes. "Unfortunately, they have decided to keep him."

"What?" I gasped.

She nodded with a frown, "I cannot believe they would do that. Now it is just going to be a fight and I am so damn tired of fighting."

"Did you have anything in writing that you were going to buy him back?"

"Of course, I did. You raised me to make sure every detail of a sale was in writing. It's in the emails we exchanged before the sale detailing they would sell him back to me at the same price they bought him on the condition I would pay them $200 a month board."

"So, you had a clear verbal agreement backed up with emails?"

"Yes…"

My phone was sitting on the small table. I found the Nuxoll's in my contacts list and hit their button.

Ray Nuxoll answered, "Hello?"

"Ray, it's Victoria Rafael-Taylor."

"Hello, Victoria," His voice was pensive, almost defensive.

"I have a driver that can be there in an hour to pick up Brownie. We'll get the money wired to the same account Sawyer has been transferring the monthly payment." My voice was calm, strong; business as usual. "My grandson is really looking forward to riding his horse again."

After a hesitation, he spoke in a low guarded voice, "I've spoken with Sawyer this morning. We've had him for a few months and used him as a backup for my ranch horse."

"What are you trying to say?" I kept my voice light and airy.

"He fits in here pretty well."

My spine stiffened, but I kept the tone of my voice even, "Ray, the only reason I can even imagine you wouldn't send that horse home is if he was injured or…"

"There is nothing wrong with him," he said quickly.

"That's great. Sawyer had full confidence you would take great care of him since she is paying you $200 a month for his care on top of you using him. I do want to thank you for helping my daughter in her time of need. I truly appreciate it and hope to return the favor if there is anything you need in the future."

I had no doubt, letting them know I would 'owe' them a favor would change their minds.

Another hesitation followed by a big sigh, "We're not home right now. Can you make it two hours?"

A wide satisfied grin escaped me, "Of course, just call when you get home and Sawyer will process the payment."

"Thank you, Victoria," His voice was firmer.

"Thank you, my grandson will be delighted to know his horse is on the way here," I tried hard to keep the satisfied drawl out of my voice. "Please don't hesitate to call if you need anything."

"Alright," He said just before the line went dead.

I set the phone on the table and sighed back into the cushions.

Sawyer sat in the chair next to me and shook her head with a smirk, "So…who is going to be there in an hour to get him?"

I chuckled, "I'll call Ari. She is in Arizona, and he did request two so she will have…"

"MOM! Where is Grandma?"

She turned to Rafe's voice echoing in the house.

"We're on the back porch," she answered.

Rafe appeared in his pajamas, cowboy boots, and with a wide grin as I opened my arms to him.

We wrapped each other in the first hug in two years. I held him close and squeezed with all my love.

"I love you, Grandma," he whispered.

It brought tears to my eyes, "I love you, too and I feel good enough today, that after breakfast, we'll go on a tour of the ranch and introduce you to all the horses."

He leaned back with wide eyes, "All of them?"

Sawyer and I shared a knowing grin. He was as much of a horse-nut as we were.

"We'll see how many we can get to today, but the babies for sure," Sawyer stood. "We have months to meet them all."

Rafe turned to me with a grin, "I'm really glad you're feeling better. Can we have breakfast out here?"

"Yes, then we'll have your mother get the 6-wheeler out of the garage and she can chauffer us all over the ranch," Just the thought of driving around the ranch made the excitement in me build. I couldn't wait for him to see my home.

Rafe turned to his mother, "Can we just have cereal so it's faster?"

She chuckled, "Your grandmother needs something hot and nourishing to help build her strength."

"We have all day," I assured him with another big hug.

As the pair of them made breakfast, I called Ari to arrange transport for Brownie. Other than being Jeff's sister, she was my ranch manager in Arizona.

After breakfast, I awkwardly wiggled my way onto the back bench-seat of the 6-wheeler. I sat sideways with my leg stretched over the seat and braced with pillows. A blanket was thrown over me since I was wearing a dress and just wore a sandal on the uninjured leg. With Sawyer driving and Rafe sitting up on the seat next to her, we began the tour.

It stopped at the first pasture.

Rafe pointed to the golden stallion grazing peacefully in the morning sun, "Mom says he is the son of the horse in your portrait in the house."

"Yes," I nodded. "The horse in the portrait is named Honey, and this is his son, Lucas."

Rafe turned in the seat so he was on his knees and looked at me; "I saw the videos of you riding both of them and some others. They were awesome, Grandma. You are such a good rider. Those sliding stops with the dirt flying and the spins and the running and then with the cows with Lucas." His eyes were wide. "Can you teach me to ride like that when the cast is gone?"

"I'll teach you to ride like that even before my cast is gone," I was pleased with his eagerness. "It all starts with basics before you start the advanced moves."

"Can we start today?" He asked.

"No," Sawyer said quickly. "Give Grandma a couple more days. It's only been three days since she broke her leg."

"We have all summer," I smiled at his huff.

The tour began again with a stop at each pasture to name the horses. When we crested the hill overlooking the pastures and the barns and clinic, I could see Lenny, Jeff, and Bubb at the large outdoor arena.

"Go to them," I instructed Sawyer.

All three men turned as we approached. Jeff was riding a daughter of Lucas, a bay named Sweet Honey Bijou Babe that at the last series of competitions had won each of her classes. It was now up to Jeff to continue the progress with the young horse that was one of the current stars of the ranch. Jeff's grin grew as we appeared, Lenny waved us to the gate, and Bubb took one look at us, walked to the barn, and disappeared. His attitude was not better and I knew the time was coming when I would need to act.

Lenny stood at the gate as Jeff looked down at me from the back of the mare.

I gave Jeff a reassuring smile, "I have all the confidence in the world in you."

His eyes rolled in exaggerated exasperation, "I don't think I have ever been so nervous."

"You will do fine," Lenny added. "He's been out here every day since you broke your leg."

I looked up at Jeff, "Where is your confidence level?"

"It's getting better the more I ride," he answered.

"You need to focus," I knew he would be riding and continuing to do his ranch duties.

"I'm trying, but there is so much…" Jeff started and his shoulder's lowered as if already defeated.

I looked at Lenny thoughtfully then back to Jeff, "I want you to pack up and go down to my place in Arizona."

"What?" Jeff exhaled.

"Damn good idea," Lenny nodded.

"But there is so much to do here," Jeff shook his head but his eyes lit up and shoulders rose again.

"I have a dozen people I can call that will help here while you're gone," I said firmly.

"I can help," Sawyer turned in her seat to look at me.

"Me, too!" Rafe leaned over the seat to me. "I can do whatever you need."

I smiled at his eagerness then looked up at Jeff, "Make arrangements to leave as soon as you can. The sooner you get down there and focus before the show, the better you will compete. That is what is important here; the horses and the competition. I'll call Ari and ask her to stock the house so you don't have to worry about that. She'll be thrilled to have you down there and will make sure you're taken care of and can concentrate."

"Well, I'm not going to argue with you," Jeff grinned, and I could see the relief on his face. "I don't have anything holding me here and you have Sawyer and Rafe, so, if you don't mind, I'll leave first thing in the morning."

"It's good with me," I smiled. "Come down to the house this afternoon and we can go over the details."

"Will, do," Jeff nodded.

I turned to Lenny, "If you'll put together a list of the chores you would like to take over and what you would like help with, then I'll decide who the best person is to call for assistance."

"I'll have it to you within the next few hours," Lenny nodded.

"There is the lady coming on Monday morning," Jeff added. "I was going to help with her."

"That," I smiled at him. "Is something Sawyer will enjoy."

"What?" Sawyer twisted in her seat.

"I'll tell you when we get home," I smiled. "Let's carry on with the tour."

"Vic," Lenny mumbled with a glance to the barn. "We need to talk…"

"I know," I interrupted. There was no doubt in my mind there had been more issues with Bubb. "Let's talk later."

"Alright," he sighed. "We have a client bringing in a horse for insemination tomorrow, but he is off work."

I just nodded and tapped Sawyer on the shoulder. With a smile and a wave, she moved the ATV forward to continue the tour. When we crested the tip of the hill that looked down over the ranch, I tapped her on the shoulder again.

"We have horses in the back pastures, but the road is rough," I said. "You can turn around here."

She did as I asked then came to a stop so we could look at the view again.

"Mom, it is so…tranquil," Sawyer whispered.

"It's so pretty here, Grandma," Rafe whispered.

"Bijou Bay Ranch is your playground for the whole summer," I sighed.

He looked at his mom then back to me, "I'm the luckiest kid in the world."

I chuckled, but Sawyer was quiet and moved the ATV forward. She stopped at the bottom of the hill to look at the yearlings running and playing along the hillside. She was turned enough I could see her eyes glistening. The last three years, since her separation from her ex-husband and his drug abuse which led to the arrest, had been very hard on her. Her main focus had been protecting Rafe and keeping him happy. Having him say those words had to be overwhelming for her.

"Sawyer," I laid a hand on her shoulder. "Why don't you show Rafe how to drive?"

"What?" Rafe gasped.

A smile appeared and she took a deep breath, "Great idea."

He nearly pushed her out of the seat in the eagerness to take the wheel. She laughed and their joy while she instructed him had me leaning back in contentment. It was a slow drive back, but Rafe's laughter made it worth it.

After I was tucked back onto the outdoor couch with leg propped back on the pillows, Sawyer placed a plate of food on the small table next to me.

"So, tell me about the training on Monday," She settled into her chair.

"Her name is Camille Madison. She started riding horses the first of last year."

"What discipline?"

"Breakaway roping and ranching; her best friend is the reigning world champion barrel racer, Delaney Rawlins."

"That is impressive, but why would she need training from you if she has someone like that?"

"She was recommended to me because she wants to learn about other disciplines, and since I have a vast array I have competed in over the years, she can do a crash course in everything but rodeo."

"So, you're training her in…?"

"I'm not training her. I'm showing her the final results in each so she can decide if she wants to try something besides roping. We'll let her ride through a course on Western Pleasure, try English, showing, versatility ranch, and a little cutting. If she rides well, then we'll try reined cow horse."

"Seriously, Mom," Sawyer grinned. "That sounds like fun, and I would absolutely love to help. It would be great for Rafe to watch and learn. I can teach her polo, too, if you have a couple horses that wouldn't mind the mallet."

"I have a few," I smiled. Her enthusiasm was refreshing to see after the last few years she had gone through. No doubt, this would be very good for her, too. "She'll be here Monday morning to Wednesday night and her boyfriend will be here with her."

"Really? You've never allowed a distraction like that before."

"This is different. Other than she is a grown woman and will have free time at night, she travels with her friend nearly every day and her boyfriend is going to veterinarian school in Colorado and lives in Nebraska. They don't see each other often, so I told her I didn't mind and they could stay in the Trophy House."

"Did you already have an agenda for her?"

"I began one…it's in my laptop. You can finish it since you will be working with her and I'll review it."

She retrieved the laptop and was going through the files when I remembered a little detail that I'm sure Sawyer would get a chuckle over.

"After I made the appointment, I looked her up online, and downloaded a photo of her. It's in her file."

Sawyer nodded then, after a moment, leaned forward to the screen, "That is quite the picture."

"It's a marketing shot for one of Delaney's sponsors."

"Which one is which?"

"Delaney is the blonde, Camille is the brunette."

She leaned even closer, "Well, Mother, with her tall slender frame, long dark brown hair, shape of her face, and brown eyes, she looks more like your daughter than I do."

"That is what I thought, too," I chuckled. "We can go through my show clothes tomorrow and choose something for her in each discipline."

"Give her the full experience," Sawyer mused.

I leaned back into the cushions and closed my eyes, "She will have her breakaway horse with her and a two-year-old."

I woke to the sound of hoofbeats on pavement approaching the house. My eyes opened to see Jeff appear around the corner riding the pretty palomino mare, Jane, and leading one of my older mares, Miss B.

Sawyer and Rafe were quickly at my side.

Jeff lowered from the horse and walked toward us, "I was thinking Sawyer and Rafe would like to take these two out for a spin while we talked."

"Oh, Mom!" Rafe gasped. "Can we?"

Sawyer looked to me with a silent question.

"Miss B is as safe as Brownie. She is the perfect project for Rafe." I nodded to Jeff.

"Project?" Rafe asked.

"She is older and is insulin resistant, which means her system has a bad time with sugars in her food," Jeff explained.

"She needs a special diet and daily exercise," I added. "With Jeff on the road, she will need some special attention."

"Can I, Mom?" Rafe looked at her.

"Let's go get our boots," Sawyer grinned.

When they disappeared into the house, I smiled at Jeff, "Good call."

"Miss B will love the attention of a young boy," He smiled then his eyes narrowed.

"What?"

"Before we discuss the trip, we need to discuss Bubb."

I sighed, "What did he do?"

"It's his attitude toward everyone; clients and staff. I tried talking to him, but he not so kindly told me what I could do with my opinion."

The door to the house opened and I glanced at a grinning grandson.

"I'll talk to him," I whispered to Jeff.

Jeff's frown turned to a smile as he introduced Rafe to Miss B and adjusted the stirrups for him. When Sawyer joined them and mounted her horse, I held my phone to Jeff.

"Here, take a picture for me."

Both riders leaned to each other and grinned happily.

"You stay here with her until we get back," Sawyer instructed Jeff.

"I will," He answered with an understanding nod.

"We'll be back, Grandma!" Rafe called out with a wave then the pair disappeared around the house.

Jeff settled into the chair across from me with a notebook and pen.

I leaned back against the cushions, "Besides the horses you're taking down to show, I've decided to take advantage of the trip and fill the rest of the trailer with two-year-olds for Ari to train."

"She will be thrilled, but that's a lot of horses to handle by myself on a three-day trip."

"I've already called her, and she is flying to Boise this afternoon to meet you for the rest of the trip."

"I'm a bit terrified of showing your horses for you, dreading the trip down, but I am looking forward to spending time with my sister."

"She was happy about it, too. Now, for the horses..."

CHAPTER ELEVEN

Sunday morning was spent making sure Jeff had everything he needed for the next month in Arizona. I repeatedly assured him I had 100% faith in him and would want no one else to take my place. He drove away from the ranch with a trailer full of horses and a mind full of confidence.

I was sitting in the ATV when his trailer disappeared around the corner. Rafe and Sawyer were standing next to me, "We didn't make it into the Trophy House or to see the other stallions yesterday."

"Oh, yay!" Rafe climbed onto the seat of the ATV behind the driver's wheel and grinned at his mother.

"Just taking over?" She teased and slid on the seat next to him.

"I am Grandma's personal driver," He grinned over his shoulder to me.

"I have no complaints," I chuckled.

He parked alongside the Trophy House and they both helped me out of the ATV and up the two steps to the porch. Two chairs were set along the side before the entrance to the building and in the far corner was a round table with more chairs for outside dining. The porch overlooked a short driveway then a few green pastures with horses roaming about and the large pine tree covered mountain on the far side. It was a relaxing and spectacular view.

Rafe was concentrating on me when the door opened and I crutched inside, but when he shut the door and turned to look into the building his jaw dropped, and eyes widened.

"Grandma…" He exhaled.

"Oh, Mom," Sawyer gasped.

To our left were a smaller bedroom and guest bathroom, then the stairs that led to the apartment on the second floor. At the far end of the room, straight in front of us, were two windowed doors. They were closed, but they led to the wide-bricked aisle of the stallion stalls. Just in front of us was a long dining table with a dozen chairs surrounding it. In the far corner was a large buffet with a coffee pot, wired tiered serving baskets, and napkins with the Bijou Bay logo on them. A long, dark leather sofa and two over-stuffed chairs set at an angle facing the fireplace.

Above the mantle was a portrait that my daughter and grandson were staring at with mouths agape. It was a large painting of me in full western attire and standing between the stunning palomino stallions, Lucas and Honey. My hair was unseen in a ponytail under the dark brown cowboy hat that was the color of the suede chaps. The intricate gold rhinestone suit-jacket I wore complimented the golden horses.

"Your father had it commissioned right before he passed away, but I didn't accept it until last year," I admitted. "It seemed a bit indulgent until Bubb and Pauline convinced me it wasn't, it was pure love from Marcus."

Tears fell from Sawyer's eyes as she slowly walked to stand in front of the fireplace and take in the painting. Rafe was at her side, so I lowered onto one of the chairs at the dining table.

"I remember that trip like it was yesterday, even though I was only ten." Sawyer whispered. "It was the AQHA World Championship in Oklahoma…Dad was so proud of all three of you…and so was I…everyone."

"It was a huge accomplishment," I smiled at the memories.

"Look at those trophies," Rafe huffed, then turned back to me. "Are the ones on the mantle in front of it the ones in the picture?"

"Yes," I smiled. "And the official portrait for the wins is there, too."

He stepped up on the wide rock base of the fireplace for a better view of the photograph.

"And these buckles and ribbons," Sawyer pointed to the center of the mantle.

"As a three-year-old, Lucas won the World Championship in Jr. Reining, and Honey won the Senior Reining Class," Sawyer told him. "And, with his placing in other events, Honey won the Super Horse that year."

"Lucas placed Reserved Champion in Jr. Trail and fifth in Jr. Western riding," I added.

"That was a spectacular competition to have both stallions winning the reining," Sawyer sighed.

"And Honey the Super Horse," Rafe walked in front of the mantle and looked at each award. "He WAS super."

"Well, the wall to your right proves that," I chuckled.

They both turned and their eyes widened. The wall to the right of the fireplace and the front wall were layered with shelving, which was full of trophies, ribbons, and buckles the two horses had won throughout their careers. There were also trophies on tables throughout the room that were won by their offspring.

"Holy heck, Grandma!" Rafe gasped.

They walked forward to take in the display of accomplishments.

"I've been competing for 50 years," I said proudly. "I'm glad I have something to show for it."

Rafe chuckled but Sawyer was transfixed. She had never seen the more elite trophies I had won all together. Until I had purchased the ranch and needed to show my accomplishments as a marketing tool, I had never placed them all in one room. It was very rewarding to see them; they gave me a sense of accomplishment.

Sawyer turned and looked around the room again. There were two large, framed prints of magazine covers that I had graced with the horses and numerous award presentation pictures. One cover had a picture of Lucas and I in the middle of a sliding stop and the article declared me a legend in my time. That had been the first time I had heard that word to describe me. I had been embarrassed, but Marcus had been full of pride and agreement.

In the corner to the side of the fireplace, was a bookshelf that held smaller trophies, ribbons, and framed pictures from when I was a teenager. At the time, there was no division of classes, so I had competed against the best riders in the nation. It just drove me to train more so I could win against them. This small collection of awards won in Western and English classes with my horse Henry were very special. After Henry's passing, I changed disciplines to Reining and showing Quarter Horses.

Sawyer turned to me with soft eyes, as if they were looking into the past.

"All of this because of Jesse," she whispered.

She had gone to the past.

"Yes," I nodded, and my lungs tightened, so I turned to Rafe, "Now you know why we call it the Trophy House." He chuckled. "So, let's introduce you to the stallions that are here."

"Oh, yes, Grandma," He grinned. "Can I come back and look at the trophies?"

"You'll be here all summer and when no one is using the apartment upstairs, you can come in whenever you like," I crutched toward the glass doors leading to the stalls.

"Is anyone up there now?" He asked and looked up the wide stairway.

"No, you can go look," I stopped.

"Me, too," Sawyer chuckled, and they jogged up the stairs.

At the top of the stairs was a long sofa with a window behind it that overlooked the stallion stalls. A wood dining table led to a small kitchen with a long island that had a wrought iron rack above it that held brass cooking ware. Decorated in brown, gold, green, with a dark wooden floor gave it a warm and inviting atmosphere. One bedroom and a large bath completed the small apartment.

"That is so cozy," Sawyer jogged down the stairs.

"I want to live here when I grow up," Rafe grinned.

I chuckled, "If you still feel that way when you grow up, you can."

"Now more horses!" Rafe opened both glass doors and strode out into the aisle.

Sawyer chuckled and stood with me as I crutched down the one step entrance. There were six stalls on each side but only three had stallions in them. The wall facing the aisle was made of strong mesh so we could easily see the horses.

"Only three?" Rafe called out as he stopped in front of a stall with a buckskin stallion looking at him.

"Two just left with Jeff and there are two down in Arizona right now in training," I explained.

"How come these three are in here and not with Lucas?"

"Lucas is very good with all horses so when it's not breeding season, he enjoys the days in the pasture. These in here are retired, moody with other horses, and need a little extra attention," I answered.

"Like Miss B?" Rafe asked and tickled the horse's nose through the stall screen.

"Yes, that is Danny," I opened the stall door, and the horse nuzzled my hand. "He is twenty-six and has arthritis, so he needs to be contained. We take him to the back pens for exercise each day but keep a close eye on him so he doesn't hurt himself."

"And this brown horse?" Rafe stepped to the next stall.

"That is Freddy, and he is nippy so don't ever get close to him," I ordered.

"How old is he?" Rafe asked.

"He is thirty, very retired, and likes to go outside and lie in the sun on sunny days," I answered.

He walked down three more stalls.

"This one is younger," Rafe said.

The sorrel horse stepped to the stall door, and I opened it. The horse immediately nudged at my side.

"This is Boudreaux, a real people lover but he is blind in one eye," I ran a hand down the horse's nose. "He is usually in the pasture with older retired horses or by himself."

"What happened?" Sawyer asked.

"Rough housing with the other horses," I sighed and ran a hand down the horse's large neck. "He had a very successful career before the injury and has a phenomenal pedigree that matches well with Lucas and Honey's offspring. Three of the horses that left for Arizona are a cross of Lucas' daughters and Boudreaux." I turned to Rafe. "Why don't you go to the room at the far end on the left and get the halter that has Boudreaux's name on it. We'll take him out into the sun."

I let Rafe lead the horse down the aisle and to the round pen at the back of the property. Sawyer and I followed behind.

"Mom," She said low enough Rafe would not hear her.

"What?"

"The Trophy House…all these wonderful stallions…all because of Jesse."

I nodded.

"You don't think there is any way of finding him?" Her eyes were pleading.

"No, we have no name or idea if he stayed with the cowboy."

"I hate to even think it or bring it up, but were there any records that the company Betty worked for had on him?"

"He said he only told them his name was Jesse, and he was someone else with the other foster families," I sighed. "His dad brought him over from New Zealand."

"Well, damn," She sighed and walked forward to open the gate for Rafe.

We were standing next to the white fence watching Boudreaux trotting around the small pasture when Lenny appeared leading the other two horses to the pens for exercise. "The client just arrived for the AI."

"Excellent timing," I smiled at Sawyer and Rafe. "You two can see the clinic and watch the procedure."

The clinic building had three rooms. The large door to the left led into the stallion station where the semen collection was completed. The center portion of the building was the laboratory and business office while the right side led to the examination room which had two pipe stalls for examining the horses and three large foaling stalls.

We walked through the center door that led to the laboratory and office. A long work-station island ran down the middle of the room and held the equipment for processing the semen in preparation for insemination on-site or in preparing it for shipping. Across the back wall and down the right was a wide counter for the computers and books. Overhead bins ran the length of the counter. The room was basically white and chrome. The color came from the office chairs and the framed prints of all my stallions through the years. Some, like Honey, had passed, a few retired, and there were those on the road and in the stallion barn. They were a testament to the bloodlines in my herd; brood mares and competition horses.

"What do you do in here?" Rafe asked.

Anna walked him around the room and described the equipment, then we walked out the side door to the examination room. Pauline had just tied the client's mare into the stall. I leaned onto the stool in the corner of the room to give my leg and arms a much-needed rest while Rafe and Sawyer watched. When Pauline slid on the long plastic glove over her arm then began to slide it into the mare, I glanced at Rafe. His eyes widened but he remained quiet.

With her free hand, Pauline pushed the buttons on the ultrasound monitor until the black and white image began to swirl.

"Come here, Rafe," Pauline glanced at him, and he was quickly at her side. She pointed to a large black spot in the middle of the screen then to a small circle at the bottom. "See that?"

"Yeah, what is it?" Rafe whispered.

"The beginning of a horse," Pauline grinned.

"What?" The client gasped. "She's already pregnant? But they told me she didn't take last time."

"Well, she did," Pauline pushed the buttons to capture the image then withdrew her arm from the horse.

The client stared at her a moment then huffed, "Well, shit."

Pauline chuckled, "She's pregnant. Isn't that what you wanted?"

"Well, yeah," The client sighed. "But now I really wanted a Boudreaux baby."

"We can work on that for next year," Paulina shrugged.

"We don't have much choice now." The client chuckled with a shake of the head and untied the horse from the stanchion.

When the client drove away, Sawyer helped me slide onto the back seat of the 6-wheeler.

Rafe looked at Pauline, "Can I ask you something?"

"Always," She answered.

Sawyer and I turned to look at him in anticipation.

"When your arm was in the horse, what did it feel like?" He asked in all seriousness.

"Warm, tight, and squishy," Paulina chuckled.

"Cool," Rafe smirked then slid behind the wheel of the 6-wheeler. "Where to now, Grandma?"

"Back to the house so I can rest, then this afternoon we'll set up the arena for tomorrow."

*****

Monday morning, I crutched out of the clinic as the truck and trailer pulled to a stop. Rafe and Sawyer were at my side while Lenny was hurrying forward to greet the guests.

A very handsome, dark-haired cowboy stepped out of the driver's side with a wide grin to Lenny. When he turned to us, his eyes widened in surprise.

CHAPTER TWELVE

Camille Madison walked around the front of the truck and I stopped. Her long dark hair was pulled back in a braid and she wore blue jeans and a yellow shirt with a large 343 blazoned on the front. In the picture that I had downloaded, she wore striking makeup that was perfect for the image. But now, she wore minimal makeup and her resemblance to me was even more evident. It was like looking in a mirror thirty years before.

"Wow," Caleb huffed as he turned from his girlfriend to me.

"I agree," Sawyer grinned and stretched a hand to Camille. "You look more like Mom than I do."

Camille smiled, "I take that as a great compliment."

I nodded, "As do I."

After the introductions were complete, Camille looked down at my encased leg, "I didn't realize you were hurt. We could have postponed."

"No need," I smiled and nodded to Sawyer. "My other daughter will be riding with you as I instruct."

Sawyer and Camille's laughter filled the air.

"I love horses," Rafe said loudly. "Can I see yours?"

"Absolutely," Camille grinned at him. "All these horses we saw driving in aren't enough for you?"

Rafe shook his head with eyes twinkling, "There can never be enough horses."

"I agree," Camille chuckled, and they walked together to the back of the trailer.

Caleb opened the trailer gate and stepped in to unload a beautiful red filly with a wide white blaze.

"This is Piper," Camille announced as she took the lead rope. "She was my birthday gift from my family."

"Nice present," Rafe grinned.

Camille wrinkled her nose with a smile to him, "That's what I thought. Best gift ever."

Caleb walked out of the trailer with a beautiful brown mare.

"What's her name?" Rafe asked.

"This is Ember," Camille answered. "She belongs to the Rawlins family, but they let me enjoy her."

"She's beautiful," Sawyer said. "…and in great shape."

"Between ranch work and roping, we ride nearly every day, and her diet is watched to maximize what she needs," Camille beamed.

"One of the most pampered horses around," Caleb added with a proud grin.

"We'll start the day with her in saddle for Ranch Versatility," I informed them. "Rafe and Sawyer have a course setup in the arena."

"I got to design some of the obstacles myself," Rafe grinned.

I crutched toward the arena with Lenny and Caleb on each side of me. Jane, the palomino horse Sawyer was going to ride, was tied to the hitching post at the arena gate. Miss B was also there for Rafe to ride. A flat-bed trailer had been pulled alongside the length of the arena. I could sit comfortably with a good view above the fence of all the obstacles in the course.

Once I was settled onto the reclining lawn chair and an umbrella set up to protect me from the sun, Caleb and Lenny moved Camille's horse trailer then disappeared.

The first part of the day was spent with Sawyer riding through the course followed by Camille then Rafe. They rode over logs, over a bridge, into a square where they spun right, then left, then continued to a gate that had been set up in the middle. They maneuvered through it by opening then closing then rode to another log that was a foot off the ground and had to side-pass down the length of it then turn a 180 and side-pass back down. Logs were placed in two different star patterns that were to be ridden at a trot and a slow lope.

Rafe's addition was a post that held a rope with a cow hide tied to the end. They had to drag the cowhide the length of the arena then lift it and trot it back to the beginning post. His favorite obstacle he created was a blue tarp laid in the corner with water on it. He had designed them from my videos that he had watched over and over again.

I had started Camille on the versatility ranch horse competition to judge her riding ability and temperament. Although her brown horse did well on most of the obstacles, there were a few she did not like, but Camille held her frustrations in check and managed to get her through each one. Rafe's horse, Miss B, had competed in trail classes most of her life so no obstacle was refused or missed. She was a good teacher for him and he, of course, had to tease his mother and Camille every time he completed an obstacle faster than they did.

There were times the three riders were silent in concentration and other times they laughed and teased each other. It was a very good start to three days of training sessions.

Through the training, the two-year old filly Camille had brought along stood tied to the hitching post outside of the arena and watched the horse and riders. She was a pretty filly with intelligent eyes and muscular but sleek conformation.

When the riders rode to the fence next to me for a break I nodded to the horse, "Tell me about her."

Camille beamed, "Last year when I met Delaney, she was going to look at a new breakaway horse named Memphis. We walked out into a field of yearlings and this little red one came right up to me. She is, literally, the first horse I ever touched."

"That's cool," Rafe grinned.

"And, for that reason, Delaney and her dad gave her to me for my birthday," Her grin was full. "I was so surprised and overwhelmed."

"Where did they get her?" Sawyer asked.

"The Parkston Ranch in Madras," Camille answered.

"Jeremy and Alana," I was not surprised.

"Yes! You know them?" Camille gasped.

"I've competed against both of them through the years in cutting and we've also bought and sold each other horses," I answered with a nod then looked out at the pasture that ran along the driveway. "There are two broodmares in that pasture that I bought from them."

"What a small world," Camille chuckled.

"Smaller if you're competing in the same discipline," I nodded. "Their children, Mason and Sammie, have been cutting since they were little. Mason is in Oklahoma I believe."

Camille shrugged, "I help them with their company websites and social media. I've never met Mason, but I did meet Sammie when she purchased Delaney's horse."

"Do you pony the filly with Ember?" I asked.

"Yes, all the time," Camille answered. "When we're home, I'm working with her and doing whatever I can to get her ready to ride."

"Have you ever taken her through a course like this?" Sawyer asked.

"No…" Camille answered.

"Well, then," I smiled. "All three of you did well this morning, but I would like to show you how a complete program would run on a well-trained horse."

"It has been fun," Camille nodded.

"Why don't you pony your two-year old around the obstacles," I said to Camille then turned to Sawyer. "And Rafe can drive you to get Lucas."

"Oh, I get to ride Lucas!" Sawyer grinned and turned her horse.

Camille rode to the filly and had her untied and started through the different obstacles. She was patient as the young horse worked through the unknown poles, the bridge, and the tarp with water. When she neared, Camille stopped the horse and ran a hand down the filly's neck while cooing to her. Her eyes lifted from the horse to me, and she leaned up in the saddle.

"I love this, it makes both of us think," she sighed. "I am going to build something like this at home so I can continue to work with her."

"That is a good plan," I nodded. "No matter what direction you decide to go with her, the basics of learning should be the same."

Camille's eyes rose behind me and narrowed, "That is the beautiful horse I saw on your website. Is she riding bareback?"

I looked over my shoulder to see Sawyer astride Lucas with a wide beaming smile. The gold horse was casually strolling down the black path with the blue sky behind them, white fencing and green trees along the sides of the path. Next to them was Rafe in the ATV.

I retrieved my phone and took a picture of three of the great loves in my life. Only my husband and Honey were missing, but I knew, in their heaven, they were walking down the path alongside their family. I could see them in my memories and my heart constricted, making my hand cover my chest. Tears welled and I had to take a deep breath to keep them from falling.

"Are you alright?" Camille asked softly.

I nodded with another deep breath, "Just spirits of the fathers."

"Can I help?"

I looked back to her to see a look in her eyes that said she understood exactly what I was feeling.

"Thank you…but…these moments…"

The sound of hoofbeats on pavement grew closer and I turned back to see the beaming smile and wonder filled eyes of my daughter.

"Is there even a bridle or halter on that horse?" Camille gasped.

"No," I answered with a pleased smile.

As if by magic, Lucas side-passed to the gate allowing Sawyer to lift the latch, step back so she could open the gate, then he turned and stepped through and moved so Sawyer could close the gate.

"Oh, my gosh," Camille exhaled. "With no tack and she didn't look like she was telling him what to do."

Sawyer rode away from us and began a slow trot around the arena. Rafe had parked the ATV and was crawling onto the trailer. He sat down on the wood slats next to me and set his feet on the fence rail. His eyes never left his mother.

"She cried," he whispered.

I didn't say anything, but my heart ached for her.

"When she opened the gate to the pasture and Lucas walked to her, Mom was crying. She hugged him real tight before I helped her get on." He continued to watch her as he spoke. "She told me they were happy tears because she loved the horse so much and missed his sire."

"Yes…he was very special."

"She said she was happy she got to ride Lucas again because she really wished she could ride Honey one more time."

"Me, too," I whispered and wiped my tears away. After a deep breath, I looked out to Camille, "Lucas is the top of the line, elite trained horse," I told her. She looked from me to Sawyer who rode the horse to the side of the arena next to us. "I want you to see what practice and belief achieves." I turned back to Sawyer. She looked proud on the stallion's back. "Remember to be two obstacles ahead in your plan as you ride."

With hands resting on her thighs, Sawyer and the horse moved over the course with ease. When finished, she moved him into a slow lope around the whole perimeter of the arena. The smile on her face made my heart sigh; she looked at ease and at peace.

"That was outstanding," Camille gushed when Sawyer stopped in front of us.

"Can I ride him?" Rafe's eyes were wide and hopeful.

"Tomorrow," I touched his shoulder and smiled. "We'll start Camille with him in the morning…"

"I get to ride him?" Camille gasped.

I chuckled because I loved that reaction from people that I allowed to ride my personal horses.

"Yes," I confirmed. "We'll clear the arena by morning, then go through a number of disciplines which will include you riding him through a reining pattern."

"Then me?" Rafe asked.

"Then you can ride him in the field over there," I pointed to the cleared area in front of us. "But, for now, we have lunch waiting for us in the Trophy House and Camille can see her apartment for the next couple days."

"I'm starving," Camille chuckled and looked over to the buildings. "But I have no idea where Caleb disappeared to."

"I'll text and let them know we are going in for lunch," Sawyer said.

All the horses but Lucas were released into the pasture next to the arena. The two women helped me from the trailer and onto the backseat of the ATV then walked Lucas to one of the outdoor pens next to the clinic. Rafe took great pride in driving the three of us women to the Trophy House.

The meal was finished and everyone was looking over the trophies when my phone rang.

"Hello, Anna," I answered.

"Um, Vic? Did you happen to go internet shopping last week?"

"I don't think so, why?"

She chuckled, "Maybe while you were on pain killers, because you just had a couple dozen packages delivered."

"Really? What is it?"

"I have no idea, but it looks like they are all from Amazon. You want me to have them taken to your house?"

"We'll come over there. I want to show Camille and Caleb the clinic."

I was quite shocked at the number of boxes, large and small, that were stacked in the corner.

"What is it, Grandma?" Rafe asked and picked up a box.

"I'm not sure," I answered and lowered onto one of the chairs with the encased leg stretched out in front of me. It was beginning to ache.

Rafe pushed a large box to me, and everyone patiently waited as I opened it.

There was a foot-long metal ranch truck with a two-foot-long horse trailer inside.

"Oh, Grandma!" Rafe gasped. His eyes were wide and questioning as he looked at me.

"I'm guessing I bought it for you," I chuckled and looked at my daughter. "I remember thinking the other night that I didn't have anything for Rafe to play with and there is a hazy memory of shopping in the middle of the night."

The group chuckled as Rafe began to take the large vehicles out of their carton. Caleb leaned down with a pocketknife to help.

"So, you have no idea what's in all these packages?" Sawyer grinned and handed me another box.

"Not really," I opened the next box to find a set of scented candles in decorative containers.

Sawyer took them from me with a chuckle and handed me another box.

By the time I was done opening the boxes, there was a large fire truck for Rafe. It was metal and at least three feet long. He also had another large truck but it pulled a flatbed trailer with a construction backhoe on the back. There were a few comforters, a bed pillow, socks, a woman's robe, a set of gardening tools, a forehead thermometer, a package containing six t-shirts for Rafe, three large boxes of chocolates, a decorative glass container filled with tea packets, and finally ink cartridges for my printer.

"That is quite the array of mid-night shopping items," Camille chuckled.

The last boxes contained even more large metal toy vehicles for Rafe; a Jeep pulling a trailer with an ATV on it, two more trucks, and the last box contained two large farming tractor replicas.

"You have a whole fleet of vehicles," Caleb grinned at Rafe as they continued to open the containers. "I'm pretty jealous."

"You can play with me," Rafe rolled one of the trucks across the floor to Caleb who grinned and reached out to it.

"Mom, are you sure you don't want to return a few of these?" Sawyer asked.

Rafe gasped and turned wide eyes to me.

"No returning," I promised him.

CHAPTER THIRTEEN

Insisting she did not need help; Sawyer was in the house fixing dinner while I was back on the outside sofa with leg propped with Camille in the chair next to me. Our conversation about the next day had trailed off as she watched her boyfriend and Rafe. The pair were in the yard with the fleet of vehicles that had arrived along with every plastic horse or cow Rafe could find. Their chuckles and engine noises filled the air.

"That man of yours is quite something," I mused with a glance to Camille.

She nodded with a soft smile, but her gaze was over the blue water of the bay. She looked like she had drifted away.

"He is a wonderful man…very true heart," she whispered.

"Your eyes light up when you see him, and his when he sees you. Is it serious?"

Her eyes cleared and she glanced at me then out to the pair playing with the toys.

"I think…I know it could be if I could just…" Her eyes began to glisten.

"What we say, is between us," I whispered. "If you need to talk, I am here."

A hesitant smile appeared, "When I was growing up, through middle school and high school, I didn't really have a boyfriend. In college, I had one, but it was never going to be serious…it was just for fun." She sighed and looked back over the water. "Last year, I had four." She chuckled and I smiled when she glanced at me. "It started with a nice young man named Matt that I had met through friends. Through no fault of his, I broke it off with him and went searching for my then estranged sister. That is how I met Delaney Rawlins and I met a tall handsome cowboy named Mark the same day. We saw each other whenever I was home and occasionally, he would travel to the rodeos with us. The first of July, we talked and realized we had different goals in life at the time. I had finally started enjoying life with the rodeos and traveling, but Mark was ready to settle down. We parted ways…sadly but amicably."

She hesitated and eyes began to glisten again, "The third was Delaney's surrogate brother…he and his father are part of the Rawlins family, so I had known him for months. He was fun, adventurous, a bareback rider with a huge future ahead of him. When we got together a few weeks after Mark, we…clicked; with family, dreams, and adventure. We talked about everything from then to up until the day we were old together raising horses and cattle."

"What happened?" I asked.

"He was killed in a car accident the day after we spent our one and only night together," A tear fell, and she wiped it away with a glance to Caleb. "I had the privilege of loving him for only two weeks."

"Oh, damn…" I sighed and felt my own tears rise.

"Hmmm," She nodded. "I lost a whole lifetime of dreams and adventures we had shared."

"Then Caleb?" I whispered.

She nodded with a sweet smile appearing, "We met in December at the NFR. He is intelligent, driven, has goals he won't deter from and encourages me in mine. Then there is the fact he's cute, sexy, and has the kindest, most sincere heart."

"There is a glow between you two," I smiled. "It reminds me of my late husband and myself when we first met."

"How long were you together?"

"Thirty-Eight wonderful years," I answered. "We met when I was eighteen, married when I was nineteen, and he passed four years ago suddenly of a heart attack."

She gasped, "That had to be devastating."

"It was," I nodded. "I sold the house we had lived in most of our lives and bought a small training facility in Arizona and this ranch; my Bijou Bay. I did not want to live in that house without him."

"I understand that," she nodded.

We remained silent and listened to Caleb tell Rafe about the bucking horses his family raised.

"And now? With Caleb?" I whispered.

"I am having a hard time letting go of Craig," she admitted.

"Of Craig, or the fear of losing Caleb if you let your heart go?"

Her breath quivered, "I haven't had the best luck with family. My mother left me with an alcoholic father when I was three. My stepmother was wonderful but she died a few years ago. My father drank himself to death 18 months ago. Lacie Jae and I had a difficult relationship until last year."

"How is Caleb's family?"

"Solid as a rock; twin sister he adores, parents that love each other more with every day. They share dreams and encourage each other. They are what every family strives to be."

"His solid foundation can very well help balance your rocky one."

Camille wiped away the tears then turned to me, "I hadn't thought of it that way."

"He knows your history?"

"All of it."

"Obviously, our pasts with men are not the same, but I have seen a lot in my 61 years," I smiled and was relieved to see her relax and the tears stop. "Are you, in some way, still holding onto the dream that you and Craig had shared? You can't have him, so you hold onto the dream you had with him?"

She exhaled, "Yes…I think I am."

"It could be that by letting go of that dream you'll be losing him again…or forgetting about him?"

"Yes, you are so right," Her tears welled again.

"Craig will always be a part of who you are now. That, you can never lose. Maybe having a short time with him prepared you for your future. You know to appreciate more what you have now because it can be gone so quickly."

"Oh, Victoria, that is so true," She looked out at Caleb. "I can't imagine there is another man out there now that can make me as happy as Caleb does. I need to let go of the past and appreciate him, love him, and cherish every moment we have together." She turned to me with a smile and eyes wide, "I cannot thank you enough for talking with me. I also can't believe I only met you a few hours ago."

Sawyer walked from the house in time to hear the last sentence, "Well, I think you two must have been mother and daughter in a past life."

"You have the best mother," Camille grinned.

"I agree," Sawyer smiled at me with love shining in her eyes and my heart sighed. "And I know that she has enough love and wise advice, so I have no issue sharing her with her daughter from another life."

Camille laughed and stood, "Well, can I help my other life's mother's other daughter with dinner?"

"Wow, that's a mouth full," Sawyer laughed. "It's all ready. We just need to bring it out to the table."

*****

Tuesday morning, Sawyer stood in the arena and instructed Camille through a simple reining pattern. Camille was riding Lucas and a wide smile had been on her face since she put a boot in his stirrup.

"Looks like you fifteen years ago," Pauline sat in the chair next to me with a coffee cup encircled in her hands.

I chuckled, "More like Honey and I thirty years ago."

"True, but I only saw videos of that," She sipped the coffee. "What are they going to do this afternoon while we're gone?"

I turned and looked at her in surprise, "Where are we going?"

"Ah, Vic," she smirked. "I knew you forgot about your doctor's appointment to get a cast put on."

"Well, hell," I sighed. "Sawyer wanted to show her polo, so I guess they can do that. With as many years as she played, she would be a better instructor at that than I would be."

"She was a good polo player. Too bad that husband of hers took her away from it."

I glanced over my shoulder to see where Rafe was riding. I didn't want him to hear any disparaging words against his father from any of us. He and Caleb were riding through one of the large pastures and their laughter carried up to us.

"Come to a halt in the middle where you started," Sawyer instructed.

"Have her do spins!" I called out.

Sawyer's hand rose in acknowledgment while Pauline and I leaned back into the chairs. The rest of the morning was spent watching everyone ride Lucas through a pattern; even Lenny, Pauline, and Anna. Bubb was somewhere in the buildings and didn't make an appearance at all. Just before we left for the doctor, Camille rode Lucas in a complete pattern, and for someone that had never ridden in reining before, she did a damn good job.

When we returned, I wore a cast that ran from the base of my toes up to mid-thigh. It was also purple. As I settled back onto the chair on the trailer, the four polo players, Caleb, Rafe, Sawyer, and Camille, trotted to the fence to greet me.

"Grandma!" Rafe grinned. "I love that color."

"It's my favorite, too," I smiled. "I figured if I had to spend five or six weeks in it, the darn thing should be pretty."

"Sounds logical to me," Camille laughed and leaned forward in the saddle. She was riding a golden palomino four-year-old mare out of Lucas and a daughter of Boudreaux. The white mane flowed down the horse's shoulder and forelock nearly to the tip of her nose. "Reining, polo, and now what?"

I loved Camille's energy, "Team sorting is next on the list. I'll call Bubb and have him bring a dozen steers into the indoor arena."

"Yes!" Caleb grinned. "I love sorting."

"Let's do it," Camille nodded.

I pulled out my phone and took a deep breath of patience. It was not right for a boss to be reluctant to call an employee because of their attitude.

"The indoor arena is already set up, and the steers are in the back pen and ready," he answered.

Well, that was a pleasant surprise. "Thank you…"

"You gonna make me stick around or do I get to go home?" Pleasant balloon busted.

"I don't want that attitude around these clients so go home and we'll talk tomorrow."

I ended the call before he could respond.

"We're all ready to go," I called out to the riders who had wandered back into the arena.

Sawyer and Camille were in a corner as Sawyer instructed Camille in teaching a horse to spin. The palomino mare was a futurity Reiner who already had more than $20,000 in earnings so she was a good training partner for Camille. Caleb and Rafe were laughing as they were tapping the polo ball back and forth.

Lenny appeared at my side with a grim smile.

"I'm guessing you're the reason the arena is set up and ready?" I asked.

"Not really, he was already working on it when I went back to help move the panels in place."

He helped me down from the trailer and into the 6-wheeler. The afternoon and evening were spent in the indoor arena as Lenny led the group in team sorting then cutting.

Anna appeared with pizza for dinner, and they all found seats around me on the bleachers that were set at the end of the indoor arena.

"What's on the line for tomorrow?" Camille asked.

"Western Pleasure and English in official wardrobe," I answered with a smile. "Sawyer went through my show closet and chose your wardrobe."

"Oh, fun," Camille grinned. "Can I use the pali mare for that, too?"

"She is a dream, isn't she?" I smiled. "How did you choose her to ride today?"

She grinned guiltily, "Lenny recommended three in a pasture, and honestly…I chose her because she looked like Lucas."

"Good reason," I chuckled. "She'll be good for tomorrow."

"Oh, good," Her eyes were lit with anticipation and excitement. That was the look everyone should have when they go to ride their horse.

*****

"I have to leave at noon today," Caleb announced the next morning at the arena as he helped me into the chair on the trailer.

"Is Camille going with you?" That would be very disappointing. I had really come to care for and enjoy the woman.

"No, I'm flying out from Spokane, and she will drive out tonight or in the morning."

"Well, I'm glad she's not missing the day, she'll have fun…besides, I've enjoyed having her here."

Caleb leaned against the fence and looked up at me, "She has enjoyed herself, too. You made her feel like family from the start and that is what she has needed in her life."

"Between the Rawlins and your family, she is surrounded by those that care."

He smiled slightly, "She is very easy to care for…when she lets you."

"It did help that she is a daughter from my past life."

We both chuckled and his eyes shifted behind me and widened.

"Holy hell…" he whispered.

I looked over my shoulder to see the woman in question strolling toward us in tan English breeches that defined her tall slender figure perfectly. Her long dark hair was curled and hung over her shoulders and down her back. To-the-knee riding boots, black helmet, a clinging white top under a dark blue blazer completed the epitome of a sexy English model.

Many times, when I wore those exact clothes, my husband had looked at me the same way Caleb was now looking at Camille. And, on occasion, it would make us late for a show.

"Probably a good thing you were out here as she got dressed," I chuckled and looked back at him.

"Yeah," His eyes were fixated on her. "And I have to leave at noon and won't see her again for weeks."

"Well, you better take a picture before she gets here."

When she saw the phone lift toward her, Camille slowed her pace with eyes staring right at him. With a slight smile she seduced him with every step.

"That's just mean," I whispered with a giggle.

"You're right," He chuckled as the camera lowered and he walked toward her.

The moment they met, my mind went back 30 years to my husband and I doing the exact same thing. So many times we would meet, and the rest of the world would disappear as we whispered to each other or just touched a hand or an arm.

As I watched the pair, Camille's words about her lost boyfriend Craig came back to me, *"I had the privilege of loving him for only two weeks"*. I had the privilege of having moments like they were having now for over 38 years with Marcus. How damn lucky was I?

"Mom?"

I pulled my gaze away from the pair and to my daughter who was astride a horse in the arena.

She whispered, "In those clothes, she looks just like you when I was young."

I smiled and my gaze went back to Camille and Caleb, "I was just thinking how lucky I was to have 38 years with your father."

"I remember seeing you and dad like that and I was so mortified you were kissing in public." We both chuckled. "Now, I truly appreciate the love you two had for each other and it seemed to grow every year."

I missed my husband every day. The first years after his death the memories hurt my heart, but now, I had moved on to appreciate every little memory, and loved moments like this that brought back the nearly forgotten ones.

The pair stepped away from each other with their eyes shining with love.

I turned to Sawyer, "We were fortunate to have him in our lives for as long as we did."

"Yes, but I still miss him and wish Rafe would have had been old enough to know him better." Her eyes glistened.

"I do, too," I sighed.

"Look at that little pali!" Camille's voice penetrated the bubble of lost memories.

We both turned to her as she neared the fence with her hand tightly held in Caleb's.

"They look so different with English tack," Camille continued.

I turned back to see the horse standing behind Sawyer.

"Wait until you see her in Mom's western show saddle," Sawyer smiled.

"We'll use the brown tooled one on the pali," I added.

"I can't wait," Camille climbed over the fence while Caleb sat on the trailer next to me.

"Where is Rafe?" He asked.

"Helping Lenny clean stalls," Sawyer answered with a proud grin. "He says he needs to work to earn his riding privileges."

"Good kid," Caleb nodded.

As the two women rode out into the arena, Caleb turned to me, "Before I leave, I wanted to thank you for talking to Camille the other day about Craig."

"I'm glad I could help."

He nodded with a sigh as he watched the riders. "Last night, for the first time, she talked about our relationship farther than just a month or two into the future. I graduate college in two years, and she was talking about how we are going to celebrate. That was big for her. I knew she was scared, but I was willing to wait. She is worth everything that is coming to her in life, and I have my heart set on making her happy every day."

"That is an outstanding goal."

"That was advice from my dad on how he keeps the love alive with Mom."

We chatted about his family's stock contracting business and watched the training.

I continued to be impressed with Camille's desire to learn. By the end of the morning, she had improved, but I was pretty sure she was never going to be an English rider. Thankfully, she admitted it with a laugh then went to change into the Western wardrobe.

The flashy palomino horse was then fitted with my western show saddle and bridle.

"Man, that it quite the vision," Caleb exhaled as Anna led the mare out of the barn. He threw his overnight bag into Lenny's truck. "Glad I stuck around to see that."

"Well, wait until you see this," Sawyer said from behind us as she stepped from the porch of the Trophy House.

We turned as Camille walked out wearing the exact show outfit I had worn for the portrait that hung above the fireplace. Her hair was in a ponytail down her back and the same brown cowboy hat completed the transformation.

Anna, Pauline, and Lenny gasped.

I was transported back to my standing for the portrait with the two horses twelve years before. It was as if it was all happening again. Silently, I watched as her eyes widened when she saw Lucas' daughter in the same saddle he had worn that day. She laughed then turned to me.

"I've seen the pictures and videos, but seeing it in person is just…stunning," Camille ran a hand over the saddle and moved to mount.

"You can't go yet," Lenny waved toward the barn. "Your competition has just arrived."

CHAPTER FOURTEEN

We all turned to see Rafe walk out of the barn leading Lucas who was wearing the same saddle his sire, Honey, had worn in the portrait. I'm not sure who looked prouder, Rafe or Lucas.

Rafe grinned and looked right at me, "Lenny said you would be OK if I rode, too."

I could barely speak from the history swirling in my mind and pride tightening my heart, "You both look absolutely handsome."

Camille turned to me, "I had Sawyer take my picture next to your portrait," She beamed. "Can I take one with you and Lucas, too?"

"Of course, but we need to keep his daughter in there." The horses were positioned, and I crutched myself between them. With a hand on Lucas' shoulder and an arm around Camille's waist, Anna took the crutches.

"That is so bizarre," Sawyer exhaled. "It's like seeing Mom now and when I was young."

Smiling on the outside as the pictures were taken, I was a bit numb inside as Marcus' memory came to life in a vision of him standing next to our daughter and looking at me with pride and love. For the thousandth time, my heart sighed at the loss of him.

"Well, I have to say," Caleb grinned. "If Vic is what I have to look forward to with Camille at that age, I'm pretty damn excited about it."

We all laughed but Camille's eyes shown with love as she wrapped her arms around him. There was an ease and acceptance from her with talk of the future.

"I would like a picture with both my daughters," I said proudly. They both chuckled and with each one at my side and a horse next to them, Anna and Caleb took pictures.

When good-byes were said, and Lenny drove Caleb down the driveway, I turned to the group, "We best get this competition going." I smiled and crutched to the six-wheeler. "Anna, you'll have to drive since my normal chauffeur has his own ride."

"Well, I don't think it is fair I have to go against the judge's grandson and favorite horse," Camille playfully pouted.

"I agree, it's not fair, but I want to do it, too," Sawyer whined.

"Go saddle, Boudreaux," I told her. "He would love the attention."

I watched my three horses as the trio rode in circles to warm up. A day would never pass that I would be tired of the quality of horses I had raised. Marcus had always been proud. My aunt and uncle who had raised me would have been proud, too. Although my parents had never shown an interest in horses, they would have been delighted with the horses, ranch, and life I had lived. In my heart, I knew I had kept my promise to Jesse.

Months would go by without thinking of Jesse until something small would happen to bring back the memory of those two days. At times, it was nothing more than biting into an apple.

"Mom, what do you want us to do?"

Sawyer's voice brought me out of the daze, and I took a deep breath before beginning the lessons that were followed by a fun competition.

*****

"Grandma?" Rafe yawned and rolled to his side on the bed.

I tucked the blanket around him, "Yes?"

"Can I ride Boudreaux?"

"Yes, he enjoyed the ride today."

"Tomorrow?"

"I don't see why not," I swept his bangs away from his closed eyes and smiled at his serene innocence. "He will enjoy being ridden. He still startles easy when someone appears on the side with no eye, so you just have to be careful and ride when someone is with you."

"I will, I promise." He sighed and his head fell forward as sleep took over.

I loved having him here and did not want the summer to end.

I crutched down the hall to find Camille standing at the double doors to the outside deck that looked over the bay. She turned to me, and her beautiful smile was relaxed and happy.

"Such an outstanding view."

"It definitely made the decision to buy this place easier." I settled down onto the sofa and she helped lift the cast and tuck the pillow underneath.

"Is the water called Bijou Bay?"

"No, but to me it is," I smiled. "Bijou is French for jewel, and this was definitely a jewel surrounded by pine trees. I was looking for something different than the sand and cactus ranch Marcus and I owned in Arizona."

She chuckled, "Are you French?"

"I was born and lived in France until I was ten. My parents moved us to the States and had planned on staying for a few years then moving back. I've taken Sawyer over a few times to show her where I lived."

"Well, I'm jealous then," Camille chuckled. "I've always wanted to go to France, but then again, who hasn't?"

"You're more than welcome to come with us next time," I smiled. "Rafe is at an age to appreciate it."

"I would love to. Your daughter is such a joy to be around and so is Rafe."

"I've seen a bit of the person she used to be come out these last few days," I sighed. "She's had a tough couple of years."

"I went through some bad years and understand needing a break from life. Delaney has given me that. Sawyer could come…"

Her words stopped when Sawyer appeared from her room with a wide smile, "Mom? Would you be upset if we did a little hot tub time tonight over the hill?"

"Perfect idea to end your week," I smiled. "You can watch the summer sun set over the bay and don't forget to take wine."

"I'm in!" Camille stood.

"You two go down and have sister time together," I relaxed back into the cushions. "I'm just going to sit here, relax, and watch a movie."

"Do you need anything before we go down?" Camille asked when they returned from changing into swimsuits.

"My little table has everything I need…so go," With a smile, I waved them away and their giggles faded as the door closed.

I listened to the silence until my body and mind became calm. I smiled at the memory of Rafe's giggles when Lucas would gallop and his adoring love for the horse when he finally slid from the saddle and gave the palomino a big hug. Everyone that came in contact with the stallion fell in love with him.

My eyes went to the portrait of his sire.

"Hello, Honey."

Officer Lucas' words echoed in my mind and my eyes closed as I thought of the day I first met the stallion.

"He's good sized for a two-year-old," Marcus said to the seller.

"Yes, sir," The seller smiled proudly.

"Not gelded?" Marcus glanced at me.

"No, sir," The man shook his head. "With his blood-lines, disposition, and looks, we didn't even consider it."

"Vic has moved from showing and is now training in reining and cutting. She has a good horse that's helped her learn, but we're looking for a horse to be the center of our showing and breeding program in the future." Marcus tucked his thumbs in his back pockets. A sign he was relaxed and confident we had found the horse.

I stood in front of the colt and took in the dark gold hide, long white-blonde mane, large expressive eyes, and the calm nature as he stood looking back at me. When my hand rose to his nose, the colt stretched out to touch my fingers. The first touch made me feel warm and safe.

"Hello, Honey," I whispered to him and the discussion between Marcus and the seller faded away. "I've been looking for you for years." I stepped to the horse, and he tucked his nose under my arm as if to say, 'here I am, take me home'.

My hand slid down the muscular neck to his shoulder and up across the wide, flat back. His head had turned to watch me, and I held a hand to his nose. His breath caressed my skin.

"I'm glad I found you." I whispered to him.

It was the beginning of 29 years with the horse. Hundreds of awards, over a million dollars won, dozens of offspring, including three stallions that I still owned; Lucas, Danny, and a six-year-old being shown in Arizona.

Every horse that I was showing came from Honey's bloodline. Lucas was officially retired, but there were still several colts and fillies in competition or in the breeding program. Lucas' foals always sold before they were a year old.

"Queen Victoria?"

"Yes, King of the Pirates?"

"You be strong and have a good life. Promise me you'll have the life your parents would want for you."

"I promise…will I ever see you again? How will I know you're okay?"

"I have Betty's card. I'll send her a letter to send to you and let you know where my adventure led me and that I'm okay."

My eyes opened to look at the apples in the bowl on the side-table, then to the large, framed painting that was the centerpiece on the wall in the kitchen. It was of an apple tree sitting peacefully by a flowing river. Big red apples hung from the limbs and the leaves were an array of yellow, green, and red fall colors. The artist had captured my memory perfectly. Of course, no one knew of that memory when I had it commissioned. Not even Marcus, who liked the painting just for its colors.

My eyes wandered the room until they stopped on a set of three framed flower prints by the front door. They were what I remembered of the pictures in Betty's office. Tucked away in the corner of my dresser, hidden by lotion and perfume bottles, was an old bobble-head doll of an old-fashioned policeman. There were times I would accidentally hit it and the head would bobble and take my mind back to Officer Lucas.

The doll looked nothing like him, except the hat; blue with that big badge on the front.

More horses had been named from that past. Other than Honey and Lucas, Danny was named after my father, and the horse Rafe was taking care of, Miss B, was actually Miss Betty. One of the mares in Arizona with Jeff was named Jewel.

No one knew where I came up with names for the special horses. Maybe, it was time to tell Sawyer the truth. I turned and looked at the bookshelves next to the fireplace. Maybe…

"Mom?"

"Yes?" I whispered and my eyes moved from the bookshelf to the two beautiful women I didn't hear come in. The sky was dark out the windows behind them.

"Are you alright, Vic?" Camille knelt next to the sofa.

"Yes, yes…" I nodded and looked at Sawyer as if in a haze. "I've never told you…"

When I hesitated, she slowly lowered onto the cushions at my feet.

"What?" She asked softly as if afraid I wouldn't tell her.

"I told you about the apple tree we ate from?" My eyes went to the painting in the kitchen.

She turned and her eyes widened, "That's why you had that painted?"

"Yes," I nodded. "And the little bobble head in my room…"

"Officer Lucas?" Her eyes were wide in wonder.

"And the flower paintings…they are what I remember of Betty's office," I looked at them then back to her. "And there is one more thing you should know."

"What?" Tears had begun to glisten.

"On that bookshelf, by the fireplace…the antique book on the easel…it's a copy of the book he read to me," I whispered.

She stood and quickly walked to the shelf and lifted the book. Her eyes widened as she gasped, "This one?"

"Yes…" I exhaled.

"Mom?" She turned unbelieving eyes to me. "The Adventures of Tom Sawyer? You named ME after HIM?"

CHAPTER FIFTEEN

"Yes…" I have no idea why I had never told her the book was why she was called Sawyer. She would never have connected it to the mystery of my past.

Sawyer stared at the book as tears slid down her cheeks.

Camille moved from kneeling on the floor to sit on the cushions at my feet, "Would I be out of line to ask who?" Her gazed moved from me to Sawyer then back.

"A young man from my past that saved me from a horrible situation," I answered with a sigh.

"She just told me about it last week," Sawyer whispered, and the book was pulled to her chest as she turned to me. "I want to find him."

"Sawyer, we talked about that. It would be impossible," I sighed.

"Why?" Camille asked, then leaned back as if she had intruded.

Sawyer looked at me with the question in her eyes, *'Can we tell her?'*

Why not?

I told her the main parts of the story, not the details and certainly not the horrible kiss from Mr. Campbell. But, I did expand on what Jesse had endured to save me from the nightmare of the foster home.

"And the letter just said a cowboy?" Camille frowned. "It didn't say rodeo or ranching?"

"It said he was a cowboy that rode horses that bucked," Sawyer answered with determination in her voice.

"Well, that would be a start," Camille shrugged.

"He changed his name," I shook my head. "We have no idea what his name is, if he is still alive, or even if he would want to be found."

"Horses that bucked could be a trainer or rodeo," Camille mused as if I had not spoken. "But what we would need is an older cowboy that would be around the same age." She rose in her seat and smiled. "I know the exact cowboy…"

"How would you go about that with no name?" I huffed in disbelief.

"We could just put out a post on Facebook with…" Sawyer started.

"NO," I sat up straighter. "A lot of people were affected by what the Campbell's did and I do not want that horrible history brought up for them."

"Oh," Sawyer sighed. "I hadn't thought of that...that is true."

"But, if we had that older cowboy that might have heard of a kid in a foster home that was adopted by a cowboy?" Camille shrugged. "Someone that knew a lot of the older people…"

"Who were you thinking?" Sawyer asked.

"Delaney's dad, Evan," Camille turned thoughtful eyes to me. "He is mid-forties but traveled with his dad when he was young, so that would put the people his father competed with about your age…doesn't it, Vic?"

"In the general area," Sawyer nodded.

"I think Evan knows just about everyone in rodeo that would have competed in the 1960's and '70s," Camille's voice grew stronger as her plan developed. "We can talk to him and go from there."

"Mom?" Sawyer's shoulders were high, and lip caught in her teeth. "What do you think? What would it hurt?"

I thought they were crazy. There was no way that anyone could find Jesse or whoever he called himself. With his adventuring spirit, I could not even fathom he would have stayed with the family of the cowboy very long.

But, what would it hurt? Not for me, but for Sawyer? She needed something in her life besides Rafe. The last few days riding, especially with Camille, Sawyer had come alive again. I wanted to see that continue. So, what would it hurt if I played along with their plan with one twist?

"I think you have to be fully accepting to the fact this may be a wild goose chase," I finally said.

"So, Camille can talk to Evan?" Sawyer grinned and pulled the book closer to her chest.

"No, you can," I answered and looked at Camille. "Sawyer knows the whole story, which I don't want to go through again. So, is there a way she can go with you tomorrow and talk to Evan?"

"Mom!" Sawyer gasped. "What about Rafe?"

"In fact," I smiled at Camille and hoped she understood what I was implying. "Can you take Sawyer for the weekend?"

"Yes!" Camille nodded and reached for her phone, "Let me text Delaney."

"Mom, Rafe?" Sawyer shook her head, but her eyes stared at Camille's fingers as they typed.

I didn't answer.

Camille's phone chimed and she smiled as she looked at Sawyer. "What do you like to drink?"

"What?" Sawyer's brows rose.

"She is going to the liquor store in the morning to stock the trailer, so what do you like to drink?" Camille grinned.

"I don't know…it's been so long," Sawyer shook her head and looked at me with apprehension in her eyes. Camille began typing again.

"Mom, I can't go…Rafe…" She exhaled.

"Rafe and I can take care of ourselves," I waved away the notion we couldn't. "We have everyone here…"

"They can't do everything for you," Sawyer huffed.

"Well, Pauline is here, and it wouldn't be the first time she's helped me take a shower," I chuckled. "I dislocated my shoulder last year and she had to help then. I helped her when she was kicked and had her arm broke."

"But, my job…?" Sawyer whispered.

"You can work from anywhere as long as you have a laptop and a phone," I shook my head at her stubbornness.

"I work in the trailer while Delaney practices," Camille added and lifted her head from the phone. "And that's it. Delaney said we'll make sure you know what alcohol you like by the time we bring you home…whenever that might be."

I chuckled. My plan had worked.

"What?" Sawyer gasped.

"We get home in time tomorrow to drop off the horses, then we're off to Prineville. Home Saturday so you can touch base with Evan, then we're on to Colorado, then Montana, Wyoming, Utah, Oregon…and maybe back and forth and maybe not in that order…and Canada for the Calgary Stampede." Camille laughed and her eyes shone with excitement and adventure. That is what Sawyer was missing.

"Mom…I can't…" Sawyer's voice trailed as her mind processed what was happening.

"You need to go pack," I smiled. When her eyes lowered to the book in her hands, I glanced at Camille and winked. She nodded back with a big grin.

"What do I tell Rafe?" Sawyer whispered.

"That you went with your sister on a bonding trip, and will be back in a week or two," I answered.

Both girls chuckled.

"He knows we're not real sisters," Sawyer smiled.

"He will be thrilled that he is in charge of taking care of his grandmother," Camille said. "And you know that is true."

"I do…" Sawyer shook her head in disbelief. "I have no idea what to pack."

"I can help with that," Camille stood. "They don't call me The Sidekick for nothing."

****

Just before sunrise, I stood next to Camille's horse trailer as Sawyer lifted her suitcases into the tack room.

"I just have to go in and wake up Rafe and tell him," Sawyer huffed with a wide grin. "I'll be right back."

Camille leaned into the front of the truck and pulled out her large purse, then a checkbook and pen.

"You've already paid for the training," I reminded her.

She just smiled, then flipped open the checkbook and hovered the pen over the paper, "I want Lucas' daughter."

I gasped in surprise, "What?"

"I love her," Camille grinned. "Ember belongs to the Rawlins and Poppy is young, so the pali will fit right in with my plan."

"Which is?"

"I don't know," Camille laughed. "As much as I enjoyed the English and Western riding…even the polo was a blast, I want to continue with cows and whether it is roping, cutting, or reined cow horse, that's the way I want to go."

"You just haven't decided on which one."

"No, but that little filly can get me any direction I want to go."

I nodded thoughtfully, "I agree, but I didn't intend to sell her."

Camille sighed, and then her eyes narrowed slightly, "Not even to your daughter from another life?" She flashed a sweet conniving smile.

I laughed, "Well…for what you are doing for your sister from another life, then I will consider it. I also would like to know that you have a horse that will not only take you in whichever cowy direction you go, I want a horse that will take care of you, and she will."

"I am so thrilled!" Camille's feet jigged. "I was wondering how I was going to sneak her off the property without you knowing."

"You are an absolute delight," I laughed.

She lowered the pen to paper then looked over her shoulder at me with a mischievous twinkle in her eyes; "Do I get the family discount?"

"Sure," I drawled. "Since I wasn't selling her anyway, why not sell her at a discount?" We both chuckled. "Depends on what you're going to call her. I have no doubt you have already come up with a barn name."

Camille nodded as she wrote, "In honor of her daddy, Lucas, she will be Lucia."

"Well then," I grinned. "As long as you keep me updated on your progress, I'll let you buy her." I told her the amount and she wrote it down without hesitation.

"Grandma! Mom says I'm the boss!" Rafe ran out of the house and threw his arms around me. When he looked up, his face glowed with happiness and love.

"On some things," I relented with a hug.

"Mom?" Sawyer turned with a frown. "What about that horse in Arizona? It should be here tomorrow afternoon."

"Perfect timing then," I nodded. "There are plenty of us here to handle that, but I think you should be the one to tell him?"

"Who, him? Me, him? What horse?" Rafe's head shot between the two of us.

"Yes," Sawyer smiled. "Brownie is coming home to live with us here."

"Oh, Mom!" Rafe cried and fell into her arms. "I thought it would be years before I got to see him again."

"No, he'll be here tomorrow. They were in Utah last night." She answered and while hugging him, she looked at me and mouthed 'thank you'.

I just nodded, "But now, we have three horses to get ready for their ride home."

"Three?" Sawyer and Rafe huffed.

"Yes," Camille purred. "I'm taking that blonde girl home."

"I knew it!" Sawyer declared with a wide approving grin.

Fifteen minutes later, the horse trailer was at the barn with Camille's horses inside and she walked back in for the palomino.

"Mom, are you sure?" Sawyer whispered to me.

We stood at the back of the trailer with Rafe holding the tailgate open in anticipation of loading the horse.

"Of course, I am," I wrapped my arms around her and squeezed tight. "You go have fun…"

"Well, aren't you a ray of fucking sunshine," Camille's irritated voice echoed from the barn.

We both turned in surprise, but she walked out of the barn with a smile that was more of a grimace. She glanced at Rafe, who was too far away to hear what she said. The palomino's head lifted, and ears perked when she saw the trailer.

Camille didn't mention the comment as she walked by and loaded the horse. I turned back in time to see a flash of

Bubb, and I knew. Irritation bubbled, but I ignored it for a moment. I didn't want to ruin the departure. After more hugs were shared, Rafe and I stood in front of the barn and watched the truck and trailer disappear with the two excited women.

I knew they wouldn't find Jesse, but I hoped that Sawyer would find herself in the adventure.

CHAPTER SIXTEEN

"So, if I'm in charge, that means it's time to ride Boudreaux," Rafe grinned at me.

I laughed, "I promised you could, but we'll have to get Lenny's help to get him saddled. Help me into the six-wheeler and we'll see if we can help with chores first."

We motored up and down the long alleyways of the barn; more for fun than looking for Lenny. We caught a glimpse of jean-covered legs just disappearing at the top of the stairway and into the loft.

"What's up there?" Rafe stopped the ATV at the base of the stairs.

"Hay storage," I answered.

"Can I go see?"

"Sure…"

He was sliding off the seat before the word was out of my mouth, which made me smile at his eagerness. His footsteps echoed as he stomped up each step, then there was silence. I waited with head tipped trying to hear him.

"Do you know where Lenny is?" Rafe's voice filtered down the stairs.

"How and the hell would I know?" Bubb's voice growled. "He does his thing, and I like being left alone to do mine."

My back stiffened, heart pounded, and nostrils flared. I slid myself across the seat, so the cast went in the air then fell to the edge of the machine. Pain shot up my leg, but I gritted my teeth and slid completely out. My hand was just reaching for the crutches when Rafe appeared from the stairwell. His normal, cheerful face was somber, and shoulders lowered.

"Get in the ATV and go find Lenny," I crutched a step away from the machine.

"But Grandma…" He said with wide eyes.

"Do as I said."

He sighed, nodded, then drove down the aisle and disappeared around the corner.

It was just moments before footsteps approached from the stairs. Bubb's brows were together, a deep frown made his whole demeanor threatening…and that was not the Bubb I had hired and loved dearly as a friend.

His eyes shot to me when he saw me standing in the aisle. They narrowed slightly as he must have realized I had overheard him.

"I don't know what you said to our client for her to call you a *fucking ray of sunshine*," I huffed. "But I did just hear what you had to say to an eleven-year-old."

He remained quiet, but his jaw worked side to side making his long white mustache twist. There was no doubt he was holding back a rude retort.

I shook my head, "I don't know what's wrong with you, but it concerns me deeply that you have gone from a man people would want to be around to this…crotchety, cantankerous, old man that people avoid. It takes a lot for the workers around here to complain about anything, but you have pushed them to the brink. Being rude to clients is unacceptable, and I see no end to it because you don't see it." I hesitated, hoping he would respond but he said nothing, so I continued. "I have no choice but to let you go, but I am worried enough about you that I will keep your insurance active until you let me know you've made other arrangements."

"A'ight…" He nodded then turned and walked away to disappear in the direction of his truck. It was a company truck, but as far as I was concerned, he could have it.

After a deep breath releasing the tension that had been building for months, I slowly crutched my way to the opening. A step before the sunlight, Bubb's truck drove by and when I stepped out, I turned to watch him drive right by Lenny and Rafe without a turn of the head. Anna and Pauline were leading two mares up to the clinic. They hesitated when they saw me.

When I stopped next to them, I blocked the disappointment and hurt and spoke to them as a boss should to their employees…strong and confident.

"I have retired Bubb," I announced.

"Grandma!" Rafe gasped and his eyes began to glisten. "Not because…"

"Not because of you," I assured him. "It's been coming for a very long time for reasons you shouldn't be worrying about."

Pauline sighed, "It was coming…"

I turned my head with a silencing stare then looked from her to Rafe and back.

"…but we'll just work through it." She quickly stated.

"I'll make a few phone calls in the morning to get summer help hired." I crutched to the ATV. "At least we're not in the middle of foaling season."

"That's true," Lenny said airily as if to lighten the mood.

The rest of the day was quiet as I reflected on the years with Bubb. My heart hurt having to let him go even if it was the right thing to do as his employer. I had to protect my employees, business, and reputation. I knew it was right, but it didn't make it any easier.

Sawyer sent a text when they arrived at the Rawlins's ranch in Bend, Oregon, then she video chatted with Rafe and I while we prepared dinner. There was no mention of Bubb. If I told her, she would insist on coming home to help. That was not going to happen.

The long day came to an end with Rafe and I sitting on the outside couch and watching the sunset while eating ice cream.

"I love it here." He whispered just as the last ray of the sun disappeared.

"I love having you here."

*****

The next morning, he cooked scrambled eggs, sausage, and toast for us for breakfast. He couldn't have been prouder by taking care of his grandmother.

We had a late arrival at the clinic.

"What do you want me to do, Grandma?"

I turned to him with a thoughtful sigh, "Brownie won't be here until after lunch. So, what would you like to do until then? Work, play with your trucks, video games, or watch television?"

His lips scrunched in the corner of his mouth as if thinking really hard.

"Can I ride Miss B?" His voice was full of hope.

"After I get done with work," I was pleased riding was his first request.

"I can check with Lenny to see if the stalls are already cleaned and the horses fed," He shrugged. "Can I…?"

The door opening stopped his question and we both turned to see Anna walk through with a wave and a smile.

"I thought you might be in here," She said to Rafe then looked at me. "Before the first appointment arrives, I'm going to take the 6-wheeler for the big loop and check the property. If you're busy, I thought Rafe would like to ride with me to see if we could spot wildlife."

"Can I Grandma?" His body rose in anticipation.

"Sounds like a perfect plan," I nodded. "But you mind her."

"I will! I promise!" He walked to the door then stopped and looked back before walking through. "Don't be walking without your crutches."

I shook my head, "I'm just going to sit here going over the calendar and horse book until you return." I set the crutches on the floor and tucked them under the desk.

He gave me a wide grin then disappeared out the door.

The room was completely silent. It was the first time I had been left completely alone since I broke my leg. Not a horse pacing in the stall, not a voice, not a peep. I looked around the white lab and relaxed for a moment before reaching for the breeding book. The book was organized alphabetically on the horse's registered name. Since they could change ownership, it didn't make sense to have it by the owner's name. In the front of the book was a daily log that kept track of each horse and the procedure as they were performed. The follow-up and outcome was then written under the horse's pages.

I took the time to go through every entry since the day before I broke my leg. Pauline had kept meticulous notes. There was no doubt she knew I would be looking through the books as soon as I was able. The more notes she kept, the less she would have to explain to me. We both appreciated the arrangement.

After reviewing the last entry, I rolled myself across the room to the refrigerator and withdrew a bottle of water, then rolled to the nearest computer. Just for fun, I rolled myself all the way around the center workstation. It wasn't an easy roll, and I was a bit exhausted when I returned to the desk, but it was a bit defiant and just fun.

Smiling to myself, I wiggled to the edge of the chair, and stretched the leg out. The cast tucked under the desk comfortably and the long blue sundress nearly covered the whole thing. I signed into my account and went right to the emails I had not looked at in a week.

There were hundreds…but I clicked on the one from Bubb that had been sent the night before.

Vic;

I want to make sure there are no hard feelings. Didn't mean to be rude to your grandson, I was just a bit cranky. It will not happen again. Retirement is probably the best thing for me. I feel you have been fair in your keeping my insurance. So as not to waste it, I go to the doctor tomorrow for a full physical. Another appointment is scheduled for next week.

Anyways, I have truly appreciated our working relationship and friendship over the last ten years. Just want you to know that. You are a fine lady, and an honest businesswoman.

If you don't mind, after a bit, I would like to meet for lunch sometime. Let me know if that is all right.

Email to Bubb:

We'll have lunch or dinner after your appointment next week. Set a time and place and I'll be there one way or another. I am glad you are taking care of yourself. I am truly concerned.

I look forward to your response.

With a sigh, I looked through the mass of emails and deleted the dozens from Amazon confirming my orders and those stating the items had been mailed. I had never splurged on shopping unless it had to do with the horses or shows. All the boxes still humored me; there was no way I would consider sending Rafe and Sawyer's gifts back. They had interrupted their life for me, so the gifts were appropriate and fun.

The door opened and I turned in the chair to see an unfamiliar straw cowboy hat over the equipment on the center island.

"Anyone in here?" A deep male voice asked.

"I'm back here," I answered and quickly glanced at the appointment calendar; Harrison Nichols. Was Harrison his hometown or his name? I played it safe. "Mr. Nichols?"

"Just call me Harrison. I brought in the mare we talked about on the phone." The door closed, then he appeared around the side of the equipment island.

He was tall, slender but looked fit, close to my age and looked totally at ease in a brown, short-sleeved, button-down shirt tucked into Wranglers and well-worn boots. His hair was nearly hidden by the straw hat and his blue eyes crinkled at the sides as he looked at me.

"Well, Victoria Rafael-Taylor, herself; I wasn't expecting you," He drawled with humor twinkling in his eyes.

I smiled in return, "Well, I do own the place."

His chuckle was deep as he stopped just far enough away from me that I didn't have to crook my head up to see him.

"Still, after you were recommended, I did a bit of research on you and this place and didn't consider you would be working in the clinic yourself."

Leaning back in my chair, I gave him a humored, curious smirk, "And what did you find in your research? It couldn't have been too bad if you still brought your mare here."

He laughed, "I'm pretty damn sure you know exactly what I found."

"Well, it depends on what sites you're looking at," I shrugged. "Some say good, and some seem to think I'm a bit of a bitch."

He laughed again, "I noticed that, and it seemed to only come from a handful of your competitors."

"Ahh, funny, I noticed that too," I chuckled. "You spoke with Pauline on the phone, and she hasn't returned from an errand, but I'm sure she made notes." I glanced over my shoulder to look for the horse book but it was on the other counter. "Would you mind handing me that blue binder on the counter there?"

He looked at the binder then at me, and after a hesitation walked to it. He didn't hand it to me; he slid it on the counter next to me instead.

"Thanks," I smiled with an apologetic glance. I hated having to ask for help and he looked a bit annoyed that I did, but I ignored it and flipped open the book.

"I drove down from Hayden Lake and am a bit early," He glanced around the room. "You never know with horses and traffic, and I hate being late."

I nodded in agreement, "Would you like coffee or water?"

"I never turn down coffee."

I pointed to the coffee center in the corner, "They are both right behind you."

There was a slight narrowing of his eyes before he turned. "Would you like anything?"

I tapped the water bottle on the desk and shook my head. When he returned with the cup of coffee, I motioned to the chair across the desk annex, and he lowered onto it then took a sip of coffee.

"Pauline's notes say her name is Willa."

He leaned back and crossed an ankle over his knee and took another sip. He looked completely at ease and natural…as if he'd been in the clinic a hundred times.

"Yes, our family prized mare," He started. "We tried to have her bred last year, but she wouldn't take."

"How old is she?"

"Just eighteen."

"Has she had a foal before?"

"Once…she bruised a leg when she was eight, so we had her bred and gave her the year off."

"How bad was the bruise?"

"My son, Jace, and the mare collided with a horse and luckily it wasn't as bad as we first thought."

My brow lifted, "How did that happen?"

"Jace is a PRCA pickup man," he smiled. "He was sliding in to help a cowboy off the horse when the bronc decided to turn at the same time. They hit shoulder-to-shoulder, and both went down."

"Was your son hurt?"

He shook his head with a slight raise of a shoulder, "Bumps, bruises…nothing serious, but Willa took a kick to the leg that side-lined her."

"Is she sound?"

He hesitated, then answered in an impatient terse tone, "Wouldn't consider breeding her if she wasn't. We've both used her for the last nine years."

"You're a pickup man, too?" I couldn't hide the surprise in my voice and felt a bit embarrassed.

He just nodded as if it didn't sound rude, "Semi-retired now. I just fill in for Jace if he gets hurt and I help with clinics and a few smaller rodeos."

"And what do you do when you're not riding in picking up cowboys?" I hesitated then huffed. "Sorry, that didn't quite sound right."

He shook his head with the smirk, "I've heard the jokes for thirty years."

"Well," I stuttered in embarrassment again. "I didn't mean to make a joke. I was asking what you did outside of rodeo." Trying to cover the embarrassment, I ended up sounding quite condescending.

He hesitated with a slight narrowing of the eyes again, "I train horses." He glanced at the pictures we displayed on the walls of the stallions. "I'm sure not to your caliber, but they are safe, good-minded, and will help rescue or save a cowboy or two."

"Every discipline is different. I have no doubt the horses you train are as high caliber in your discipline as mine are in mine." That sounded awkward, forced, and still too snobbish.

He stared at me a moment too long and his foot hit the floor and the coffee cup was placed on the counter.

CHAPTER SEVENTEEN

The door opening broke the awkward silence.

Rafe appeared with a big grin, "Grandma! We saw a bunch of deer."

His happy aura helped ease the tense atmosphere.

"Any fawns this time?" I smiled a welcome.

"Yeah, but they disappeared too fast," He answered with a curious look to the man he had never seen before.

Harrison stood and smiled down at him, "They hide in the grass really well."

"Rafe, this is Mr. Nichols. He brought a mare in for us to evaluate." I smiled up at him in hopes of easing the tension between us.

"Nice to meet you, Mr. Nichols," Rafe stuck out a hand for him to shake and my smile of pride replaced the uneasy one.

Taking Rafe's hand, he shook it firmly, "You can call me Harrison."

"Like the town? That's funny. I'm Rafe," He chuckled and grinned at me then looked back up. "I love horses, can I see yours?"

"You can help me get her unloaded," Harrison answered and with a 'polite' tip of the head to me, he turned to the door.

Rafe looked over to the other counter and back to me, "Grandma!"

His emphatic tone had Harrison stopped and looking back.

"You aren't supposed to be walking without them," Rafe admonished with a frown. "Where are they?"

"I promise I did not walk without them," I pushed myself away from the counter while dragging the cast along the floor. The purple around the foot was the only part of the cast visible. "I wheeled myself around." To prove my point, I pushed myself across the floor until I was right next to Rafe.

Harrison's eyes widened and he turned back, "I had no idea."

Rafe huffed as he retrieved the crutches from under the counter, "She's not supposed to walk without them."

"And, like I said," I smiled at my protective grandson. "Wheeling myself in the chair is not walking, and I was perfectly safe from falling and hurting myself."

When I positioned the crutches to stand, Harrison was at my side with a hand to my elbow.

"Thank you," I smiled after getting the crutches set under my arms.

"She fell," Rafe said without prompting. "Broke her fibula and tibia." He walked ahead of me to open the door while Harrison remained at my side. "That's why I got to come here." Rafe continued. "I'm taking care of her while my mom is traveling with some friends."

I glanced at Harrison with a bit of grandmotherly pride, "I couldn't ask for a more protective helper."

Rafe turned as he opened the door and pushed it with his back with a proud grin to me then a look to Harrison, "Most the time she's pretty easy to take care of. Sometimes though…" He teasingly shook his head and grinned.

"You little smart-ass," I chuckled and crutched out into the sunshine.

The six-wheeler was to our left but there was no sign of Anne.

"Where is Anne?" I asked Rafe.

"Pauline texted and asked for help with one of the broodmares," Rafe answered.

"I'll stay on this side while you get the mare," I told them and crutched over to lean against the 6-wheeler.

"You be careful, Grandma," Rafe hesitated and looked from Harrison's truck back to me.

"Willa is very gentle and won't be a problem," Harrison smiled down at him with a glance to me. "I promise."

Rafe looked at him thoughtfully then nodded, "Grandma knows her horses, so I guess you know yours."

I chuckled as they walked to the back of the trailer together. Curious brown eyes peered through the slats of the trailer and watched them approach. She stepped out of the trailer and onto the pavement. Rafe was tucked securely to the edge of the trailer and his head tilted way back to look at the mare's head.

"Wow," Rafe huffed. "She's really tall."

Harrison smiled proudly as he ran a hand down the mare's neck, "She is 16.2 hands tall."

"Most of Grandma's horses are 14 to 15," Rafe told him.

Harrison looked impressed, "Reining horses are usually smaller than horses used for pickup men."

"What is a pickup man?" Rafe asked.

The pair started walking toward me as Harrison explained. I concentrated on the tall bay horse walking calmly next to him. My horses, in the closest pasture, were whinnying and bucking behind them, but Willa ignored the ruckus they were making. I'm sure she was well practiced at ignoring rodeo commotion as she did her job.

Anne and Pauline walked out of the barn and toward us just as Rafe and Harrison stopped in front of me. Both women were frowning with sharp whispers between them that stopped as they neared.

Pauline looked right at me, "We need more help."

I nodded with a sigh.

"With you down, Jeff gone to the shows, and now Bubb retired, we need help," Anne added.

"My focus needs to be with the breeding, not helping in the barn," Pauline huffed.

"I agree with you both," I said firmly. "I'll make a few phone calls, but there is no reason to discuss this in front of a client."

Both women startled as if they hadn't seen the man and horse standing right in front of me.

"I'm so sorry," Pauline stammered. "That was very unprofessional of me."

"No problem," Harrison nodded with a polite smile.

"Can I watch you examine Willa?" Rafe asked Pauline.

She nodded, "Of course, how are you going to learn if you don't see and listen?"

"I have no idea," Rafe answered seriously.

We all chuckled, and Pauline motioned to Harrison, "We'll take her around the side."

Rafe looked at me, "Are you coming in Grandma?"

"Yes, but I'll go through the clinic," I answered with Anne opening the door for me.

I leaned against a stool in the corner of the breeding room. Rafe and Harrison were standing close to the ultrasound monitor while Anne was at the horse's head and Paulina was examining the horse at the back. She had been quiet for a few minutes with everyone waiting for her to speak. The ultrasound monitor showed the black and white warping images, and I knew from what I could see and Pauline's silence that there was something wrong.

"She's had one foal a few years ago," Pauline finally glanced at Harrison who nodded. "Live cover or AI last year?"

"Live," he answered.

The screen stopped on a large black hole.

"That is a nice follicle, and she looks like she may cycle within days," Pauline took measurements of the black circle then slowly slid her arm from the mare and took a step back. Without glancing at anyone else she looked right at Harrison. "Did anyone ever tell you that she only has one ovary?"

He huffed in surprise, "No, we've never had an ultrasound on her before."

"Does that mean she can't get pregnant?" Rafe asked with narrowed concerned eyes.

Pauline shook her head, "Just means it can be difficult to get her pregnant."

"But it's possible?" Harrison asked.

"It is, but we need to watch that follicle's growth," Pauline slid the glove from her arm and tossed it in the waste basket before pointing to the screen. "It measures 32mms now and will go to 40 or so as she nears ovulation. The tricky part is catching that ovulation."

"So, examine her daily?" Harrison asked.

"At least every other day," Paulina suggested. "Were you wanting to do live cover? Do you already have a stallion chosen?"

"Yes, and yes, but they only do live cover," He frowned at the screen.

"I'm not saying she won't take with a live cover, but with an AI we can time it and place the semen at the best possible place."

"From what you said, I have only days to decide on a new stallion," Harrison sighed as an arm rose to rest across the horse's rump.

"Keep in mind the shipping time also," Anne added. "Collection and shipping, depending on the company, may take time."

"Many breeders will stop collection in June," I added. He turned to me with a frustrated gaze. "The good news is, there is a good chance she can get pregnant," I reminded him with an understanding smile.

His shoulders lowered as he nodded.

"Grandma has stallions," Rafe looked up at him. "Won't one of them work?"

Harrison stared at him for a moment, then turned to look at me.

In these situations, I never pressed my own horses. The breeding facility was for everyone that needed help regardless if they were using my stallion or mares.

"There is no easier way than to use one of the stallions here," I told him honestly. "But, if you don't want to worry about shipping, there are many breeders within a few hours' drive that might have a horse you would prefer for your discipline."

"I appreciate the honesty," Harrison said. "But I'd be lying if I told you I didn't look at your stallions online when I was referred here. Every one of them is top stock."

"All are cowy," Pauline nodded. "A few are in Arizona, but we do have frozen semen from them."

"Boudreaux …" Anne started.

"I love Boudreaux!" Rafe's eye lit as he looked at Harrison. "He's one of my project horses while I'm here."

Harrison's eyes flickered with doubt, "What does that mean?"

"He lost an eye while playing with the other horses in the pasture," Rafe answered, his innocence unwavering by the doubt from Harrison. "I am in charge of taking him from his stall to the exercise pen twice a day."

"He has done a fine job taking care of him," I smiled proudly at Rafe then looked to Harrison. "Boudreaux is smart, great temperament, and he did fairly well in reining cow horse before he lost his eye."

"At the level he was competing, he couldn't do it with one eye," Anne added.

"But his offspring are doing well," Pauline said proudly.

The horse was a favorite with everyone at the ranch.

"Wanna see him?" Rafe asked. "I'll drive you up to the stalls so you can meet him."

"We don't want to rush a decision," I told Rafe.

"I don't see any reason why I can't be introduced to the horse," Harrison nodded to Rafe. "I'll take you up on that ride."

Rafe grinned and strode to the door with a quick turn back to me, "You coming, Grandma?"

There was no doubt Boudreaux would sell himself so I shook my head, "You can go, and I'll load a few videos of his competitions for when you get back."

"I'll put Willa in one of the pens here," Anne walked the horse from the stall as I stepped into the clinic and crutched to the nearest computer.

It was an hour before the pair walked through the door of the clinic. Both were smiling and it was easy to tell they had fun together.

"He liked Boudreaux, too," Rafe marched up to me with a wide grin. His eyes searched the area around me and stopped on the crutches I had tucked under the desk. He didn't say anything, he just turned back to Harrison.

"Who wouldn't like him?" Harrison chuckled, then turned to me. "I hope you don't mind, Rafe had to let him loose in the pasture so I could see him run."

"I knew he would," I rolled the chair back away from the computer. "Would you like to watch his videos?"

Harrison smirked with a wink, "Rafe told me I had to."

I chuckled and wrapped my arms around my grinning grandson's waist and pulled him close. We watched the videos of Boudreaux and I reining, cutting, and running the cow down the wall for a fast turn.

"Damned impressive," Harrison whispered as the horse turned the calf again then pushed him into the middle of the arena to circle the calf to the right and then to the left. When the run was finished, I brought the horse to a stop and dropped over his shoulder to pat him on each side. Boudreaux walked proudly out of the arena as I sat up with a wide grin to my husband and daughter cheering us from the stands.

"You look so awesome," Rafe whispered.

I squeezed him tighter, and the door opened behind us.

We turned to Anne walking through the door.

"I'm bringing in a few mares for preg tests," she said to Rafe. "I could sure use a driver."

"Sure!" He turned to me. "Is it OK?"

"Absolutely," I nodded.

When they disappeared out the door, I turned to Harrison. "I do not want you to feel an obligation or pressure to use one of my stallions."

He lowered onto the chair next to me, "I don't feel obligated, but I do have an offer for you."

I laughed, "Now, I know you're a true cowboy."

He chuckled, "Hopefully, this will be beneficial for both of us."

"Alright, I'm listening."

"I've been a hand since I started helping my uncle buck bales when I was seven."

"I have no doubt you're quite the hand," I said honestly. "The fact that you've been a pickup man for so long shows that."

"According to your website, Boudreaux's fee is twice the amount I was paying for the other stallion," He hesitated with a serious look. "My offer to you is, I'll give you the amount I was going to pay for stud fees, then, since you need help around here until your cast is removed, I'll work off the difference."

I gasped, "Really?"

He nodded, "You interested?"

"Am I interested in hiring someone that knows everything we need help with, and I don't have to go searching for him?" I grinned with a relieved sigh. The crew was going to be thrilled to have him working with us.

He chuckled, "I don't know about the breeding."

"Pauline, Anne, and I have that covered. It's all the manual labor, maintenance, grounds keeping, moving panels when we need, and helping exercise horses…basically everything that Bubb was doing plus a little of Jeff's chores."

"Whatever you need," He stretched out a hand. "Deal?"

I very happily took his hand to seal the deal.

*****

My body was tired as we drove to the house for lunch, so, after Rafe made us lunch, I lay down on the couch for a short nap. When I woke, there was no sign of my grandson.

CHAPTER EIGHTEEN

"Rafe?" I pushed open his bedroom door, but the room was empty. I crutched back to the garage to find the 6-wheeler in its place, so I made my way out to the patio. He wasn't playing with the multitude of toy trucks and trailers. With a huff, I crutched out the door to the top of the hill above the bay.

He was sitting on top of the covered hot tub looking out at the water: legs crisscrossed, elbows on knees, and chin resting on his fists. He looked deep in thought. It was very out of character for this bubbly boy, so I accessed the stone stairway and my ability to go down them without falling and breaking another bone. One more look at my melancholy grandson and I took the first step. Not bad…so I continued.

The skin under my arms and the palms of my hands ached from the crutches and a light sweat covered my brow by the time I arrived at the hot tub. Rafe turned his head slightly and I could see the tears glistening.

"You shouldn't come down here, Grandma," he whispered.

Without responding, I crutched in next to him so I could put the crutches to the side and rest my elbows on the cover of the hot tub. I had no idea what was bothering him and since he had gone to the effort not to have me see him this way, I didn't ask. Instead, I looped an arm through his bent leg, leaned forward, and kissed him on the cheek. Gently, I lay my head on his shoulder and his head tipped onto mine. He sniffed, turned his face into my hair, and a quivering breath escaped him.

I waited.

Five minutes went by before he lifted his head and wiped away the tears.

"I'm sorry, Grandma," He whispered.

"And what are you sorry for?" I asked in surprise.

"For making you come down here."

"You did not MAKE me come down here. I saw my grandson needed some comfort, so I came to him."

He nodded and looked out at the water, "I love it here. I love the water and the trees, and how quiet it gets."

"Me, too, and sometimes, when it's really quiet, it makes your thoughts louder."

After a pause, he sighed, "I miss my dad."

"Well, that is understandable. I would be surprised if you didn't."

"He got really…sick…is what mom said. I'm not sure what made him sick, but I know Mom was really upset about it."

"Did you ask her?"

He shrugged, "She said when he got in that car accident, it hurt his back, and he needed pain killers to feel better. But the pain killers made him act weird and sell stuff so he could buy more and act weirder." He sighed again. "It happened over and over again until…well, until Mom told him not to come back to the house. She thought someone would try to hurt us, so we went to her friend's house. She tried to make it sound like a vacation since they had a pool, but I knew."

I wondered if he knew about the arrest and the break-in at their house, but I didn't ask.

"Then we came here," he continued.

"I'm very glad you did."

"Me, too," He sighed again. "Do you think I'll see my dad again?"

"Yes," I answered without hesitation. "It may take a while, but you'll see him again."

"But, if I do, and we move back, I won't be here," His voice was low and full of anguish.

"No one knows what tomorrow brings, Rafe. There is no guarantee at this point where you will go at the end of the summer, but I will be here, and you can be here. You and your mother always have a home at Bijou Bay."

"Do you think that's why Mom went with Camille? So, she could figure it out?"

"Yes, she needed some time away to just be a woman and get her life straight again. That doesn't mean she doesn't want to be with you or that she doesn't love you. It's just that she needs a vacation, and she was wise enough to let you take care of me while she takes care of herself."

A slight smile escaped, "You think she's partyin' and drinkin'?"

I chuckled and leaned back, "Yes, I have absolutely no doubt that Camille and her friend Delaney are making sure she has a really good time."

His legs fell forward over the edge of the tub, "Well, it's a good thing you broke your leg then." We both chuckled. "Except, I do miss that pool her friend had."

As he slid off the hot tub, I reached for the crutches. "If you like pools, we need to get you to Silverwood."

"What's that?"

He walked next to me with a hand at my elbow as if he was going to help if I fell.

"It is an amusement and waterpark."

"I'd love to go."

"I'll check with Anne and see if I paid for their tickets, if she would take her kids and you this week."

"But, if you're not going, what would you do without me?"

I laughed, "I have no idea."

As I crested the hill next to the patio furniture my phone alert binged.

Text from Anne: Brownie has arrived.

I turned to Rafe as I lowered to the outdoor couch, "Would you retrieve the old red photo album that is at the bottom of the bookshelf in the living room?"

"Yep," He chirped and disappeared into the house. He returned and set the book on the table in front of me. "What's in it?"

"These are pictures of the first horse I owned," I opened the cover to reveal the dark brown horse. "His name was Henry, and he taught me patience, love, how to heal, and most of all, he taught me how to be a team with a horse."

Rafe leaned over the picture, "He looks like Brownie."

I chuckled, "And that is why I bought Brownie for you." And, why I was so irritated with my daughter when she sold him. "Henry was almost 17 hands tall and when I got him I didn't know how to ride. He was trained in Western Pleasure, showing at hand, and English. He helped teach me about those disciplines."

"How long did you have him?"

"I was eleven when he came to live with us, and he passed away when I was twenty. We had to compete against the very best in the business, so I practiced and took lessons until we began winning and placing. We travelled all over the country together. Henry taught me so very much, just like Brownie has taught you."

"I loved riding Brownie. I've missed him."

"Well, you need to go get the six-wheeler, because Brownie is here."

"Yeah!" He jumped from the couch and ran for the door. He held the door for me then put his hand on my elbow as I stepped down into the garage.

Even in his excitement, he was taking care of me. I adored my grandson.

Brownie was tied to the transport trailer when we arrived. Rafe had barely stopped the six-wheeler when he was jumping out to greet the horse. Lenny, Anna, Pauline, and Harrison were there with the driver.

I sat quietly on the back seat of the ATV and watched Rafe with the horse. I had been just as eager at eleven-years-old when Henry had arrived on our property. Since my aunt and uncle did not know horses, our neighbor, Mrs. Shelby, took over my training from the moment the horse was delivered. She had also helped us find him so she knew what disciplines he could manage. I spent every moment I could with Henry and Mrs. Shelby so I could learn and improve. There was no way I would be able to find Jesse in my local hometown; I would have to become good enough we could travel.

And I excelled. From the first blue ribbon at the first show I competed in, and every show after. I became obsessed with training. Within two years, I had improved enough that I was beyond Mrs. Shelby's ability. She found another trainer for me and by the time I was sixteen, we were travelling across the country. I looked for Jesse at every arena, gas station, or restaurant where cowboys were gathered. I may have only been with him for two days, but I would never forget what he looked like.

It wasn't until I met Marcus that I eased in my search for Jesse. I was eighteen and it had been seven years. I was beginning to realize just how big the cowboy world was. Marcus and I were married when I was nineteen and he encouraged me to become the best competitor the industry had ever seen. I began to train and compete for Marcus instead of Jesse.

It was a trip back east for a competition that had me stopping at a library in Gatlinburg. I knew they would have the area's newspapers on the new computers. I was right, and my heart ached when I read Betty's fate. It was the first time I had learned that neither my name nor Jesse's was attached to the story.

"How do you want to handle this?"

I turned to Lenny and frowned, "Handle what?"

He smirked, "You weren't paying attention to me."

"No," I admitted. "I wasn't."

Rafe was walking Brownie from the trailer toward us.

"Do you want to let Rafe ride…?" Lenny started.

"No," I whispered. "We'll let Brownie settle in today and you can ride him first thing in the morning to make sure he is still safe for Rafe. I'm sure the Nuxoll's treated him well, but I would prefer to know that no bad habits developed after he was out of Sawyer's care."

"And not tell Rafe," Lenny nodded.

Harrison stood next to him and had heard the conversation and was nodding in agreement.

"I'll delay our arrival in the morning to give you time to ride." I turned to my grandson.

"Grandma, he looks really great." Rafe grinned as he stopped in front of us. "He remembers me, too."

"Of course, he does," I ran a hand down the horse's neck.

In just the short walk from the trailer, I could see the horse was in excellent condition. There was no doubt the Nuxoll's had been riding him regularly.

"Can I ride him?" Rafe asked with wide hopeful eyes.

"No," I smiled in understanding. "We'll put him in a pasture and let him get settled in for today and run off that long trip in the trailer." I turned to Harrison. "Would you walk with Rafe to the pasture behind the back pens and put him in with the cattle? It is across the path from my stallion and geldings. There is plenty of room for him to run and they will be able see each other but not touch yet."

"And I can see him from the house!" Rafe added with a grin. "Come on, Harrison. I'll show you."

The man smiled at me with a nod, "We'll stay there just a bit and make sure Brownie doesn't hurt himself in his excitement." He turned to follow the boy and gelding.

I looked to Anne and Lenny, "Let's put together a duty list so Harrison knows what is expected of him."

Lenny nodded, "I took him on a tour of the buildings, and he has already pointed out a few things that need repaired. He was a good hire, Vic."

"I will always miss Bubb," Anne sighed. "But I have a good feeling about Harrison."

I glanced at the man walking with my grandson and his horse then turned to the clinic. I had a good feeling about the man, too.

At the end of the day, I started a video chat with my daughter but instead of Sawyer, it was Delaney that appeared on the monitor. Her long hair cascaded over her shoulders and new highlights made it look a lighter blonde than her pictures. She was grinning broadly with eyes twinkling mischievously.

"Hello."

"Hi," She giggled.

Camille suddenly appeared and leaned into Delaney. Her grin was just as mischievous.

"You two look very guilty." My brow rose in anticipation.

They both laughed, then leaned slightly apart from each other to make room for my daughter's grinning face to appear between them. Sawyer's hair was now cut to the top of her shoulders and layered causing a feathering effect around her face which made her look softer. She rarely wore more than just mascara but now, her green eyes were highlighted in browns and her lashes were thick and full. But the most startling change was the brown hair was now a deep auburn red.

Sawyer laughed, "We decided I needed a change, and since we had a blonde and brunette in the truck, I went red."

"Isn't it stunning?" Camille grinned and fluffed Sawyer's hair.

"It is absolutely stunning!" I gasped and couldn't stop the proud smile. "Sawyer, you look…alive."

Her head leaned back with a laugh and my heart filled with joy.

"I can't wait for Rafe to see it. Is he there?" She asked.

"No, he is out checking the horses with Harrison," I answered.

"Who is Harrison? I haven't heard that name before," Sawyer eyes narrowed in concern.

"Harrison Nichols, I hired him this morning to help around the ranch," I explained.

"I know Harrison," Delaney grinned. "Great choice."

Sawyer turned to her, "How do you know him?"

Delaney chuckled, "My brother, Brodie, is a saddle bronc rider, Harrison and his son are pickup men. He is a damn fine hand, and Rafe will be very safe with him." She assured Sawyer.

"I wouldn't have let him go riding with him if he wasn't," I informed my daughter with a smirk. "So, where are you ladies tonight?"

"In Prineville for the race," Delaney answered.

"Then we go to Colorado tomorrow," Sawyer grinned.

Camille nodded, "Sawyer had some time with Evan this morning."

"It was more of an introduction," Sawyer added. "We didn't get into any detail yet."

"We will be gone to Montana then Cody then back to Montana then Utah this week." Camille said. "Next Saturday, the race is in St. Paul, then Calgary, so we'll have more time to spend with him and ask for his help."

"But for now," Delaney smiled. "We'll let you have time with your daughter before she goes on the road with us, and we corrupt her."

All three women laughed as Delaney and Camille waved, and then disappeared.

Sawyer looked at me with a sigh and a bright smile.

"I am so glad you went," I whispered.

"So am I."

CHAPTER NINETEEN

The next morning, Pauline and Harrison met us at the clinic door.

"I just examined Willa, and she is ready for the AI," Pauline said.

I turned to Harrison, "And you're still wanting to use Boudreaux?"

"Yes, ma'am," He nodded.

"Anne went over to get him," Pauline added, and we all turned to see her and the horse walking down the road between the buildings. "I've already cleaned Willa and wrapped her tail in preparation and Lenny has Abilene, the teaser mare, in the room."

"Can I watch?" Rafe turned to me.

"I asked your mother last night and she agreed you get to watch and learn the whole process," I nodded then turned to Harrison. "Have you ever seen the process?"

"No, ma'am," He shook his head.

"Alright," I nodded. "You two watch this time. Lenny will handle the teaser mare while Anne handles the stallion. Then, while Pauline is processing the semen, they will put the horses back and get Willa ready."

"How long does it normally take?" Harrison asked.

"After collection, about 20 minutes or so," Pauline answered and lifted the long soft leather collection bag from the counter. "We call this the AV bag and use it for the collection."

We walked into the collection room to join Lenny as he tied the mare into a padded pipe stall. The moment a snorting, excited Boudreaux appeared at the door, Rafe, Harrison, and I stood back into a corner and out of the way. The mare squealed as her tail rose to show the stallion she was ready. Boudreaux pranced excitedly, then lifted his front end to mount the dummy horse-body that was next to the stall. Pauline slid the collection bag over the horse's erect penis. After a few moments of thrusts, whinnies, and grunts, she slid the AV bag off as the stallion dismounted.

"The good thing about a stallion of his age," Anne smiled. "He is well trained for the dummy mare, so it doesn't take long," Anne smiled then walked the proud, prancing stallion out the door again.

We followed Pauline into the lab and watched as she removed the semen collection jar from the AV bag.

"There is a little cloth that the semen will flow through first to filter any gel or debris from getting into the collected semen," Pauline tipped the jar for them to see. "We toss that and pour the semen from the collection jar into this large, sterilized tube." She pulled a smaller glass tube from a sterilizing container. "We pour a small amount into a smaller tube and set aside for now. We'll use it to verify the sperm count to make sure there is a viable amount to fertilize the egg and we like to track each collection to chart the data." She lifted another glass tube filled with a white fluid from a container filled with warm water. "The seminal plasma is toxic to the raw semen so we have to use what is called an 'extender' fluid that will dilute the toxicity and help the semen stay alive longer."

"So, the semen is toxic to itself?" Harrison asked.

"Yes," She answered. "Seminal plasma is the liquid that binds the sperm together. The plasma is toxic to itself and will quickly kill the semen."

"That white stuff makes it less bad?" Rafe asked.

"Correct," She poured the extender into the large tube of semen. Harrison and Rafe were watching her closely as she put a cap on the larger tube and set it in a holder.

"Now, we'll process the smaller tube quickly to check the sperm count." She squeezed a few drops of another fluid into a tiny cup in a small machine that was in front of her. "This liquid will basically kill the sperm once we add it so it will stop moving and our little machine here can count it."

"How does it count it?" Harrison asked.

"A small beam of light will be shot through it for density," She answered and used a long spear like device to draw a portion of the semen from the small tube then squeezed it into the small cup. She pushed the green button on the small machine and all three leaned over the top to look at the digital screen.

Pauline turned to me with a smile, "It reads 596."

"Which means what?" Harrison asked.

"That is 596 million per milliliter," I answered. "Which is a pretty concentrated sample."

"So that is good?" Rafe asked.

"Yes, very good," I smiled.

"And that is the data we chart," Pauline added. "It may be low the first collections of the year as it cleans out dead semen but should increase with each following collection. If it goes down or up dramatically, then we may have health issues."

She collected another sample from the larger tube and placed it in a clean small tube, "Now we check mobility." She placed the sample on a slide on the microscope then turned on the small monitor above the counter so we could see small black dots moving across the screen.

"Are those dots the semen?" Rafe asked.

Pauline nodded, "The mass is called semen. When you look at them individually, they are called sperm. The ones going fast across the screen are moving well and the more we have of those in a collection the better chance of the sperm reaching the egg." She pointed at a small dot moving in circles. "This little guy is getting nowhere. So, even if there are a good portion moving, if they are all just going in circles, it is less likely they will travel up to the egg."

"Damn, that's interesting," Harrison muttered.

"Let's get back to the big tube that has our large sample," Pauline stated.

"Even though we aren't shipping it today," I stated. "Show them the process as if we were so they can see the whole program."

She withdrew a syringe from a cupboard and after adding a bit more extender to the large tube she filled the syringe, "We seal it, put a label on it, then write the stallion's name on it immediately so there is no mix-up." She completed the process then lifted a white Styrofoam container from under the counter. "Then we secure the syringe in here, place a thin piece of Styrofoam over it then place a cooling pack over that to prolong the life of the semen for the shipment. Place the top on, tape it, then put it in an overnight package and get it out the door."

Harrison huffed, "So, it really takes less than twenty minutes to have it collected from the stallion to out the door on the way to the mare."

"Correct," Pauline nodded.

"Now for Willa?" Rafe asked.

"Yes," Pauline nodded. "We collect the semen we will use in these large syringes." She collected the semen then handed them to Harrison before we made our way to the examination room.

I leaned on the stool in the corner and sent a text to Lenny.

Anne had tied the mare into the bar stall, "I already sedated her, and we cleaned the area around the opening to keep it as clean as possible." She told Rafe. "We wrap the tail so it doesn't get in the way and helps keep the skin clean."

Pauline walked into the room with a plastic glove over her left hand and up her arm. "I'm going to put my hand inside to make sure everything is OK but first we use this lube so my hand and arm slide easily and we don't hurt her." She pumped the lube from the container on the shelf then slid her arm into the relaxed mare. She pulled her arm almost all the way out and took a long, tiny clear plastic tube from Anne. "This is called a pipette and we'll use it to get the semen from the syringe and into the uterus." She inserted it by sliding her arm back into the mare. "OK...I'm finding the ovary you saw yesterday that looked good. There it is and we're ready." She said to Anne and the syringe was attached to the pipette.

Anne slowly pushed the top of the syringe, and the semen was inserted into the mare. The room was quiet as Pauline removed the glove and Anne cleaned the mare one more time.

"Rafe, look here," I pointed to a poster on the wall that had a diagram of a mare's reproductive system. He and Harrison turned to look as I used my fingertip to follow the process. "The semen was placed here and when it fertilizes the egg, which is called a zygote, it then travels down the fallopian tubes and enters the uterus around day six to seven. It migrates throughout the uterus until about day 16 and typically attaches onto the uterine wall at 16 to 17 days.

"When do we know if she's pregnant?" Rafe asked.

"We'll check in 14 days and if she took, we'll check again at 30 days to make sure the pregnancy is still viable by checking for a heartbeat," I answered.

Pauline looked at Harrison, "If you can, and it is included in the cost, bring her in for another check between three to six months to make sure it didn't slough away."

"Come with me," I stood and turned back to the lab to crutch through the room and out the door.

A grinning Lenny was waiting for us with one of my mares and the youngest foal at her side.

"And, hopefully," I smiled at Rafe then Harrison. "In 360 days from now, we will have one of these little babes next to Willa."

"From your lips to God's ears," Harrison sighed.

"So, we just made a foal," Rafe's eyes were wide. "That is just the coolest thing, ever, Grandma."

I chuckled, "I agree, but once the foal is born, we keep him healthy for a few years and let him play in the pastures. Then, there are years of training and, if all goes well, we are in an arena either winning awards, or in Harrison's case, out saving cowboys from bucking horses and bulls."

Rafe sighed and shook his head while quietly watching the foal prance next to his mother. He slowly turned to me. "Grandma, that is just the coolest thing. I can't imagine anything neater."

"Me either," Harrison grinned.

*****

At lunch, Rafe prepared tuna sandwiches and a bowl full of chips for myself and Harrison. Then he started a video chat with his mother, Delaney, and Camille. He told them about the insemination process, and they hung on his every word.

"How many live covers do you do here?" Harrison asked in a low voice.

"I have a few mares that I trust with my stallions, but other than that, none. After I had a stallion kicked by an outside mare and she broke his penis, I don't take the chance anymore."

He stared at me for a moment with squinted eyes, "Damn, that had to hurt."

I chuckled slightly, "He let us know it did." I cringed again for the poor horse.

"How long did it take him to heal?"

"He was ready for the next season, but the break happened with the first session, so we didn't have any foals from him for a year."

"I think it would take longer than a year for me."

We both chuckled as he picked up the plates and started to walk them to the kitchen sink.

"Hey, Harrison!" Was yelled from the computer.

He stopped and grinned at the monitor, "Well, hell. If it isn't THE World Champion Barrel Racer Delaney Rawlins saying my name. I feel so honored."

They all laughed.

"How is your dad doing?" Harrison asked.

"Just an obnoxious, wise old man," Delaney grinned, and Harrison laughed. "He is the best there is." She finished.

"You are pretty lucky," Harrison agreed. "Tell him hello for me."

"Will, do," Delaney nodded. "Are you going to be at the Coeur d' Alene rodeo?"

"Wouldn't miss it," He answered.

"Great! I'll buy you a beer." Delaney smiled.

"Can I go?" Rafe asked.

"Of course!" Sawyer answered. "But she's not buying you a beer."

We all chuckled then the call ended.

"What now, Grandma?" Rafe shoved a handful of chips in his mouth.

"There is a big brown horse in the pasture that needs to be ridden," I informed him with a grin. "I'm sure we can find a horse for Harrison so he can go on a ride with you."

"Yes!" Rafe grabbed the whole bag of chips and ran for the ATV.

The next few days were uneventful as everyone settled into a routine. The pain in my leg diminished and my only issue was the inconvenience of the damn cast. More than once, Rafe caught me trying to maneuver my way down a counter or across furniture without crutches. The hardest thing was introducing Harrison to my best set of horses then watching him saddle and ride off into the trees or arena with them for exercise. I began cursing at the cast every time Rafe was not within earshot.

We took videos and pictures every day to send to Sawyer and they chatted on the phone once or twice a day.

On Wednesday, Lenny drove me into town so I could have lunch with Bubb while he shopped at the feed store.

I was already sitting at a table when I saw Bubb drive into the parking lot. The moment he opened the door of the truck, I knew he was different. The lines across his forehead had eased and his eyes were relaxed. There was even a slight smile lifting the edges of the long mustache. He walked to the restaurant door with wide, peppy steps.

My smile was wide and honest when our eyes met. When his grin appeared, my heart soared.

"You look like my old friend again," I sighed as he sat in the chair next to me.

"I'm feeling that way, too." He chuckled. "I'm sorry it drug out so long and ended the way it did, but your persistence has changed my life...no matter how much of it is left."

"Oh, Bubb," I exhaled. "What...?"

CHAPTER TWENTY

"Technical term is andropause which basically concerns my testosterone levels. Then there is arthritis in my hips which was causing a bit of pain, and just the frustration of being old added to depression."

"Getting old sucks," I nodded with a sigh.

He nodded, "The doctor gave me a prescription for depression and testosterone then amped up what I was taking for the arthritis." He smiled with the light twinkling in his eyes. "Vic, I feel a hell of a lot better and a bit of a fool for letting it go for so long."

"I am just so relieved it wasn't anything worse," I sighed with a grin. "What are your plans now? Do you want to come back?"

He smiled again, "Maybe after the summer. Tomorrow, I fly down to Sacramento to meet up with my daughter and her family then we're driving to San Diego to catch a two-week cruise to Hawaii."

"Oh, my!" I laughed and tears of joy rose. "Bubb in Hawaiian shirts and shorts...I want a picture!"

His laughter rumbled through the restaurant, "I'm not sure that will happen, but if it does, I'll send ya' one."

We talked nearly non-stop for an hour before my phone beeped an alert.

Text from Ari: We have arrived in California, Jeff is nervous, could use a call, practices have been outstanding, and he is ready. First class is Friday Morning

Text to Ari: I have what he needs

"Scoot over here next to me," I told Bubb. "We're going to take one of those selfie pictures to celebrate this moment and I'll send it to Jeff to lift his spirits."

Bubb chuckled, "I hate those damn things. I swear I look older in each one."

"That is because we are."

We were both grinning when I took the picture.

Text to Jeff with picture attached: His smile is back, headed to spend a few weeks in Hawaii with his family. Who doesn't want to see Bubb in a Hawaiian shirt?

I sent the text to Ari, too. I loved the brother-sister team. Although Jeff was always focused on competing, Ari focused on training. They were a perfect pair for an outstanding business in the future.

Lenny returned to the restaurant to pick me up and Bubb watched over me as I made my way to the truck. When Bubb grinned at Lenny, I saw the same relief and happiness in his face that I knew I had in mine.

The mood at the ranch rose as we told everyone about Bubb, and they saw the picture. While Rafe disappeared to help his new best friend, Harrison, repair fence, I printed the picture and hung it on the wall just before I accepted the video chat from Ari. She was tall, slender, very fit, and always wore her black hair in a short pixie cut above her ears and, most of the time, she wore a straw cowboy hat that covered it.

"I need to clarify something," There was clear concern in her eyes.

"What?"

"Are you coming down?"

"I hadn't even given it consideration," I said honestly but a bit of worry ebbed into my stomach.

"Good, don't," Ari grinned.

She had always told me the truth and been straight forward with me. That is why, even as young as she was, I didn't hesitate in putting her in charge of the Arizona estate and horses.

"I wouldn't have sent him if I didn't have confidence that he could show my horses as well as I could."

"And that confidence from you has really changed him this week. I've seen a difference in him and for the better. I was worried if you came down it would shake it a bit."

"I would not do that to him," I nodded in agreement. "If I went down there, then my daughter would cut her vacation short to come here. I will not do that to either of them. I will watch from the monitors here, but I expect video chats from you."

"I can do that," She smiled. "We brought a groom with us to help prepare and care for the horses."

"What did you think of the two-year-olds I sent down?"

"That black is one of the smartest I've ever ridden," She grinned, and her eyes lit up with excitement. "I've been calling him Briggs."

We chatted about each horse until her eyes quickly shifted away from the screen, "Here he comes. I don't want him to know I called and told you not to come."

I grinned, waved, and ended the call.

****

Friday morning, the entire Bijou Bay crew stood in front of the monitor anxiously waiting for the competition to start. Riding the dark red bay mare with long black flowing mane and forelock, Jeff made the slow walk to the center of the arena.

"Here we go!" Ari grinned then turned the phone to show Jeff riding into the arena for his first reining competition of the next three days.

"What horse is that?" Rafe whispered.

"Sweet Honey Bijou Babe," Lenny answered before I could.

"She is out of Lucas and a daughter of Boudreaux," I added.

"We call her Sweety," Pauline said softly.

"She's striking," Harrison stated.

The room went silent as Jeff nodded to the judges to begin his run.

"Beautiful"

"Perfect"

"Outstanding"

"It doesn't get better than that"

"Look at his confidence"

"A strong run for both of them"

"Stunning"

The words were breathed in utter awe from myself and Ari. Pride and sheer admiration dripped from each word we spoke. Whoops and hollers echoed in the building with each flying lead change, spin, rollback, and the final three sliding stops with mane and dirt flying.

If it wasn't for the damn cast, I would have been jumping up and down for him when he rode out of the arena with a hand sliding down both sides of the bay horse's neck.

Ari hurried to his side but was stopped by a reporter that already had a microphone in front of Jeff.

"Outstanding run," the reporter huffed with a smile.

"That is the best I have ever felt in the arena. I walked in with so much confidence in this horse that I tried my best to live up to her." Jeff's breath came out in excited pants.

"It takes a hell of a team...what...did you hear that score?" the reporter gasped. "You have set the bar extremely high for the rest of the competition with an outstanding 237.5-point run."

"I take it, that's a good," Harrison glanced at me.

"Absolutely," I sighed in pride. "Best he has ever scored."

"Comes from that horse talent and the confidence he had riding into the arena," Ari added. "And both of those are because of Vic."

Jeff beamed with tears filling his eyes, "When you have a mentor and friend like Victoria Rafael-Taylor, you do nothing but succeed. She has an outstanding work ethic and breeding program that produces horses like Sweety here and the other three we brought. Wait until you see the new stallion, Dreaming of Honey. He is the grandson of her World Champion, Honey, and the son of the National Champion, Lucas. He is spectacular and I am so honored to be his rider."

"The legend herself, Victoria Rafael-Taylor couldn't be here due to a broken leg, but I have no doubt she was watching and beaming with pride for you," the reporter said to Jeff then shook his hand.

Jeff turned to Ali and his eyes widened when he saw the phone. His eyes fixed on me, hand to chest, and the other holding up the reins toward the camera, "You are my hero."

"I knew you could do it," Goosebumps rose on my arms. "It was stunning, flawless, beautiful. You are an amazing team to watch."

"I truly wish you were here for Dreamers' debut," Jeff sighed with a wide smile.

"He is in good hands, and I cannot wait to watch you compete. Take your time and stay focused. Take the momentum from this ride into the next, but do not go at him too excited or he will get anxious."

"What? No, she is already gone," Ari's voice interrupted, and the screen went dark.

"What happened?" Rafe asked.

"Someone wanted to talk to me, and Ari didn't want to just hand the phone to them without warning me first." I leaned back in the chair and sighed. "She is a bit protective."

"You bring that out in people," Anne smirked as she walked to the door.

The next day, we reconvened in front of the computer to watch Jeff and my golden stallion, Dreamer, ride with all the confidence I had in them. They rode away with a spectacular win sealing the future of both horse and rider.

*****

Sunday morning, Sawyer's video call came just as Rafe and Anne drove away from the clinic to bring broodmares in for pregnancy tests.

"Hello, my beautiful daughter," I grinned at her.

"Hi, Mom," She smiled, and it was a bright, eye-lighting smile.

"You look wonderful."

"So, do you."

We talked for a good half hour before she smiled at someone off the video then looked back at me with a pensive light in her eyes. I could see the blush paint her cheeks.

"What's going on?" I asked.

"I met someone," She whispered and looked around her. "Well, actually it's who I came here to meet."

"Who?"

Another glance around and a secretive smile, "Evan Rawlins."

"Really? Isn't he…older?"

She giggled softly, "About ten years. I'm at an age between him at 46 and his son at 27."

"His son the steer wrestler?"

"Yes, and engaged to the most cheerful young woman named Lacie Jae. Isn't that a cute name?"

"Yes, but I want to hear about this man that makes your eyes light up."

"He is so kind, Mom," She glowed. "Smart, caring, and so damn masculine," She giggled with a scrunch of the nose. "We talk for hours about everything. He loves his kids, and you should see him with his best friend's grandchildren. Evan has been so patient with all the questions I ask."

Her eyes twinkled in humor, and I knew her leaving with Camille was the right decision.

"And have those questions led to any answers?" I asked.

"Not yet. Yesterday, Evan and I sat at their kitchen table and went through boxes and albums full of old pictures. He thought looking at the men he was around while on the rodeo trail with his dad might shake loose some memories. It didn't, but, my goodness, this family has had a full life."

"I hope he isn't minding the intrusion."

Her slight smile let me know he wasn't. "Since we don't want to ask via social media Evan came up with an idea."

"What?" I asked cautiously.

"All three of his kids are competing at the Calgary Stampede and the Wyoming rodeos are going on at the same time. The Wyoming rodeos are very historic, and all the old cowboys go there. Evan is taking a couple horses down for Delaney and Logan so they can fly between Calgary and Wyoming and compete at both."

"Wow, that's a lot of miles."

"They are chartering a plane to get from Canada to Wyoming then back if they make the finals. Anyway, instead of going to Calgary, I'm going with Evan to help him with the horses."

I smiled, "And Evan needs help with the horses?"

She nodded, "He was in a farming accident a couple of years ago that broke his back. He's in a wheelchair 90% of the time."

"Oh," My jaw dropped in surprise. No comment from Camille or Delaney had let me know Evan had been injured.

"He can stand for a couple minutes at a time, but it gets really painful," she continued. "Plus, we're going to inconspicuously investigate the older cowboys."

"Just the two of you?"

She giggled with eyes twinkling, "Yes, just the two of us and tens of thousands of people at the rodeos."

"It sounds like a wonderful adventure."

"We're leaving tonight for a race in St. Paul, Oregon before they leave for Canada."

"I am so happy you decided to go and have fun."

"Me too, Mom. I feel more like myself than I have in years." She sighed with a beautiful smile. "When Evan kissed me, it was...it...I felt so alive again. I felt like a whole woman again. He is such a wonderful man, and everyone loves and respects him. I can't believe he is even interested in me..."

"Sawyer!" I gasped. "You're worth..."

"I know, Mom. Camille has thoroughly chewed me out for even thinking I wasn't worth a man like him."

"I knew that sister from another life came into your life for a reason."

"I wouldn't have come here if it wasn't for her. I wouldn't have met Evan." Tears rose in her eyes as her cheeks reddened. "I find it a bit of a miracle that you broke your leg, and we came to Bijou Bay just as she got there."

"Well, this is the only time I am happy I broke it," I chuckled.

"What about you, Mom?"

"What about me?"

"Every call with Rafe, he talks about Harrison...a lot about him and he says you laugh and smile a lot when you're with him."

"What?" I huffed. "As far as I know he is happily married."

Sawyer sighed with a slight smile, "Delaney said he was single, and has been for years, Mom. Dad would not want you spending the next 20 to 30 years by yourself."

"Sawyer!" I was shocked.

"If Rafe has noticed how much Harrison makes you smile, then you have to be attracted to him."

I shook my head in stunned amazement, "Well, he's not...he is...well..."

Sawyer grinned with a chuckle, "You DO like him."

"I can't believe you're even saying this," I huffed with another shake of the head.

She just smiled, "If the situation were reversed, you wouldn't want Dad to be by himself for the rest of his life either. So, since Harrison makes you smile, what would it hurt if you took a chance? Just know it is all right with me that you begin exploring the option."

"I don't think...or don't know that I could." I said honestly.

"Mom," Sawyer smiled. "I want you to feel what I'm feeling with Evan. You cannot go through another 20 or 30 years without moving on. Seriously, Dad would not have wanted that."

My stomach fluttered and heat rose up my back and flushed my neck and face.

"Mom, if the opportunity rises, don't be scared, just go for it."

I waved a hand as if to wave away the conversation. "I'm going to go check on Rafe."

"...and Harrison," she giggled. Her eyes were twinkling mischievously when the screen went black.

*****

"Is Jeff coming home?" Pauline asked Monday morning as she peeled away the plastic that was wrapped around the cast.

The shower had been refreshing and I sat on the bed in a long blue summer dress and brushed my hair back, "I told him to stay with Ari for now. Since I can't ride, it is logical to leave the horses down there and have Jeff and Ari train, work, and show them until this damned cast is off."

Light tapping on the door had Pauline walking to open it. Rafe stood with a rope in hand and his small red wagon sitting on the floor next to him.

"Took you long enough," He teased with a smart-ass grin.

"I didn't know we were in a hurry," Pauline chuckled.

"I got something to show Grandma," He said and walked into the bedroom while pulling the wagon. His eyes were lit with excitement. "I was thinking about you being here by yourself while we went to Silverwood. Since you can't carry anything, I was thinking you could put what you need in the wagon, and we tie it to your crutch, and you can just drag it behind you."

"Oh, my heaven, you are a thinker," Pauline laughed.

I grinned proudly, "Well, let's give it a try."

Once I stood and the crutches were in place, he tied the thin rope around the crutch and to the handle of the wagon. We chuckled as I slowly made my way into the living room with the wagon following.

"Perfect!" I hugged my proud grandson.

They left after lunch to drive to Silverwood to spend the rest of the day at the park. I would be on my own for hours for the first time since breaking my leg. I assured Rafe I was doing nothing more than sitting on the sofa and watching a horse auction the whole afternoon.

I placed a thermos of soup into Rafe's little wagon and added a bag of grapes, crackers, and two bottles of water. When I crutched forward, the rope tightened and began to pull the wagon. Giggling to myself and to my grandson's ingenuity

I made my way to the sofa. Half-way there, Harrison appeared at the glass door, and I waved him in. He stepped in with a brow lifted at my little red wagon.

I laughed, "Rafe's idea on how I can transport items and not have to carry them."

"That boy is quite something," Harrison nodded and hurried to my side.

"He is going to love that I used it." I sat on the edge of the sofa and reached for my phone to take a quick picture of the full wagon attached to my crutch. When I glanced up at Harrison, he was frowning.

CHAPTER TWENTY-ONE

"What's up?"

"Just came by to suggest a farrier come out sometime next week."

I nodded, "They will be here Thursday on a regular 3-week assessment. They are usually here the whole day."

"Ah, good," He sighed. "I figured you had something scheduled but thought I'd mention it."

"If you have any particular horse suggestions, please let Lenny know so he can put it on the work order."

"Sure, no problem."

I leaned back on the sofa and looked up at him. His usual bright eyes were now narrowed, and his shoulders were high. "What's going on?"

He exhaled and his shoulders relaxed, "Just a lot on my mind and I haven't been sleeping well."

"You need this sofa then," When he gave me a curious glance, I chuckled. "Every time I sit on this damn thing, I fall asleep."

"Could be the pain killers," He smirked.

"Maybe, but I don't take many of those anymore," I smiled and suddenly realized Rafe was right. I did smile and laugh a lot around Harrison. *What would it hurt if you took a chance, Sawyer had asked.* Maybe she was right, too. So, I smiled to hide the nerves and looked up at him. "Come over and sit with me for a while and relax while I watch this auction and see how much my young mare sells for." It was an innocent enough request but still made my heart skip a beat.

He looked up at the large screen on the wall where a sleek young black filly was being led around the auction ring.

"Sure," He mumbled.

I wiggled down to the middle of the sofa to give him room in the corner and pushed this opportunity we had alone together just a bit further. "Do you mind if I use your shoulder for support?"

"Not at all," He chuckled, and my nerves eased.

He helped lift my casted leg up onto the pillows, then pushed the little wagon next to the sofa so I could reach it easily. When he sat down, he turned enough that I slid under his arm and came to rest in the crook. His arm came to rest along my hip. I could easily reach the grapes and placed the bundle on my lap.

"Comfy?" He asked.

"Hmm, yes, are you?"

"Yes, sitting here on a soft sofa with a stunningly beautiful woman in my arms...I am very comfortable."

I chuckled. What woman doesn't love being called beautiful? Even better, stunningly beautiful at 61 years old.

"How far out is the mare?"

"She is two out from the black filly on there now," I answered and relaxed against his side. He was very comfortable to use as support. I thought of Sawyer's comments about him, and I felt my whole-body flush. I had to swallow the inkling of guilt for sitting with another man that wasn't my husband. Marcus would never be back and sitting innocently on a sofa with Harrison was not cheating. I repeated it to myself a dozen times before I relaxed into him a little more.

"Why did you sell her through the auction?"

"I'm not. I sold her before she was born. She has lived the last two years in Oklahoma."

"Why are they selling her?"

"Because her value for someone else, is more than what they have experience to live up to."

"Makes sense. With their experience they might win 20 or 30 grand on her in competitions. But they can sell her now for more than the 30 to a professional that can make over 100 during her career."

I giggled, "Glad you understand, because I have had to explain that too many times in my career. But she will bring more than that."

"How much do you think?"

I felt and heard him yawn. There was something about this sofa.

"If I was in the market, I would pay up to 150 for her."

"Seems to me, a person like you, is always in the market for a new horse."

I could hear the humor in his voice and grinned.

"You are correct. There are so many beautiful horses for sale every time I turn around or open the damn laptop. I have had to restrain myself from buying on a whim. The horse must be a bloodline I don't already own or one that could live up to my current and past herd."

"Like that stallion over the fireplace?"

I looked up at the proud golden stallion. He resonated masculinity, intelligence, and superiority. The horse had known he was special.

"His name was Honey, and no horse will live up to him, although Lucas comes close, and I think his son, Dreamer, will be up to their caliber."

"Rafe showed me the videos of Honey. You are impressive and he was spectacular."

I couldn't pull my eyes from the portrait that stirred so many wonderful, exhilarating memories.

"How did he pass?" Harrison asked.

"He went in his sleep at the age of thirty-one. I didn't find out why, it was just his time."

We grew silent as the auction on the monitor continued. After a few moments, Harrison's body sunk back into the sofa and his legs relaxed. The weight of his arm on my side and hip grew heavy. I watched the little mare sell for $145,000 to one of my competitors in the arena. I knew that mare was going to have a big career.

Harrison's breathing became deep as his chest rose and fell. By the time the next horse sold his whole body melted into the sofa. When the first low rumbling snore escaped, I carefully leaned away from him and managed to get myself to a standing position without disturbing him. I picked up the soft green blanket and laid it over him. Then, I watched him sleep and thought of Sawyer's encouragement to 'move on'.

I missed my husband every day, but I would never get him back and I did miss having a man in my life. I knew I didn't NEED a man in my life, but I did WANT one in my life. As Sawyer said, Marcus would want me to move on, and he would have liked Harrison. That meant a lot to me. The only man I had ever kissed was my husband, but watching Harrison, I wondered what it would be like to kiss him.

I had been around hundreds of men since my husband died and had dated a handful and turned down a dozen. But Harrison did the one thing that no other man had come close to; he didn't just make me miss my husband, he made me miss the whole life with my husband.   A blush warmed my cheeks, so I crutched my way back into the kitchen with the little wagon in tow.

I looked back at Harrison sleeping soundly on the sofa, "*Dad, would want you to move on.*"

A sudden desire for some equine therapy struck me, so I unhooked the little wagon from the crutch and made my way out the back door. I stopped long enough to grab a small bag of horse treats. I was half-way to the first pasture when the golden Lucas' head rose from grazing and looked right at me. His body rose in excitement, and he trotted to the fence to greet me. His head bounced in anticipation when he saw the treats.

The stallion melted my heart. He was more rambunctious than his father had been, and he was a bit taller, but he was just as beautiful and intelligent. As I crutched my way to him, I thought of his namesake, Officer Lucas. I had researched him, too. He had a long career in the police force; thirty-five years with many citations of bravery before his retirement. After another fifteen years, he had passed at the age of 74 of natural causes. From everything I had read, he had a very good life. That warmed my heart.

The other three horses in the pasture waited patiently while I rubbed down Lucas across the fence. Once he went back to grazing, the trio came forward for their attention. When they returned to grazing, I turned to crutch back to the house. Halfway there, I received a text.

Text from Anna: We were going to stay until after dark so the kids could see the park at night, but Rafe is getting concerned about you. May end up coming back soon.

Text to Anna with the image of the wagon attached to the crutch: Show him this and tell him it worked perfectly, and I am doing fine watching the horse auction. If he needs, he can call me, but tell him I want him to stay and enjoy the park.

Harrison was still sleeping with his head back, mouth slightly open, and chest heaving in deep breaths. The sun was just beginning to lower to the horizon, so I crutched out the back door and started the fire. After making sure there were no spiders or bugs on the cushions, I settled onto the sofa and watched the sunset begin. Other than being with the horses, watching the summer sunsets over the water and trees was my favorite thing to do.

As I lay quietly watching the sun lower with the fire flickering beside me, I thought of Sawyer and Evan going through hundreds of pictures. I didn't believe she could find Jesse, but this search and adventure with Camille, Delaney, and now Evan, was what she needed to do.

As the sun dipped behind the horizon, I thought of Jesse with his long blonde hair swishing around him and the ever-present smile. Even after his first beating by Mr. Campbell he had been smiling. The memories of the young adventurous thirteen-year-old made me sigh. Our swinging sticks in the air as if they were swords made me smile, then the image of his eating the raw fish with a teasing grin, made me grimace.

Jesse…he would always be that happy adventurer in my memories. But, in reality? The thought made my stomach hurt. There were so many possibilities of what could have happened to him. I wondered if he had tried to send me another letter.

The sky had darkened as I reminisced, and the lights of Anne's car caught me by surprise. Rafe appeared from the car and greeted me with a wide grin. I waved at Anne just before she backed out of the driveway.

"Hi, Grandma," He placed a balloon and his small bag on the chair then sat down in front of me.

"Did you have fun?"

"Yes, but I'm kind of cold now and I got really tired on the drive back."

"Well then, it's time for bed and you can tell me all about your day in the morning. Harrison came over to watch the auction with me and fell asleep on the sofa. I'll sleep in my own bed now…"

"But that is so far away from mine," he yawned.

I hugged him tighter, "It's not that far. You can help me settle in, then scurry off to your own bed."

Five minutes later, I was lying on the bed with a pile of pillows bracing my casted leg.

"How's that?" Rafe yawned again.

"Perfect, and I love being in my own bed," I hugged him. "Be real quiet and turn off all the lights except for the hallway so Harrison can see if he wakes up."

"Ok," he whispered, yawned, and then walked out of the room.

I turned off the light and sighed into the sheets. It felt good to be back in my own bed and it didn't take long for my eyes to close and my dreams to drift to the past.

"You didn't see Kathy?" Betty gasped and her face paled.

"It was just me and Jesse," I answered as she gently wrapped her arm around my shoulders to guide me toward the front door of the building.

When I was in the chair in front of her desk, she began pacing back and forth.

"Are you hurt? Did they...?" Her voice trembled.

"No, I'm OK. Mrs. Campbell was going to chop off my hair and I screamed. Jesse got me away from her, then we waited for dark so we could get to you."

She stopped and knelt next to me, "Do you know where Jesse went?"

I leaned back in the chair as tears filled my eyes, "No, he said he didn't want to go to another foster home and that I would never see him again."

The eyes that had been so soft and caring when I first met her were now narrowed, filled with worry, and red from crying. "He was hurt...he needs a doctor."

I shrugged slightly, "He is pretty beat up, but we ran through trees and down beaches and even crossed the river twice to get here before the Campbell's did."

"Oh, Lord, Victoria," She gasped. "What have I put you through?"

"You didn't do it," I frowned. "The Campbell's did."

She stood and began to pace again, "But, where is Kathy?"

Before I could answer, the main building door opened with my aunt and uncle appearing. They briskly walked down the hall toward us and both gasped when they saw me.

Betty's whole body trembled, and her hand gently cupped my face, "I am so sorry this happened." The tears rose in her eyes that were filled with true sorrow. "I have to go find them." She whispered and turned to my aunt and uncle. "I'm sorry...I have to go." She ran past them as they looked at my dirty, torn dress, long tangled hair that had leaves and pine needles stuck in it, and long red scratches over my face, arms, and legs.

I leaned around them and watched Betty disappear out the door.

My eyes opened into the dark bedroom as I thought of Betty's eyes. They had haunted my dreams for years after my aunt and uncle had whisked me away from the center. Even as young as I was, I understood what a wonderful, caring woman Betty was and just how traumatic it was for her to realize what Jesse had gone through, what could have happened to me, and the unknown of what had happened to Kathy.

I thought of what lay ahead of her when she walked out those doors. Why? Why did that happen?

It suddenly occurred to me that I could hear someone breathing. If Harrison was still in the living room, he was too far away for me to hear him, but the breathing was coming from beside me.

CHAPTER TWENTY-TWO

I slowly turned my head, and the moonlight allowed me to see Rafe curled on the opposite side of the king-size bed. He was wrapped in his blanket and laying over my covers.

Watching him sleep, I thought of the overnight trek Jesse and I had endured to get to Betty. I was eleven, the same age as Rafe was now. I couldn't imagine him having to run into the night and cross the swift running river. As an adult now, I could understand the horror that Betty felt and the anger from my aunt and uncle. I couldn't imagine how I would feel if Rafe had appeared in front of me with dark blue and purple bruises around his entire torso and the swollen eyes and scraped chin. My heart pounded at the thought.

Taking deep breaths, I closed my eyes and tried to fall back to sleep.

I woke when Rafe moved and when I opened my eyes, he was looking back at me. His guilty little grin made me smile.

"Good morning," I whispered

"You were too far away if you needed something," He explained.

"I am so lucky to have you taking care of me," My heart filled with love.

"I love it here, Grandma," He whispered. "I love the horses, and people, and you, but you really need a dog."

I chuckled softly, "Where did that come from?"

"Anne's boys have one and they were telling me about him. His name is Dodger. Have you ever had a dog?"

"Lots of them through the years. Jazzy passed away last winter. She was a smaller mixed terrier that was full of energy but a good traveling companion."

"How did she die?"

"She was twelve and I woke up one day and she had passed away in her sleep."

"That's sad..."

Footsteps on hardwood floors echoed toward us but they stopped just outside the open bedroom door and out of sight. My hand instinctively went to finger comb my hair and adjust the covers.

"Can I get you some coffee?" Harrison asked.

"I don't like coffee," Rafe grimaced.

Harrison chuckled, "Apple juice for you then. Coffee for you, Victoria?"

"Every morning," I smiled.

"As a thank you for letting me get a good night's rest on your couch, I'd like to make you breakfast." Harrison said.

"I'll help," Rafe kicked the blankets to the side and rolled off the bed. "All that swimming last night I am starving to death." He grinned at me then disappeared out the door.

"I guess that is a yes," I chuckled.

"Do you need help?" Harrison asked softly.

My skin warmed and stomach fluttered at the thought of him helping me out of bed. Then a wave of guilt washed over me. "No, I can manage."

"Alright, I'll get the coffee started."

His footsteps faded away just as my phone beeped.

Text from Camille: You awake?

Text to Camille: Yes

The video chat alerted me to her call. When I pushed the button, her beautiful smile greeted me, and her eyes held a bit of mischief.

"Good morning my daughter from another life," I answered and we both grinned.

"I am so glad you're awake," The phone shook to indicate she was walking.

"Why is that?"

"We flew in from Calgary overnight and met up with the family for breakfast, and I wanted to show you what happened while we were gone."

"You're in Wyoming with Sawyer now?"

Her grin widened, "Yes, and, well, I'll let you see for yourself. They think I'm talking on the phone with a client so I'm going to reverse the camera so you can see them, and they don't know."

"Alright...but why...?"

The image changed from Camille to a small group of people in front of a living quarters horse trailer. They were sitting at a round pop-up table enjoying coffee and conversation. It was my daughter that drew my attention. Her smile was wide as she listened to a tiny woman with short white-blonde hair. Sawyer's eyes were lit with pure joy as she turned to the man sitting to her right. Her arm encircled his with their fingers comfortably interlaced. But it was the shine in his eyes when he looked at Sawyer that made my heart skip a beat and my breath catch. The man was just as smitten with my daughter as she was with him. The pair radiated happiness.

"Oh, my," I whispered.

"That's what we thought!" Camille giggled. "While we were in Canada, magic happened with those two."

"I am so happy for her."

"Delaney and her brothers are just as happy with this as I am. Evan is one of the best men I know, and I adore Sawyer. She has really stepped up and helped with the horses and arrangements."

"She grew up traveling with me and horses to the shows and her polo matches."

"They have so much in common and have just clicked like best friends since they met. Everyone could see it."

"You would have to be blind not to," I sighed. "This trip was the best thing that could have happened to her."

"I agree." The image flipped back to Camille. "I just wanted to share that, but I do need to go."

"Thank you, Camille."

Her smile brightened, "You have a beautiful day."

"You, too."

"We're in the majestic state that is Wyoming, and all three Rawlins made the championship round in Calgary, so we get to fly back on Saturday in a private jet. It's gonna be good."

I laughed as she waved, and the screen turned black.

The warm feeling of happiness was in my heart as I crutched into the kitchen. Rafe was setting plates on the outdoor patio table while Harrison lifted a sheet filled with biscuits from the oven. The comfortable 'family' scene made me smile. When Harrison turned to look at me and my first thought was how ruggedly handsome he was with a bright smile surrounded by whiskers on his strong jaw, the wave of guilt swept through me again.

"We may have over done it," Harrison chuckled. "But I slept through dinner last night and Rafe swam all day yesterday so we're hungry."

"And you need warm hearty food to get your strength back," Rafe added with a grin as he walked back into the house.

"That sounds like your mother talking," I teased and slid onto the chair he held out for me.

"And SHE sounds like YOU...so there is that," Rafe gave me a smart-ass grin.

The alert chimed on my phone.

TEXT from Sawyer with an image attached: I wanted to share but don't show Rafe. We'll video chat once things have calmed down here. This picture says it all right now. Thank you for pushing me into coming.

With Rafe on the opposite side of the kitchen island with Harrison, I pushed the button to open the image. It was Sawyer and Evan with their arms entwined, her head tipped intimately into his shoulder and their eyes shone with happiness as they looked into the camera.

TEXT to Sawyer: You both look so happy. Love you my darling daughter.

We were just finishing breakfast at the patio table when Pauline appeared around the corner. Her brows rose in surprise when she saw Harrison.

"Any food left?" She asked Rafe.

"Lots more, I'll get you a plate." He slid from the chair and ran into the house.

"And I'll need a cup of coffee," Pauline's eyes darted between myself and Harrison as she followed Rafe into the house.

I turned to Harrison, "If you don't mind my asking, why are you having such a time sleeping?"

"Just a lot on my mind," he sighed. "Jace is a bit upset that I'm not home working the horses every day and he'll be needing a few of them for the upcoming rodeos."

"Hmm," I sighed. "Is it just the riding?"

"Conditioning and training," He nodded.

"Is there anything keeping you at home besides the horses?" I asked.

He shook his head, "Just, Trouble, my dog and the half dozen horses."

"Well," I smiled. "There are three pastures empty right now next to the Trophy House. Why don't you save time and bring the horses here and stay in the upstairs apartment? It is empty right now. And, as for the dog, Rafe was just saying we needed one here." Harrison's eyes narrowed. "That will save you driving time and the mountains are wonderful for conditioning horses."

Harrison began to nod, "You're sure?"

"It would be like a little mini- vacation. I don't expect you to work seven days a week and you'll have the indoor arena available for the upcoming hot days. Occasionally, we take the pontoon boat out on the bay and you're welcome to join us." I smiled at him. "There is a kitchen in the apartment with a washer and dryer in the large bathroom."

He took a deep breath and exhaled sharply, then turned and looked at Rafe and Pauline in the kitchen. His brows were furrowed.

"What?" I asked.

"As much as I would like to say yes, there is another issue."

I leaned forward in concern, "Something I can help with?"

He shook his head with a smirk, "And that's the problem."

"What?"

He glanced into the kitchen and then to me, "We're grown adults, Victoria, so there is no sense in playing games."

"I agree," My skin warmed and stomach fluttered.

"I like you, Victoria," He stated with a slight smile. "Not just like you, but I admire you. From everything you have accomplished in your life, to your sincerity in helping others, and even your years of a happy marriage to Marcus." He leaned forward so we were just inches apart. My whole body flushed, and tingles of guilt rose up my spine. "Over the last couple of weeks, I did feel you liked me too, but after your inviting me onto the couch with you last night, I am convinced of it."

"I do," I admitted in a whisper.

"I look forward to coming here every morning and spending time with you and Rafe. You make my days brighter."

I leaned back with a hand to my chest, "Rafe says we smile and laugh a lot together...and I do look forward to seeing you."

Laughter filtered out of the house and we both turned to Rafe and Pauline. She glanced at us, and it became clear she was keeping Rafe in the kitchen.

I turned back and looked at Harrison. Sawyer had told me to take a chance. It was OK with her, but it didn't help the ache in my heart and the tingles of guilt.

Harrison smiled, "If I accept the offer to stay in the Trophy House, then it is with the understanding that we see where this relationship goes."

His eyes and voice were sincere and hopeful.

I took a deep breath and nodded, "Alright, but you should understand that when I think of you...that way...I feel like I am cheating on my husband. It will take some time to work through those feelings."

He nodded with an understanding smile. "When I spoke to Pauline yesterday to get her opinion, she thought you liked me, were ready to move on, and as long as I didn't ask you to forget Marcus, that I should take a chance. I understand you have a past with a man that was taken from you, not one you left. So, we start slow. Just hanging out here together, then a dinner alone together here and there."

I nodded with another deep breath, "Thank you for understanding." I smiled as my stomach settled. "And once this damn cast is off, I look forward to going on rides together."

He grinned and leaned back in his chair. It must have been a signal to Pauline that our private conversation was over as she led Rafe out the door.

"Can we check to see if Willa is pregnant today?" Rafe asked and Harrison turned to look at her in anticipation.

"Not until Friday," Pauline answered with a grin to both.

"What is today?" Rafe asked with a tilt of the head.

I had no idea, so I turned to Pauline.

"Thursday," She answered. "And, no, we are not cheating by one day."

"Does it really make that much difference?" Harrison asked.

"The last thing we want to do is rush it and get a false test," Pauline nodded. "So, we wait to the fourteenth day, which is tomorrow morning."

"Well, fine then," Harrison stood with a teasing smile. "I need to run home, but I'll be back in a couple of hours."

"Something I said?" Pauline teased with a chuckle.

He laughed and I smiled at the sound then turned to Rafe.

"You were just saying we need a dog here, so I asked Harrison to bring his dog and the two of them can stay in the Trophy House apartment while he is helping at the ranch. He'll also be bringing his horses here for conditioning and training. I think it's the least we can do for him jumping in to help us around here while we are shorthanded."

"That's awesome!" Rafe grinned. "What kind of dog?"

"A golden lab...more pale yellow than gold," Harrison answered. "His name is Trouble."

Rafe laughed, "Mom calls me that all the time."

We chuckled with him as Harrison set his hat on his head, nodded to Pauline, then smiled at me before walking away.

"What are we doing this morning?" Rafe asked.

"After swimming all day yesterday, you need to go shower off all that chlorine then get dressed," I answered. "Then, maybe a drive around the property to start. I'm getting a bit stir crazy being cooped up all the time."

Rafe disappeared into the house and Pauline turned to me with a raised brow. "He stay with you last night?"

"He slept on the couch, and I was in my room. But honestly, we just talked about a possible relationship."

"And, how are you handling it?"

My gaze wandered out over the pastures, trees, and the distant water of the bay. "I feel like I am cheating on my husband."

"You're not, you're just moving on."

"I'm sure my mind will wrap around that soon enough."

"Well, Marcus would have liked him. It could be that he sent Harrison to you at the time you need to move on and to Rafe at a time he needs a father, or grandfather role model in his life."

Sawyer was right, if I had left first, I wouldn't have wanted Marcus to be alone for the rest of his days and I would have wanted to choose the woman he would be with to finish his life.

"I like that thought," I smiled at Pauline. "In a way, it makes it a bit easier to accept Harrison in my life going forward."

"In fact," Pauline leaned back and grinned. "I think Marcus broke your leg."

I laughed, "He what?"

"However you broke it, I think Marcus did it," She chuckled. "Just think about it. You breaking your leg brought Sawyer here when she needed you most, and Rafe who needed his grandmother and a great male role model in his life, like Harrison. And! If you had not broken your leg, after your training session with Camille, you would have traveled to Arizona to get ready for the shows and you would not have been here to meet Harrison and Sawyer would not have been here to go traveling with Camille and find Evan."

I stared at her for a moment before slowly nodding, "Maybe you're right."

"So, how did Marcus make you break your leg?" Her eyes twinkled in humor.

I just smiled and pushed myself into a standing position, "Let's get this shower over with so I can go enjoy Bijou Bay."

CHAPTER TWENTY-THREE

I was leaning against the 6-wheeler watching Harrison unload his horses from his horse trailer when the alert beeped on my phone. My horses were running across the green pastures in anticipation of the new arrivals, and I couldn't pull my eyes away from the mares with prancing foals at their sides. Such a wonderful sight; one that Marcus and I had enjoyed for years at the Arizona equine center we had run together. I closed my eyes to hold onto the vision of him standing next to me, hand-in-hand, watching the horses run. The loss was heavy on my heart as my eyes opened and I turned to Harrison.

My mind changed Harrison into my husband. It was sad that Marcus missed moments like this with his grandson. I felt the pull at my heart for the loss of him and the memories that would never be. Every ounce of my soul wished that Rafe could have had the time to make more memories with his grandfather.

I never saw my father's parents again after he died, but I had wonderful memories of my mother's parents. They joined my aunt and uncle quite often on their small farm in Arizona. My aunt created beautiful turquoise jewelry that was sold across the country. I still had a jewelry box full of pieces that she had hand made. She was also a holistic healer, and my uncle grew herbs and vegetables for her. It was a simple life of jewelry making, farming, and my horses. We got along well even though I never thought of them as parents, and they never tried to replace them.

"Grandma!"

My mind jolted back to reality to see Rafe leading a pretty chocolate colored horse.

"Isn't he pretty?" Rafe yelled.

"His name is Mocha," Harrison said, and their voices faded away as they walked the horses to the pasture gate.

My phone beeped again.

Text from Sawyer: We have a lead on what happened to Jesse!

Text from Sawyer: We should know in just a couple of hours.

My breath caught and skin tingled, *what happened to Jesse*. My hand lay over my suddenly tumbling stomach. I closed my eyes and took a deep breath to hold back the nausea. I never thought they would find him. Jesse needed to remain that thirteen-year-old boy I had known for less than two days yet had changed my life. I did not want to know that his fate was as bad if not worse than Betty's.

"Victoria? Are you all right?" Harrison asked from right beside me. I hadn't heard him approach. "You look..."

"I'm fine," I exhaled and forced a smile. There was no reason to focus on Sawyer's text. There was a good chance that it was a false lead. I could only hope. I wanted Sawyer to find herself, not Jesse. "So, introduce me to your herd."

Sawyer's text arrived as we made our way into the Trophy House but I ignored it...I wasn't ready.

"Can you show me videos of you being a pick-up man?" Rafe asked Harrison as the man carried his bags up to the apartment.

"Sure," Harrison answered.

"Grandma's got a great monitor downstairs for watching videos," Rafe continued.

"Well, let me put my bag in the bedroom," Harrison's voice faded away.

I was anxious to see the videos, too. As I made myself comfortable on the recliner, I took a deep breath and read the text.

Text from Sawyer: That fell through. He didn't recognize your last name.

Text to Sawyer: Which last name did you use?

Text from Sawyer: Rafael

Text to Sawyer: That is my maiden name, I had not taken my uncles' name yet. Jesse would have known me as Moreau.

Text from Sawyer: OF COURSE! What was I thinking? Everyone we've talked to I said Rafael and not Moreau...now we have to start over. Damn it.

Text to Sawyer: So, you have to spend more time with Evan? After seeing that picture, it doesn't seem to me that would be a problem.

Text from Sawyer: LOL, you're right. Love you, Mom. We'll call and video chat in a bit so I can introduce Rafe to Evan.

Text to Sawyer: We're settling in to watch rodeo videos of Harrison, so he will have a lot to talk about.

After an hour of watching videos of Harrison riding bucking horses then a few of him riding Willa as a pickup man, the video chat began. The introduction of Rafe and Evan could not have been better. The two men told him story after story and Rafe hung on every word.

After we returned home, and I was sitting on the outside couch while Rafe played with his trucks he turned and looked at me with serious eyes.

"What?" I asked.

"Did Mom introduce me to Evan because he is her boyfriend now?" His voice was low.

I nodded, "Yes."

His gaze went to his trucks, and he sat quietly a moment before turning back to me, "So, she won't be going back to Dad?"

I sighed and smiled in understanding, "Even if your mother wasn't with Evan, she would not go back to your dad."

"Ever?" He whispered.

"Sometimes, when too much negative happens in a relationship, it is just too much of an obstacle to get over and ever be happy again."

He nodded with a sigh, "She did seem happy with Evan."

I pulled out my phone and opened the picture Sawyer had sent me of her and Evan together. He stood to walk over and look at the image.

"Look how happy they are," I smiled.

"I really like it when Mom smiles that much and he looks happy, too."

"Someday, your father will find someone that makes him that happy, but it could never be your mother."

He nodded with a sigh and turned back to his trucks.

*****

The next morning, Rafe, Pauline, Lenny, Anna, and I stood in front of the clinic as Harrison walked his mare, Willa, down the asphalt path toward us. His expression was unreadable which I understood. There were dozens of times I had prayed for a mare to take and the apprehension leading to the test was unnerving.

"I sure hope she's pregnant," Rafe whispered.

"If she's not, we still have a few different procedures we can try," Pauline assured him.

"But, I agree," I whispered as Harrison neared. "It would just be nice if she is pregnant, and we didn't have to try any of those."

Five minutes later, we held our breath as the black and white image on the sonogram screen appeared. The black follicle appeared, and my eyes desperately searched for the small circle indicating the foal.

"There!" Rafe pointed to the screen.

"No," Pauline sighed, and the image swirled then held steady to the large black circle again. "But, right there is the beginning of a foal."

"Pregnant?" Harrison huffed.

Pauline nodded with a grin and hit the button to print the image, "Yes."

"Yay!" Rafe bounced and turned happy eyes to Harrison. "Your Willa is going to have a little baby Boudreaux!"

Harrison's eyes brightened and grin widened, his shoulders lowered as he exhaled in relief. He was chuckling softly when he pulled his phone from his pocket to take a picture of the screen, "Now, I can't wait to let Jace know." He turned to me with a happy, relaxed smile which made this handsome, rugged cowboy look ten years younger.

CHAPTER TWENTY-FOUR

The day was filled with bookkeeping for me, preg testing mares for Pauline and Anne, and trail rides for Rafe, Lenny, and Harrison. As a beginning to our 'dating' and in celebration of Willa's pregnancy, Harrison drove Rafe and I to the steakhouse in Coeur d' Alene for dinner. When he dropped us off at the house, Rafe immediately made his way to his trucks and trailers.

Harrison retrieved my crutches from the back seat, then helped me slide gracefully from the front seat of his truck. We stood side-by-side for a moment with his hands resting on my hips while I leaned into his chest.

"You alright?" he asked softly.

"Yes," I let the nearness and intimacy of the moment settle in my system. *One step at a time,* I told myself and hesitantly looked up into his eyes. They held an understanding of how hard this moment was for me, and yet a yearning for a kiss to happen. I tilted my chin up in an invitation of the kiss. His eyes softened as he lowered. It was a soft kiss, just long enough to send warmth throughout my body but not long enough for the guilt to make an appearance.

"Next time, a little longer," He smiled and handed me the crutches.

I was still standing at the end of the driveway as he turned the truck around and drove away. My eyes immediately fell to the large driver's side mirror. I could see Harrison looking back at me through the mirror and our eyes briefly met and we smiled.

"You hurry home," I stepped onto the running boards of Marcus' truck and leaned into the window to kiss him again. It wasn't a short kiss; it was filled with the passion of 38 years of love. Our morning had run late as we had spent the extra time in each other's arms. No matter how long we were married, the passion between us would never cease.

"You keep kissing me like that," He whispered with our lips barely apart. "And I won't be able to leave."

I leaned back and looked into his loving eyes, "Maybe I should go with you, and we can find another side road to drive down again."

"And now I'll be thinking of you and me in the backseat of this truck for the whole damn trip."

We both chuckled and I reluctantly stepped away from the truck.

"Love ya, Beautiful," He winked and drove away.

My eyes went to the large side mirror and, like a thousand times before, our eyes met, and we smiled.

An hour later, the police were knocking at my door. My breath slowly released from my lungs as Harrison's truck disappeared over the top of the hill.

In that side mirror, I had seen my past and my future. There were millions of memories of Marcus, but those last few minutes were how I remembered him most. Harrison and I had just started making memories together, but the look on his face when it was confirmed his beloved family horse was carrying a foal would be a cherished one.

I had always envisioned Jesse as that 13-year-old boy I had shared the dramatic adventure. He would always be the 'pirate' that danced around the fires, waved stick swords in the air, and fed me apples. He was always that hero that delivered me to Betty. I didn't want that to change.

What if he was dead? What if he had moved on from being a cowboy and had died when he was hitch hiking around the country? What if he had been put into another foster home or orphanage and came to the same horrible fate as those children at the Campbell's house? If I found out what happened to Jesse, would that destroy that adventurous boy?

My trembling hand lay over the ache in my stomach that had formed as Harrison drove away. My lungs were tight, barely able to take in a breath. Sweat formed on my brow and the desire to burst into tears was overwhelming.

I did not want to know what happened to Jesse. I wanted to keep that 13-year-old adventurous pirate alive. With trembling fingers, I pulled my phone from my pocket. I didn't know if I could speak coherently so I typed a text instead.

Text to Sawyer: Stop looking for Jesse

Text from Sawyer: Why? Is everything OK?

Text to Sawyer: I don't want to know

Minutes passed before the phone alert rang.

Text from Sawyer: OK, I understand. We can talk when I get home.

Text to Sawyer: Do not hurry coming home. Enjoy your adventure.

When my eyes opened the next morning, I felt rested. More than I had since before I broke my leg. There were no dreams of Mr. Campbell charging me, Betty's desperate eyes, or the bruised and beaten Jesse. Falling asleep with the memory of Harrison's soft kiss must have eased my mind.

Rafe was still asleep across the bed from me, so I carefully rose and was crutching out of the room when I heard him snore. I chuckled softly. The morning before they had travelled to Silverwood, he had still been up early helping feed horses and clean stalls. I decided he needed the morning off.

Text to Lenny: Rafe is sleeping in today.

Text from Lenny: Boy needs it. He is a great worker, but we all need a morning off now and again.

Text to Sawyer: Rafe is sleeping in today. I'll have him call you when he wakes.

Text from Sawyer: We are on the road to Cheyenne so have hours to drive.

It was just after six in the morning, and I had no doubt Harrison was awake.

Text to Harrison: Rafe is sleeping in this morning. Would you like to join me on the back patio for coffee?

Text from Harrison: Just got down from the top of the mountain. I'll put the horse away and be there in 30 minutes.

I started the pot of coffee then pulled out a box of cinnamon coffee cake mix.

With cup of coffee in hand, I sat at the back table and looked across the blue water of the bay surrounded by green pine tree covered mountains. The sky was a bright blue with white puffy clouds on the horizon. A deep breath filled my lungs with the aroma of both the trees and the water. Sawyer was happy, Rafe was happy, my business was solid with Pauline in the breeding clinic and Jeff and Ari taking the reins on competitions. Then there was Harrison, who was the promise of a future. I took a deep contented breath, and a peaceful sigh escaped.

"You are beautiful."

With a warm smile, I turned to Harrison. His smile was wide, eyes lit with happiness to see me, and his low straw cowboy hat and worn boots added to his rugged handsomeness.

"You're not too bad yourself," I chuckled.

"Little sweaty and smelling like a horse," He stepped in next to me and slowly bent to give me a quick kiss.

"Just like I like it," I admitted with a smile, and he lowered in for another kiss, just a bit longer but not too much.

He rose, looked out at the bay, and took a deep breath, "Love the air here."

"Me, too," I sighed. "It's one of the reasons I chose this place. The coffee cake in the oven should be ready."

When he returned with the cake and his cup of coffee, he looked relaxed and content.

"Sleep alright?" I asked.

"Like a baby," He sighed. "Bed was comfortable, and the mountain air just lulled me to sleep."

"Where is your dog? I thought you were bringing him, too."

"My neighbors had taken him to the lake. I'll pick him up later today."

"Would you mind taking Rafe with you? He needs a break away and I'm sure he would enjoy it."

"Love to take him. I really enjoy that young man."

"Me, too," I sighed. "Another couple of months, and I'm afraid he'll be headed to Oregon to start the school year."

"It wouldn't surprise me. Your daughter and Evan looked pretty happy together. And, knowing Evan for thirty years, he wouldn't and hasn't ever made a woman he was seeing public. I'm not sure he even let his kids know he was seeing anyone. His first marriage, to the kids' mother, was pretty special."

"What about you? Have you been married?"

"Twice, the first one was about six months and was a bit my fault. Jace's mother and I split after he graduated college and we were left to just the two of us. We raised him just outside of Seattle and she wanted to move into town and I was not moving away from the horses and the country. So, we both got our wish and we're both happy."

I noticed he had skipped over the first marriage and glanced at him in curiosity.

He smiled slightly and shrugged, "We were married at 19 and for some reason she thought I was going to stay home and not rodeo. As you saw from the videos yesterday, I was a bronc rider before becoming a pickup man and traveled a lot. She didn't want to go on the road, but every time I came home, she accused me of cheating on her. Not once did I cheat on her, but after months of her jealous anger and accusations, I'd had enough. I was young, stupid, and drunk when I figured if she was thinking it, accusing me of it, then I might as well do it. The next morning, I felt horrible about what I had done and knew I couldn't look her in the eye, so I divorced her. Went through an attorney and didn't ever see her again."

"Youth," I leaned back and sighed. "I think going through what I did with my parent's loss and my focus and discipline in training the horses, I was a bit mature for my age. I was lucky to find Marcus when I did, and never went through those rocky years that test a marriage."

"Jace's mom, Kellie, and I were happy through most of it. Once he and I were on the road a lot we just drifted apart. She nursed me through hip surgery, and I was there for her during a cancer scare. We still respect each other but want different lives."

I took a bite of the cake and nodded, "Marcus broke his back. That was a rough six months. But he was there for me during all my injuries."

We talked of injuries we and our children had throughout the years. He was a comfortable man to talk to and I thoroughly enjoyed myself.

"Grandma?"

I looked at my phone, 8:47; two and a half hours later than normal

"We're outside," I called to him.

He appeared with a major case of bedhead, red cheeks, and wide eyes when he saw what was left of the cake.

"Why did you let me sleep so long? I have stalls to clean." He slid onto a chair and pulled the cake platter in front of him. With a chuckle, Harrison slid a clean fork to him so he could eat directly from the platter.

"You are having a day off," I explained. "We all need them."

"But I want to ride at least." He said before shoving a large piece of cake in his mouth.

"We can ride after we get back," Harrison said.

"Where we going?" Rafe asked around the mouthful of cake making Harrison and I cringe.

"Victoria said you can ride with me to get supplies for my apartment refrigerator and pick up my dog," He stood. "I'll get you a glass of milk to wash that cake down."

"Thanks," Rafe grinned at him then turned to me. "What are you going to do?"

"I may take the day off, too, and just sit here enjoying the view while reading a good book. Pauline can handle the clinic on her own today."

"OK, but be careful," His eyes twinkled in mischief. "You don't want to be picked up in the middle of the driveway again."

"Smart butt," I teased with a laugh. "Eat your cake then go take a shower to get rid of that messy bedhead."

He chuckled and his eyes twinkled while another large piece of cake was shoved in his mouth.

An hour later, he was crawling into Harrison's truck, "Be good, Grandma!" He called out with a laugh as the door closed.

Harrison grinned and stepped into the truck, "We'll be back in about an hour."

"I'll either be reading or taking a nap," I chuckled.

The truck moved away as I began to crutch toward the house. At the last moment, I turned and looked at the side mirror of the truck. Harrison was watching me, and he smiled.

My body flushed with memories, but I continued to the back patio couch. A bottle of water and a book were on the side-table, but I didn't want to just sit and read and was relieved when my phone beeped.

Text from Camille: Do you have a minute to watch a video then talk with me?

Text to Camille: Absolutely

Within minutes, she sent me a video. I leaned back in the chair at the table and watched her ride Lucia, the palomino she had purchased from me. They were in a large arena riding a basic reining pattern. I watched it twice before she called.

"Thank you, so much," she gushed.

"You decided to go with reining?"

"Yes, I really enjoy it. Maybe somewhere down the line I'll add the cutting for the reined cow horse but right now I want to just focus on the reining."

"You're young, take your time," I nodded to myself. "Over the last fifty years, I have slowly conquered each discipline I put my mind to."

"And that is why you are a legend in the horse industry," Camille chuckled. "I've talked to a number of people about Lucia and where I got her and most of them know you from one discipline or another."

"Well, I guess I've been called worse things," I smiled. It wasn't the first time I had been called a legend and it made me proud. I had worked hard through the years, and it was obvious people had noticed.

"Haven't we all!" Camille laughed. "I'll do the learning and training around Delaney's race schedule. Nothing will take away from our adventure for a year or two, so I have time."

"Good, I'm glad you're taking your time. The video is good, but you do need training."

"And I was calling to see if you would be my trainer...or coach."

"I would love to," I said honestly. "You have a future with Lucia. I will help you every way I can. In fact, after the cast is off, I can meet you at my ranch in Arizona during your travels and we can get a good foundation started."

"Oh, I just love you!" She giggled. "I'm so excited."

"To start..."

We discussed her video and the future plans for another half hour before she needed to go.

When the call ended, I looked across the bay and sighed. Helping Harrison's mare be bred and continuing her legacy and helping Camille is exactly what I wanted to do with my life going forward. I wanted my stallion's offspring to be successful and help them bring joy to their human families.

A sudden urge to visit Lucas had me standing with a bit of levity and crutched my way through the house and to the front door that faced the horses. When I arrived at the fence of my golden stallion, he didn't approach the fence, instead, he and the other horse's heads had risen, and they were looking up the slight hill of the road. I turned to see what had captured their attention.

There was a movement, a bobbing of something just over the rise of the hill; it looked like a horse was loose on the asphalt trail or it could be a turkey or deer. But then it began to appear over the top of the hill, and it was clear it was a cowboy hat tilted down and covering the face of the person. I didn't recognize the hat as one of the workers of the ranch and it wasn't the one Harrison had been wearing when he left. The figure continued up and over the hill and it was clear it was a man walking along the path. My hand went to my pocket and over my phone.

But, as the man grew closer, his head tilted back and the cowboy hat that had blocked the view of his face rose. My hand went from my pocket to the fence...my fingers curled around the panel.

I looked past the wrinkles at the sides of his eyes, the scruff of a greying beard and past the last fifty years to see the pirate king dancing by the river.

CHAPTER TWENTY-FIVE

With the numbness of the shock, I leaned against the fence and let the crutches fall so I could hold my hands out to him. When his slid into mine, I felt like the scared little eleven-year-old girl trying to crawl out the window of the Campbell's home. The memory of sitting on the beach, crying at the loss of my parents while he held my hands made my legs tremble.

I was so numb, "How?" was the only word my mind could form.

He smiled and a small scar around his left eye was mixed with the laugh lines. A scar along his jawline was nearly hidden by his whiskers. "I received a phone call from an old friend that said he remembered I had been in a foster home when I was young and wondered if the name Rafael was familiar. I said no, but he called back the next day and said the Pirate Queen was looking for her Pirate King and wanted to know if Moreau was familiar." His smile widened, "I didn't tell him yes, I just said it sounded familiar then when I put the two phone calls and names together, I looked up the name Victoria Rafael." His hands tightened around mine. "When I saw the name of your ranch, I knew. Bijou...jewel, it was the name your father called your mother. Then, when I saw your picture? All I had to do was imagine your hair black, messy, and with twigs, leaves, and pine needles in it."

The memory made me laugh and the numbness eased.

"Jesse, after all these years," My voice shook. "I told my daughter to stop looking for you. I didn't want to know if you had left the cowboy and...and..."

"No, I stayed with Dad and the family until I was eighteen," He smiled warmly. "I thought of leaving a number of times, but I grew to love all of them as if they were my true family, because they are. You have no idea what this kid off the streets put his new mother through."

"I want to know your story, where you came from and how you came to this moment." My hands tightened over his, "And, I want to know the truth about what happened to Betty after she left me at the clinic. I have a gut feeling you know."

He nodded with a sigh and leaned over to pick up the crutches, "Let's get you sitting down first."

Before I took the crutches, I wrapped my arms around him and held him close. The tears began to rise and my body trembled when his arms held me tightly. Fifty years had gone by and so much history in that time, but those two days with him had been the beginning of who I was without my parents.

I leaned back and smiled, "I am so thankful you are alive."

He laughed and his eyes sparkled like the pirate king, "It was close a few times, but I scrambled through."

"I got your letter saying you were with a cowboy that rode horses that bucked," I was near tears. "Did you write more?"

"I wrote three, with the second two coming back to the ranch so I stopped writing."

I took the crutches and led him toward the house, "We can sit on the back deck while we talk but there is something I want to show you."

"I read on your website that you were raised in Arizona where you met your husband and had a ranch there. What led you here to Idaho? Was it your search for me?"

"The pine trees. My parents loved the mountains and forests with all the pine trees. The day of the accident, we were just going for a drive to enjoy them. This place reminded me of them and as soon as I saw this ranch from on top the hill, I felt like I was home. Why would it be from the search?"

He chuckled and shook head, "I was raised about 2 hours south of here in a little town called Kendrick."

I gasped, "No...are you still there?"

"I moved...actually the whole family moved. They are all still involved with the rodeo life and once us kids graduated high school, they moved to where it was simpler for them."

He opened the front door for me and as I crutched by him our eyes met again.

"It is so good to see you, Vic," he grinned.

I nodded with the tears rising again, "You were the first person to ever call me that. I wanted to know about you, but I was so scared that what we found would destroy that pirate on the beach."

"Well, let's hope what I have to say doesn't," He sighed and shut the door behind him.

I let the comment pass for now, and pointed to the coffee table, "Can you bring that green box out to the back with us?"

He picked up the box and hurried ahead of me to slide the door open. When I sat on the outdoor couch, I didn't lay across it like I had the last few weeks, I sat normally with my cast braced on the ground. Much to my surprise, and pleasure, Jesse didn't sit in the chair, instead, he sat down next to me with the box on his lap.

"Open it," I whispered.

He lifted the lid and his eyes changed; narrowed as if going into the past.

"After all these years," he whispered and lifted the old blue blanket out of the box and set it between us as his thumb caressed the material. After a moment, he took my hand, a deep breath, and began.

CHAPTER TWENTY-SIX

JESSE'S STORY

"Go in and buy a new road map." Jesse's father handed him a twenty-dollar bill for what he knew was a sixty-nine-cent map.

From the moment he had met his father, Jesse had been in charge of reading the maps and getting his salesman father from one job to another. By travelling with his father and waiting in the car for hours when his dad had a meeting, they could stay together. His dad had even taught him to drive so when he was tired, Jesse could get them to the next job.

Jesse was six years old and living in New Zealand when his mother passed away. He spent years with his grandparents on their small farm helping with the fields and bird hunting with his grandfather until they tracked down his father in the United States. His father had been a soldier when his parents met and was only passing through New Zealand when Jesse was conceived.

At nine-years-old, Jesse flew with his newly discovered father to North Carolina in the United States. His grandfather had told him that the secret to a happy life was making that life an adventure. Travelling with his father to his new home and then through all the coastal states as his father sold encyclopedias had been an adventure. It was a good life for the first year, until his father met Patty who would unfortunately become his stepmother.

Patty did not like Jesse from the moment she met him and the older he became and the more outspoken of her treatment of him, the less she liked him. At the time, Jesse didn't know that he was putting his father between him and the evil stepmother; that someday his father was going to have to choose a side.

Today was that day.

"Today", Jesse had heard Patty say the word at least a dozen times as they prepared for the trip down to the beach. It was whispered twice in the car.

And now, as he took the twenty-dollar bill from his father and looked up into his face, Jesse knew his father was doing as Patty demanded. His father didn't even look him in the eye; he just walked away to pretend he was going to the restroom at the side of the building. Instead of going into the gas station, Jesse sat down on the bench next to the door to the gas station and waited. His father appeared within a minute, and without a look back, he walked straight to the car.

Jesse didn't see Patty when his father got in the car, but when he began to pull away, he could see her looking at Jesse. She smiled with a "got you, you little bastard" look she always gave him when his father would take her side in an argument. But Jesse didn't mind seeing her for a final time, because he could do the one thing he knew she hated. He held up the middle finger of one hand, while the other hand waved over the top of it. It was his way of telling her to 'fuck off'. Her face scrunched in distaste which made Jesse grin.

It pleased him that her seeing the gesture and his grin was the last thing she would see of him. He would never see his father again, which Jesse didn't mind. If the man didn't have the guts enough to stand-up to the woman and tell her he was not abandoning his child at a gas station, then Jesse didn't want anything to do with him. Instead, Jesse would focus on what his grandfather had told him; make life an adventure. At eleven years old, Jesse had started his life.

He sat on the bench and decided on a plan. He bought the map his father told him to because he was going to need it. When they left, his father had driven back toward town, so Jesse walked down the road to the beach.

He swam and played in the sand all day without a care in the world. No one asked him where his parents were and a few people even offered him food. When the sun went down, he wandered the beach and looked for items left behind. He found three beach towels which became a pillow and blanket that night as he slept on the beach for the first time. He also found a small pair of scissors he used to make his long jeans into shorts.

In the morning, he stashed the towels behind a large rock and mingled with the tourist, beach combers, and the multitude of kids. As the sun went down on his second day on his own, he sat on the beach and stared out over the blue water and sky as far as he could see. This was a much better life than living with Patty.

Jesse stayed at the beach the whole summer and stole food from unsuspecting people who spent their days there. In the summer, there were people there all week. When the temperature began to lower and school started for the kids, the weekdays were long and the food scarce. Adults seeing him alone on the beach began to question him. The evenings became colder and his nights sleeping outside would soon come to an end. He needed to go somewhere warmer, so he pulled out his only possession; the map.

He stood at the side of the small restaurant by the beach and waited for the fruit delivery truck he knew was going south where the weather would be warmer. Once the driver had taken the boxes of fruit out of the back of his truck and walked into the building, Jesse seized the moment and crawled into the back of the truck. He hid between boxes in case the driver looked in, but he didn't. The man crawled into the truck and started down the road; south like Jesse had wanted. His adventure at the beach was over, so now he was on to his next.

When the truck pulled into a motel, Jesse tucked himself deeper into the boxes and watched the driver take out a suitcase and walk into the building. Jesse sighed in relief then looked at the signs. They were in Savannah, Georgia. Perfect, they were right along with his plan of going to south Florida for the winter. It would be warmer there and he could live on the beach. Since he had taken food from the beach goers over the last few months, he still had nineteen dollars and change from the purchase of the map. Like his grandfather had taught him, Jesse did not keep his money all in one spot. Half of it was in his jeans pocket and the other half in his shoe.

His cut-off shorts were getting tighter around the waist, and the hem was getting pretty high up his legs. He would be needing new clothes soon and didn't know how much they cost.

As the night grew darker, Jesse fell asleep tucked between boxes and with a stomach full of oranges from the boxes.

He woke to the slam of the truck door and roar of the engine. But the driver did not continue south. The first sign Jesse saw said they were heading inland to Montgomery, Alabama. When they stopped at the gas station, Jesse slid out of the truck. He was sitting on a large boulder reading the map when he saw someone approaching. He slowly turned to see a police officer walking toward him and thought of running but didn't think he would have a chance in outrunning the man.

"How are you doing?" The officer smiled.

"Fine." Jesse mumbled.

"And where are your parents?"

Jesse stared at him and wasn't sure what to say. He was twelve now and could take care of himself. "At home."

"Little young to be out here by yourself."

"I manage." Jesse had a sinking feeling that this was the end of this first adventure.

"Well, according to the man that saw you sneak out of the back of the fruit truck, you look like you're a runaway."

"I'm not a runaway." Jesse huffed and puffed out his chest because it was the truth. He hadn't run away from anything or anyone.

"Yeah, well, for now you'll need to come with me until we get ahold of your parents." The officer leaned down and gripped Jesse elbow.

He didn't fight because there was no sense in it. He'd just use his head when the time came.

"What's your name?" The officer asked as he opened the back door of the car.

If they didn't know his real name, they wouldn't know who his parents were and couldn't make him go back.

"Jack," Jesse answered.

"Alright, Jack, I'm Officer Greenfield," The police officer smiled. "I'm going to take you to the station, get a good meal in you, and see if we can't find you some clothes that fit."

That didn't sound bad, Jesse thought, and the idea of running away as soon as he could was dismissed.

Three hours later, Jesse finished the last of three hamburgers and the pile of French fries. He had nearly finished a full gallon of milk. He was also sitting in new jeans that were almost too long for him, a new black T-shirt, and had new black and white sneakers on his feet. Somewhere during that time, he had also given Officer Greenfield his new full name and where he lived; Jack Johnson from Montgomery, Alabama. From the look on the officer's face, he didn't believe him.

"No one is missing a Jack Johnson," Officer Greenfield leaned back in his chair and smirked.

Jesse just shrugged and ate the last fry.

"That means, you'll have to go to the orphanage if we can't find a foster home to take you until we can find your parents."

Jesse was not surprised. Many nights on the beach he had wondered what would happen to him if he was caught by himself. He had read about orphanages and knew it wasn't where he wanted to be. He would escape the first chance he could.

He was surprised how many kids were at the orphanage. He saw at least twenty when they first arrived and a few more after that. Everyone seemed nice, at first, then, as night approached, the kids became quiet and a few of the girls hid in corners and closets. Jesse had no idea why.

When he lay down on the small bed in the dormitory room, he was looking forward to sleeping on a real mattress for the first time in six months. The first sign of trouble started with a whimper from one of the beds. Jesse turned to see the tall figure of an adult pulling one of the kids from their bed and out of the room. He had no idea who it was or why they took them. He was still awake when the kid walked into the room and to their bed. Within moments, he heard crying, so he slid from his bed and followed the sound.

"Go back to bed before you get us all in trouble," He heard whispered from someone in the room.

Jesse ignored them until he found the girl in her bed crying. She was younger than him.

"Are you OK?" He knelt next to the bed and whispered.

"What?" She gasped and shrunk away from him while pulling her blankets to her chin.

"What's your name? I'm Jack."

"My name is Linda."

"Are you OK? Why are you crying?"

"I don't like what he does to me, and it hurts."

Jesse's stomach ached and his breath caught; he had seen enough movies and heard stories at school to know what she meant.

"Did you tell anyone?"

"Yes, and no one cares."

"I…" He had no idea what to say. "Your parents?"

"My mom died last month, and Dad didn't know how to take care of me, so he brought me here," she whispered. "And that man has done that every night. I tell him I hate it and it hurts but he just laughs and does it anyway."

"Why don't you run away?"

"Where would I go?" She whispered and the tears began again. "Maybe, someday, I'll get adopted and get away from him."

"I hope so," Jesse whispered. "I'm sorry…"

He lay awake most of the night and heard one more kid pulled from their bed. They didn't return.

The long tables in the dining hall were full when they gathered for breakfast. Jesse could see Linda sitting at the second table. Her head was down, and her shoulders slumped. They were fed oatmeal and bread. It reminded Jesse of a book he had read at school and decided he had eaten better at the beach.

"See that guy by the door?" A boy leaned over and whispered to Jesse.

The man in question was older with a large stomach and a scowl on his face as he watched the kids eat. "Yeah."

"Stay as far away from him as you can."

Jesse sighed and looked around at the kids. He hadn't seen it the night before, but now he could see they all looked scared and most had bruises. He did not want to be here.

After breakfast, they were escorted to the back of the building where there was a large yard with swings and balls. The kids ran out of the building as if it was on fire.

Jesse had hesitated at the door and when he turned, the man he was supposed to stay away from was right behind him. Jesse barely managed to duck the large hand that was swinging toward his head. He ran out to the mass of kids, through them, and just continued until he ran into a tall fence that was thirty yards in the trees. He scrambled up the nearest tree and leaped over the fence to his freedom, then took off at a run.

When he looked over his shoulder, there were no adults in sight, but two boys were running right behind him. They reached the road, looked at each other, and without a word, ran in different directions.

Jesse swore he would never let himself get caught again, but he still walked toward town. When he arrived, he stood in the parking lot of the police station for an hour waiting for Officer Greenfield. When he finally appeared and walked toward his car, Jesse stood up but made sure he was a good distance from the police officer so he could make a safe escape.

CHAPTER TWENTY-SEVEN

Officer Greenfield turned and shook his head with smirk, "Aren't you supposed to be at the orphanage?"

"No, I was never meant to be there," Jesse said honestly because he truly believed his adventure did not include an orphanage. "But there is a little girl there named Linda."

"And?"

"One of the adults is taking her out of the main room and hurting her every night. She's younger than me." The officer's eyes narrowed, and his chest rose. Jesse knew he understood what was happening. "I can take care of myself, but she needs help, and the other kids do, too."

They stared at each other a moment before the officer spoke, "You need help, you call this department and ask for me. I'll go get Linda."

Jesse nodded then turned to run back into the trees. He ran to a phone booth and picked up the phone book. He tore out the page that had the phone number of the police station, folded it carefully, and tucked it into the pocket of his new jeans. Every day, he repeated the number to himself until he had it memorized and knew he would never forget it.

It was three months later when he was walking along a road in Jacksonville that a car pulled to a stop next to him.

"Are you out here by yourself?" The woman driver asked him.

"No, my parents are waiting for me up the road."

"There is nothing up the road for miles," she argued. "Get in and I'll take you to town."

Jesse hesitated, but decided if she took him to the police, he would just get away again...and, she took him to the police station. He glared at the woman as the officer took his arm and walked him into the building.

"What's your name?" The man asked.

"Jack Johnson, you can call Officer Greenfield in the Mason Police Department to confirm." Jesse smiled innocently. "And I'd like to ask him a question."

The officer hesitated, then reached for the phone. "I'm looking for an Officer Greenfield." His brows rose and he turned to Jesse. "This is Officer Munson and I have a runaway named Jack Johnson here. He wanted me to confirm with you that was his name before I take him over to the foster home. He also wants to ask you a question."

He handed the phone to Jesse.

"Hello?"

"Well, Jack, how long you staying at the foster home this time?"

Jesse smiled, "Not long."

"Make sure you get a good meal…what was it? Three hamburgers and a large plate of fries?"

"Yeah, I will, but did you find Linda?"

"I did, Jack. I not only found her, but my wife and I are in the process of adopting her."

For the first time since he had been abandoned, Jesse wanted to cry. "Thank you."

"Thank you. The adults who were hurting her and the other kids are now in jail and will be going to prison soon."

"Oh, good," Jesse sighed. "I guess there was a reason for the slight detour on my adventure."

"You changed her life…probably saved her life."

"Make sure she has the life she deserves," Jesse sighed. "I'm on another detour right now."

"Yeah," Officer Greenfield chuckled. "You know how to reach me when you need me."

"Okay," Jesse handed the phone back to Officer Munson who had been watching him closely.

It was just three hours after being dropped off at the foster home before the foster father threw a punch at Jesse because he didn't want to take off his shoes when he went to bed. Other than he had what was left of his money in the shoe. He needed his shoes to run away.

The first fist hit him in the left side, but Jesse ducked the second and third swings. It just seemed to anger the man even more. Jesse didn't even make it to bedtime before he was running out the back door of the house and down the road.

He was going to have to make sure that he wasn't seen walking down the road by himself. At least he got to find out that Linda was okay and had a new home.

On a particularly cold day, Jesse walked into a store just before a rainstorm started. Thunder, lightning, and the downpour had him wandering around the store for hours. He tried to stay out of sight of the people working there so they didn't realize how long he stayed. He was standing next to the book display when the announcement over the speakers said they were closing in five minutes. His eyes stopped on a book; The Adventures of Tom Sawyer. If this Tom could write about his adventures, then maybe, someday, Jesse could write about his own. When the lights began to turn off, Jesse realized they didn't know he was there. Taking the book from the rack, he hid until he saw the employees leave and lock the door behind them.

For the rest of the rainy night, Jesse found a chair in the back of the store and read the book; twice. When the store opened, he stuffed the book in his back pocket and calmly walked out the door. He had made up his mind; his next adventure was to go to the Mississippi River to become a pirate.

It was a small bottle of milk that detoured his adventure again, but it was how he met the woman that would change his life; Betty Sanders.

*****

He was sitting in the back of the police car, when a little white car drove in next to them. A woman with blonde hair pulled back into a ponytail and covered with a dark red scarf emerged from the vehicle. She seemed too young to be a children's counselor. And, she was pretty. Her smile was aimed at the police officer at first but when it moved to Jesse, he sighed.

"Hello, young man," Her voice was warm and soothing. "What's your name?"

"Jesse," He whispered in a bit of awe and instantly knew he had made the mistake but couldn't just suddenly change his mind and say 'Jack'.

"Well, Jesse, my name is Betty Sanders and I'm here to help you."

"I don't need help."

"I'm going to guess that anyone stealing milk from a store is in the need of some kind of help; especially when they are so young." Her eyes twinkled as she teased him.

"I'm eighteen," He said in a strong, deeper than normal, voice.

Her smile widened letting him know she didn't believe him, "Come on over and get in my car. I'll take you to a warm house and you can sleep on a clean, soft mattress tonight."

That did sound good. Months at the beach and hitch hiking across states made him yearn for a soft bed. He stepped out of the police car and into hers.

"Is it your place?" He asked with a hopeful smile.

She just laughed, "No, I'm not a foster parent."

"So, a foster home instead of an orphanage?" He sighed.

Betty glanced at him as she pulled out of the parking lot, "You've had experience with both?"

"Briefly."

Her lips pursed and wiggled back in forth, "Did you have a bad family?"

Jesse was surprised at her question because no one, in the 18 months he had been on his own, had asked him about his family. "My mother died when I was six, I lived with my grandparents before my dad showed up. Then, after he got married and she didn't like me, he left me at a gas station." He had no idea why he was telling her the truth.

"Oh, I'm so sorry, Jesse."

From her concerned eyes, and slight frown, he knew she was telling the truth.

"Not all families are bad, Jesse, and there are parents looking for children that they will take care of and love."

"Even at my age?" He huffed.

"You mean eighteen?" She teased. He chuckled and nodded. "I'll admit it is harder for teenagers, but I'll try my best to find you a home where you can have regular meals and a soft bed at night." She glanced at him and smiled. "We'll start with the Campbell's house for the next couple days. Will you stay long enough to give me a chance to find you a home?"

He didn't want to say yes, so he didn't say anything. It wasn't his fault if she took it as a yes.

From the moment Betty left him with the tall old couple, Jesse was basically ignored. He was told to stay outside and was only allowed in the house for breakfast, dinner, and to sleep. The wide, fast flowing river behind the house and barn encouraged his imagination of being a pirate. He didn't care about the Campbell's at all. He ignored them in return, and spent his time at the river fishing, picking apples, reading his book, and dreaming.

On his third day, Betty arrived with a young girl named Kathy. The woman was pleased to see Jesse had stayed. Kathy was ten and her parents had left her with her grandmother.

When the grandmother died, Betty had been assigned to find her a home until she could find the absent parents.

Jesse and Kathy spent the first day at the river. She didn't talk very much, but Jesse didn't mind. He was used to silence, but the morning after her first night when Kathy was in tears at the breakfast table, he became concerned. Mr. Campbell had left for work, and Mrs. Campbell was sitting on the couch watching television as they tried to eat the grey oatmeal.

"What's the matter?" Jesse whispered.

Kathy turned and looked at him. Her eyes were dazed and the skin on her cheeks and lips were red as if she had a rash, "I just can't."

"Can't what?"

Tears fell, "I'd rather be dead."

"Kathy? What…?"

She rose to take her bowl full of grey oatmeal to the sink and washed the dishes as they had been instructed to do. Jesse hurried behind her then followed her as they walked to the river.

"Kathy? What's the matter?"

"I can't do this, Jesse."

"Do what?"

They were standing on the beach with the rushing river next to them.

"I can't be his wife."

Jesse gasped, "You aren't his wife."

Tears slid down her face, "He told me last night that I was going to stay with them and be his other wife." Her body convulsed and she turned away to throw up in the river.

"No!" Jesse growled. "That is not going to happen, your parents..."

"It already did." She fell to her knees, with chin to her chest as she sobbed.

Jesse held back the scream and just stood and looked out over the water. Mr. Campbell did that to her while he was sleeping in the room right next door and Jesse had no idea what was happening.

"I'll protect you until your parents get here," He promised her. "I've been getting ready to leave and have a pillowcase full of biscuits and apples. We'll go find Betty."

Kathy didn't say anything, she just looked out at the river as the sobs began to slow down.

"I'll go get some more apples upriver, then we'll leave."

Still, she said nothing.

"I'll be right back." Jesse ran to the brush and pulled the pillowcase out of the trees then ran upriver. Another dozen apples were added to the pillowcase before he ran back to the beach, but Kathy wasn't there.

He tossed the supplies back in the brush, then ran up to the house and looked inside the back window. Mrs. Campbell was sitting on the couch eating a sandwich and watching television. He turned and ran back down to the river, to the last spot the crying girl had been. Kathy's shoes were at the edge of the water and her footprints were there in the wet sand.

He gasped and ran into the water as his eyes desperately searched for her, but she wasn't there.

"I'd rather be dead."

CHAPTER TWENTY-EIGHT

"Kathy!" Jesse cried out and ran down the edge of the river. He desperately searched for her; calling her name but knowing she wouldn't hear it over the rumble of the river and worse, under the water.

She was nowhere to be found, so he turned back and ran for the house. To his surprise, Mr. Campbell's car was in the driveway.

Jesse burst through the back door and both adults swung around in surprise, "Kathy went in the river."

"It's too damn cold and swift to be swimming," Mrs. Campbell grumbled, but from the look in her eyes, Jesse knew she knew why Kathy went in the river. "Didn't you tell her that?"

His body tingled in shock. They were going to blame him?

"Why would you let her swim in the river?" Mr. Campbell yelled and rushed at Jesse. He had just enough time to duck into his bedroom before the older man got to him. There was a bang on the door and the man yelled. "You let her die!"

Without hesitation, Jesse ran to the window and slid it open. He was leaving. There was no way Betty would believe him with the couple saying it was his fault. He would probably go to jail!

He had jumped out of the window but stopped when he heard a car drive in. He peeked around the corner of the house to see Betty's car. That was why Mr. Campbell had come home from work.

Jesse's heart dropped. There was no way he could survive in jail, so he started to turn but stopped when he saw the back door of the car open and heard the front door of the house open. A girl with tangled long black hair and a blue blanket wrapped around her appeared. When she looked at the Campbell's, her eyes were wide and dazed. When they spoke, she shrunk back into Betty. The girl was already scared of the old couple.

With a sigh of dread, Jesse realized he couldn't leave her alone with them, but if he went out and talked to Betty, they would accuse him and he would go to jail. He jogged to the back door and made it into the house before the front door was open. Mr. Campbell had locked Jesse's door from the hallway and Jesse quickly opened it and stepped inside. He left the door open enough he could eavesdrop.

When the adult's voices faded, indicating they had walked into the kitchen, Jesse stepped into the hallway. The black-haired girl was sitting on the couch and staring at him. He lifted a finger to his lips to keep her quiet, then tip-toed down the hall.

"Her parent's died in a car accident just hours ago," Betty whispered. "We've got a call into relatives but we're not sure how long it will take for them to get here."

"Oh, the poor dear," Mrs. Campbell whispered.

"Hopefully, we'll be back tomorrow," Betty sighed.

Jesse could hear footsteps, so he rushed back down the hallway to his bedroom and closed the door. Leaning back on the wall, he knew he couldn't leave yet. The Campbell's didn't tell Betty about Kathy, so maybe he could last long enough to protect the girl, then leave before they had him arrested.

He jumped out the window again and made it out to the barn before the back door opened and the girl stepped out. She glanced around with eyes wide and scared.

"Come on," He waved to her. "We'll be out here until the old guy comes home from work."

Wanting to keep her calm and try to calm his own nerves, Jesse jumped up on top of the first un-chopped log and then to the next. "Come, have a seat in the queen's chair," He dramatically swung out an arm.

Her brows came together.

"Imagination," Jesse chuckled and jumped in the air and landed with both feet on the ground, then dramatically flopped onto the log next to the 'queen's chair'.

Her fingers gripped the blanket tightly. It seemed to give her a sense of security.

"I'm Jesse, well…this time anyway." He tried to cover the mistake and make sure no one knew it was his real name. She just frowned so he laughed. "I've been to one orphanage, and this is my second foster home and each time I give them a new name. What's your name?"

"Victoria Moreau," she whispered.

"That's a beautiful name, fit for a queen, but do you have an accent?"

"I was born in France," she nodded. "We just moved here last year."

"Cool, accent," Jesse said honestly. "I was born in New Zealand. My dad brought me here a few years ago."

"Where is he?"

"Don't know."

"Jesse?"

"Yeah?"

She looked right into his eyes and took a deep breath, "Are my parents dead?"

This was the worst day ever. After one girl kills herself an hour before to get away from Mr. Campbell and they accuse him of killing her, he had to tell this one her parents were dead. The air rushed out of Jesse.

He sighed, "I'm sorry, Victoria. I heard Betty tell the old people that they were killed in the car accident and found you 20 yards away."

She buried her face in the blanket and cried.

Jesse just wanted to leave. He looked down the river to where Kathy's body had disappeared, then down to Victoria who was trying to stop crying because of her parent's death. He thought of Linda who had been in danger but was now a policeman's daughter. Life can change so fast. He needed to protect Victoria, and, luckily, she was only going to be there one day then he could leave.

So, he spent the day entertaining her with stories from his book and fishing. The dreaded moment came with the old woman at the back door yelling for "Vickie".

"My name is Victoria." She said to Jesse with a frown.

He smiled and looked over his shoulder, "I know that, but it's the old lady calling you."

"But, I didn't tell her my name."

"Someone did," He whispered and picked up the pillowcase of apples, slid the book into it, then tossed it into the bushes.

"Vickie!"

Victoria grimaced and her body tensed.

"She'll come stomping out here," Jesse whispered and slowly turned.

They walked to the house and followed the grumbling woman down the hall to the kitchen. The old woman began stirring something in a pan then swirled around and looked at Victoria and growled, "Say something now or you can go to your room for the rest of the night."

Victoria backed up so fast she bumped into Jesse then she turned and ran to the room. The old woman didn't even acknowledge he was there and went back to stirring. With a sigh, he jogged down the hall, out the door, and around the side of the house to peer into the girl's bedroom. She was leaning back against the door crying so he tapped on the window. Falling to her knees, she scrambled to get to the window and slide it open. He had to push her back into the window and try to keep her calm.

Jesse held her hands tightly to reassure her everything was going to be all right, and he would be there to protect her. He meant every word.

"I want my mum...." She cried and Jesse felt his own tears rise for her. But, he had to be strong.

He stayed with her even when Mr. Campbell came home, and his wife began arguing with him. When the house became quiet, Victoria came up with the idea of spending the night in the barn. She was a tough girl.

The next morning, they returned to the window to find it closed and the bedroom a mess.

"Why would they be in there already?" She whispered.

"He was…" Jesse shook his head and thought of Kathy. "You need to be with Betty."

"I agree, but what do we do until then?"

"Let's go down to the river and just pretend we went fishing early and like nothing happened."

She ate apples on the fallen log then suddenly stood and walked to the river's edge.

"What are you doing?" Jesse gasped and ran to her. She knelt in the same spot Kathy had knelt the day before.

"Just washing up a bit," she smiled. "One night in the woods and another on a dirt floor in the barn and I'm a bit dirty. I don't think I have ever been this filthy."

Jesse couldn't get himself to leave her side until she was back on the log trying to comb her hair, then he went back to fishing. He had just caught one when the Campbell's appeared and stomped across the yard.

"Jesse," Victoria cried.

"You'll be, okay," His voice was low and smoothing, then rose in energy, "Look what we caught this morning!" Jesse held up the fish and cheerfully showed the older couple which caused them to glare at him, but they turned to Victoria.

"Vickie! Why aren't you in your room?" Mrs. Campbell growled.

Victoria's eyes widened and she said nothing.

"You damn child," Mrs. Campbell stepped forward and Jesse knew she was going to hit her.

"We just came fishing," Jesse hurried to Victoria's side with the fish dangling from the end of the line. "Before sunrise is always a good time to fish."

"It was…" Mr. Campbell started gruffly then stopped. He glowered at Jesse.

"I have never seen a child more addicted to fishing than you," Mrs. Campbell grumbled at Jesse and took the pole and fish from him. "Get it on up to the house and we'll have it for dinner tonight."

Jesse followed behind Victoria to protect her from Mr. Campbell but when they walked down the hall, something hit him from behind and he was suddenly falling into his bedroom. A fist on both sides had him falling backwards and he hit his head on the dresser. Everything went black.

Somewhere in the hazy darkness, Jesse heard his name being called. Hand to head, he tried to open his eyes. When he tried to sit up, pain shot through his body. He remembered the two punches Mr. Campbell had landed on his ribs, but he was sure that when he was unconscious, the man had kicked him in the back. His whole body hurt, and he fell back onto the floor.

After taking deep breaths to clear his head, he finally managed to sit up. As he was pulling himself to a standing position by using the bed frame, an ear-piercing scream echoed down the hall. Victoria!

CHAPTER TWENTY-NINE

Forgetting the pain, he ran out of the room and down the hall. Mrs. Campbell's fist was raised toward the screaming girl. As if he were a football player, Jesse ran right into the old woman making her crash to the floor. He grabbed Victoria's arm, but her eyes were closed, and she screamed again.

"Vic, it's me," Jesse gasped.

"You damn…" Mrs. Campbell yelled from the floor as she scrambled to stand.

Jesse pulled Vic out of the kitchen, down the hall, and they burst out the back door. They were halfway to the barn when the woman yelled.

"Wait until Mr. Campbell gets home, you little son-of-a-bitch!"

They ran toward the river with confidence the woman would not follow. Jesse stopped and his arms went around his waist to try and relieve the pain. "She won't come out here," he groaned.

"Jesse? Are you hurt? What's wrong? What happened?"

"I'm okay," he grimaced and turned toward the river. "He got me before I realized what was happening."

"What do you mean?" she cried.

"He just got a couple blows in before I could get away, then, I guess, I hit my head," His hand went to the back of his head. "It hurts like hell."

"I saw you through the window. You were lying on the floor. He must have knocked you out."

They stood silently for a moment as he rubbed his head with one hand; the other was wrapped around his side.

"Are you sure you're okay?" She whispered.

"Yeah, I will be," He huffed. "I've been hit harder, but I've never been knocked out before."

"Oh, Jesse," She started crying.

"It's been a long morning, Vic," Jesse whispered and put a hand on her shoulder. She flinched away and he jerked his hand back. "Sorry, Vic, I didn't mean anything."

"No," She cried. "Mr. Campbell…he…he…"

Jesse growled, "Did he hurt you? Touch you?"

She looked mortified…just like Kathy before she walked into the river. "He grabbed my shoulder and he…kissed my head…"

"Oh, damn, Vic. Betty better show up today." He shook his head then moaned with a hand going to the back.

"She called…they aren't coming until tomorrow."

His body slumped and eyes widened, then he turned and looked out at the river where Kathy had died, then to the house.

"Maybe we should try and call," She held out Betty's card. "I found this, but the phone is right next to her."

"Well," Jesse huffed. "Then we head upriver until we find a place we can make a call or find Betty."

"Okay, let's go."

"Nah, can't in the daylight. One thing I've learned, if adults see kids walking by themselves, they'll call the cops on ya. That's how I got caught and thrown into the first foster home."

"So, what do we do now?"

"Did ya get something to eat?"

They ate and stayed at the river reading his book until the sun started to go down. Jesse knew he needed to go back in the house for supplies, but Victoria was scared and started crying. Once he made her promise never to go to the house again, no matter what, he hid her in the brush, then walked up to the window on the back door. The old lady was sitting on the couch. She looked asleep so he went to the side window that led to the kitchen.

Jesse slid the window open and glanced into the house. He could barely see the woman's feet, so he pulled himself up through the window. Pain shot through his ribs and back and he grimaced to keep from making a sound.

When he slid into the kitchen, he remained still and looked to see the woman had not moved. He tip-toed through the kitchen to the cabinet where he knew she kept extra blankets and linen. He found another pillowcase and carefully slid open the drawer where he had seen a map. There was also a flashlight, so he dropped both into the pillowcase. He glanced over his shoulder and the woman was still sleeping, his eye caught something blue. It was Victoria's blanket stuffed into the garbage can, so he slowly lifted it out and was stuffing it into the pillowcase when the front door suddenly opened.

Jesse and Mr. Campbell looked each other in the eye for a moment before Jesse bolted and had just enough time to throw the supplies out the window before the man hit him from behind propelling him over the table. His jaw scraped down the side of the table as he slid off and onto the floor. His head hit the floor with a thump, but he rolled away from the charging man. Jesse turned to look back as a fist slammed on his left cheek. Then another hit him on the other side. He was dazed, but he thought of Victoria hiding in the trees. He had to get to her before the Campbell's found her.

A loud growl had Jesse turning to see the old woman standing in the doorway to the kitchen with a shotgun in her arms.

"Get out of the way," she yelled at her husband. "I'll take care of that son-of-a-bitch."

Jesse dove through the window as the blast from the shotgun rang out. He felt stings in his leg but the slam against the ground shook his whole body. He knew they would expect him to run across the yard, so he grabbed the bag of supplies and tucked under the brush next to the house.

He heard the back door slam against the house then Mr. Campbell yell, "You son-of-a-bitch!"

Jesse leaned around the side of the house enough to see the couple running toward the river and at Vic. As he scrambled to his feet and kept tucked into the trees along the side, he prayed Vic would remain hidden. He made it into the barn and found a pitchfork to use as a weapon if they found Victoria. He stood at the barn door as moments passed with his body aching, breath in gasps, and eyes watching for any movement. He could feel the skin around his eyes tightening as they began to swell.

Finally, the woman appeared walking toward the house and was soon followed by the man, but there was no sign of Victoria. Jesse waited until the couple were in the house before stepping through the barn to the back door.

"Vic," He whispered but there was no answer. Was she still there? "Vic the victorious, it's me."

"Where?"

His body exhaled in relief at the sound of her voice.

"Edge along the back of the barn. Don't go into the open in case they are watching."

She finally appeared and their journey began upriver through unseen brush and limbs. It was dark out, but Jesse could feel the skin around his eyes burning and his left eye began to ache. He held back the cries of pain when the branches hit his throbbing face or his ribs and back. As they ran across beaches the stings in his legs worsened.

She told him the Campbell's were going to blame him for her disappearance. Combined with Kathy's death in the river, he had no choice but to get to Betty first. They forged on and filled the silence with her teaching him French words. It entertained Vic, and kept him from thinking of the pain.

On one of the beaches, she fell to the ground and cried about her lost parents. That was worse than the physical pain, so he held her hands until she stopped. They ventured across the river to an island with the cold water giving his legs some relief. Each time he fell, he splashed the cold water into his face. It burned and he could feel sweat trickling down his face and across the jaw.

When they crested the hill on the island, and he saw the shallowness of the next river crossing and the lights of town in the distance, the relief was nearly overwhelming. Jesse cried out, "Oh, Victoria, Queen of the Pirates, look what lays ahead."

The exhilaration of seeing the lights of their destination eased the pain coursing through his entire body. They laughed and ran through the water and into the trees. When they made it into a clearing, Victoria finally saw his swollen face. From the look in her eyes, Jesse knew it was bad, but they had no choice and continued forward. They found a road with signs, and he was able to find their location on the map. When we finally made it to Betty's office, he leaned against the back of the building in exhaustion and pain.

"We did it, Jesse."

"Yeah, we did, and Queen Victoria was strong and brave on the journey."

"Only because the mighty pirate led the way."

They both chuckled, but the energy was draining.

"Now what?" she asked.

"We wait until she gets here, then you can go with her."

She gasped in disbelief, "Jesse? You're not coming with me?"

"I'm on to my next adventure out west as soon as you're safe with Betty."

"But...I don't want you to leave."

Jesse sighed, "You have a family waiting for you, and I have an adventure waiting for me."

He leaned against the wall, then slowly slid down to stretch his legs out across the ground in front of him. He couldn't keep his eyes open.

"You sleep," she whispered. "I'll wake you when she gets here. I remember she drives a white car."

"I'm leaving as soon as she gets here, so she can't put me in another foster home." He succumbed to the darkness.

"Jesse, she is here." He heard Victoria's voice as images of Kathy and the Campbell's filled his nightmare.

He tried to open his eyes, but one wouldn't open, it was swollen shut. He peered at her through the slit of the other and began to sit up when a deep moan escaped. It was hard to move as the pain shot through him, but he forced himself to stand. He had to get away before Betty tried to put him in another foster home or orphanage.

His book lay on his lap, so he stretched his arms and legs as he slid it into his back pocket. When they finally saw Betty, she was just walking into the building, but her car door was still open.

"She's coming back out for something," Jesse whispered then turned. No eleven-year-old could have been stronger than this girl at his side. "Queen Victoria?"

"Yes, King of the Pirates?"

"You be strong and have a good life," He whispered and brushed the hair away from his injured face. He could barely see out of his left eye. "Promise me you'll have the life your parents would want for you."

"I promise…will I ever see you again? How will I know you're okay?"

"I have Betty's card. I'll send her a letter to send to you and let you know where my adventure led me and that I'm okay."

Tears slid down her cheeks, "So…this is the end of Jesse's adventure. Who will you be tomorrow?"

"No matter what name I am called in the future, I will be your Jesse."

Betty appeared out the door and walked toward her car.

"She needs to at least see what that horrible man did to you."

"Yeah, okay," He sighed, no matter what happened next, at least Betty would see his injuries and hopefully she could convince the police he did not kill Kathy or kidnap Victoria. He thought of the Campbells and his body felt cold. "I'm going to make sure it never happens again."

When Betty walked toward them, they walked toward her. She glanced up with a startled smile, then stopped. The keys in her hands fell to the ground as her eyes widened and jaw dropped.

"Victoria? Jesse?" She took a step and stopped as if they were an illusion.

"I brought Vic to you so she was safe," Jesse announced and pushed Victoria toward her.

"What? What happened…?" Betty's voice shook and legs trembled as she slowly walked toward them.

"He beat Jesse," Victoria said.

"He was going to hurt, Victoria," Jesse added.

"We left last night and walked here so they couldn't say Jesse made me run away with him," Victoria huffed.

"Mr. Campbell did this?" She cried and cupped Jesse's cheek gently as her face paled.

Jesse was relieved to see that Betty was truly distressed and shocked. He would have hated if she had known what the Campbell's were doing.

"Yeah, and this," He carefully untucked his shirt and lifted it high to show the red, black, and blue ribs. The bruising nearly wrapped around his whole body.

"Ahhh," Betty gasped as the first sob escaped her. Tears slid from her horror-filled eyes. "The manager said they were good people…good foster…I would never have…if I had known…" She sobbed again and turned to Victoria. Jesse took his chance and turned to disappear around the building and jog to the nearest gas station.

In their travels, his father had taught him to drive, so Jesse waited until a man walked away from a little blue car to go into the gas station then he walked right up to the car and slid onto the driver's seat as if he owned it. The keys were still in the ignition. Within minutes, Jesse was driving down the road with anger overwhelming him.

CHAPTER THIRTY

He parked in the trees around the corner from the Campbell's home and no other cars or people were in sight. As he walked toward the house, he could see Mr. Campbell's car parked in front, so he hid in the brush and trees as he made his way to the window at the back door. Neither Campbell was in sight, but he could see the shotgun lying on the couch. He knew they were keeping it handy in case Jesse returned. There was no doubt it had been reloaded.

Jesse slowly opened the front door and peered inside. There was no one there so he tiptoed to the gun. During his years staying with his grandparents, he used to hunt turkey and ducks with a shotgun, so he knew how to break open the gun to look at the shells inside. They were new, so he slammed the gun back together. The sound echoed into the room and Mr. Campbell walked out of his bedroom as Mrs. Campbell appeared at the kitchen door with a long butcher knife in her hand. They both glared with a snarl.

"What are you going to do? Shoot me?" Mrs. Campbell spat.

"Why not?" Jesse huffed. "You're blaming me for killing Kathy when you know it's because of what he did to her." Jesse snarled at the man. "She said she'd rather die than have you touch her."

The old man took a step forward and Jesse lifted the gun to his shoulder.

"You think you scare us?" The old man growled.

"How many kids have you put in the river?" Jesse glared. They had taken the news of Kathy killing herself too easy for it not to have happened before.

"In the river, in the ground, who the fuck cares?" Mrs. Campbell huffed a contemptuous laugh. "It sure as hell weren't any of the parents. You and them, are nothing more than throw-aways."

Jesse's stomach tightened and his finger quivered on the trigger. "If I'm going to be arrested for Kathy's death, then I might as well go to prison for killing the people responsible. You're not going to stop unless I stop you." He snarled at the old woman. "I heard you tell him to put the room back together. I wasn't sure until then that you knew what he was doing to the girls...what he did to Kathy and was going to do to Victoria. You're as nasty and evil as he is."

"You're nothing but a fucking throw-away garbage kid," Mrs. Campbell lifted the knife and charged him.

The blast made Jesse step back as the front of her black shirt shredded, blood spewed, and she fell backward hitting the wall. The knife bounced on the ground as her body fell next to it. Mr. Campbell charged and was only a few feet away from the end of the barrel when the blast ripped through his white shirt that instantly turned red. With a large thud, he fell to the ground in a heap.

Then, Jesse heard the car door slam.

"JESSE!"

He looked over his shoulder to see Betty running to the house. Her face was white, eyes horrified, and mouth agape. "What did you do?"

"They weren't going to stop." He set the shotgun down on the couch as she gasped at the two dead Campbells.

"Oh, Jesse," She cried and looked at him with eyes in a bit of a haze.

He felt nothing. If he was a garbage kid, then it didn't matter. He looked between the couple, then to Betty.

"Where's Kathy?" Her voice shook as if fearing the answer.

"Mr. Campbell told her she was going to be his wife and he hurt her the night she got here. She walked into the river and killed herself, so she didn't have to be with him. They said they were going to blame me for it."

Betty's eyes filled with tears, as her hand went to her stomach.

"They said there were kids in the river and in the ground and who cared because we were just throw-away garbage kids that no one cared about." His chin rose in defiance. "I ain't garbage."

"No…Jesse, you aren't," She wiped away the tears. "And neither was Kathy nor any other child they harmed." She took in a shaking breath. "I had no idea, I swear Jesse, no idea."

He just nodded with a sigh. "I've seen bad and those two were beyond that; they were evil."

"Stay here," She whispered and jogged down the steps to her car. He watched her lift her purse out of it then toss it back in. She rushed past him and walked to the kitchen where

Mrs. Campbell's purse sat and took all of the cash out of it then put a couple dollar bills back. "If there's a couple dollars in there, no one would think she was robbed."

"What?" Jesse frowned.

She glanced at Mr. Campbell's body and her whole body shook at the sight of the blood. She turned to Jesse and held out the cash, "Take this and leave."

"What?" He gasped.

"Take this cash, find somewhere to go and disappear." She shoved the money into his hands. "I shot them in self-defense when I came to confront them about you, Kathy, and Victoria."

He stared at her in disbelief, "But my fingerprints are on the gun...yours aren't."

"Then we fix that," She stepped to the gun and used her dress to wipe the barrel and stock. "I'll need your help."

Together, they carefully placed the gun in the hands of the dead bodies.

"Hopefully, since I'm confessing, they won't even test them," Betty's hands shook as Jesse showed her how to hold the gun so her own fingerprints would be visible. She dropped the gun on the floor and turned to him, "Jesse, go now, because I have to call the police and you need to be as far away as possible." Betty turned him and pushed him through the door. "Go, before anyone sees you."

"Are you sure?" He whispered.

"Jesse, they will throw you in jail and toss the key if they knew what happened," She huffed. "If they think I did it, they won't even arrest me since it was self-defense."

He stared at her then shook his head, "Alright, but…"

"No, buts…just go and make sure you have a good life."

"I won't let you down." He promised, then turned and ran.

He found a barn a few miles from the Campbell's home and hid in it until his face healed enough people wouldn't wonder what happened to him. He stole a stack of old newspapers out of the farmhouse garbage to read and found the announcement of Victoria's parent's death; Juliette and Daniel Moreau died in the car accident but there was no cause of the crash announced. Their daughter, who survived, would be in the care of Juliette Moreau's sister.

It took Jesse three weeks to hitchhike across the states and end in California. He had planned on Las Vegas but didn't complain when the trucker's route didn't take him there.

He was sitting at a truck stop in Sacramento watching television and trying to find another semi-truck driver to take him to Vegas when a larger man walked in and struck up a conversation with him. They chatted for an hour before Jesse asked for a ride. The man agreed with a grin on the condition Jesse stayed the night with the man in his trailer. With a loud 'no', the man left.

The next man to walk in the door was shorter, narrower, walked with bowed legs, and wore a cowboy hat. The more the pair talked, the more Jesse liked him. His name was Carl Nichols, and he wasn't just a cowboy, but he was a bucking horse rider; a bronc rider in the rodeo. Jesse loved sitting with him as he told him stories.

"And what's your name?" Carl finally asked.

"Jesse," Jesse answered and nearly groaned. Why did he keep giving out his real name? How was he going to cover it up? Then, he thought of Victoria's dad's name. "Jesse Daniels, but everyone calls me J.D." He was pleased with himself that he had covered his tracks so fast.

"Well, J.D., Vegas is a hell hole for runaway kids," Carl shook his head. "You're sure you want to go there? You're pretty small for your age and that city can just eat you up."

"I can handle it," Jesse nodded. "I can live off the streets until I find a job."

Carl sighed, "Alright, I'll take you there."

Halfway there, just after filling up the fuel tanks for the last leg of the trip, Carl decided Jesse was too young and small for Vegas. He told him he liked Jesse and was going to take him home to Idaho with him.

Through the winding roads of the mountainous state, Jesse knew he made a mistake and was going to be murdered. The man was going to take him to a remote mountain to torture and kill him. He had failed Betty.

CHAPTER THIRTY-ONE

For hours, Jesse talked with the man as if nothing was wrong. Maybe if he liked him enough, he would change his mind and not kill him.

They drove through a small town that was next to a narrow river then turned up a dirt road. Jesse began to sweat. He decided that as soon as the truck stopped, he would just take off at a run back to that small town and the cowboy wouldn't be able to keep up.

His plan changed when they drove into the driveway of a small ranch. A woman and two young girls walked out the door of a barn where three horses were corralled. Maybe Carl had spoken the truth. Maybe Carl's promise to give him a family was really coming true. Maybe Betty had been right.

"Who is that?" He whispered as the truck stopped.

"My wife and daughters, and now your mother and sisters."

Jesse exhaled in disbelief and relief.

A week later, Jesse walked into town to the nearest pay phone with a handful of quarters. His new sisters walked with him but were playing in the park when he made the phone call.

"I'm calling for Officer Greenfield," Jesse told the woman at the police department.

"Who may I say is calling?"

"Jack Johnson from Montgomery, Alabama."

"Just a moment."

The line went silent, and Jesse's heart raced.

"Well, Jack, it is good to know you're still with us." Office Greenfield answered.

"I am sir, barely, but I am."

"You alright?" There was true concern in the man's voice.

"I am, but I was hoping you could check on someone that may not be."

"Alright, who is it?"

"Her name is Betty Sanders."

"I've read the papers, so I know the name."

Jesse wasn't sure what that meant and was afraid to ask. "Officer Greenfield, Betty is…good. She may be going through a rough time, but she is honest and really cares about the kids."

"I know you understand what you're saying, so what do you need?"

"Can you watch over her for me?"

"Jack, were you…? Never mind," he sighed. "If you say she's one of the good ones, I'll believe you. I'll do what I can."

"Thank you, sir. How is Linda?"

"She and my wife are best friends. We honestly couldn't love her more than if she was born to us instead of gifted to us."

Jesse sighed in relief. "I may call again."

"I hope you do."

After he hung up the call, Jesse walked to the post office and mailed his letter.

Dear Victoria;

I promised I would write and let you know I am safe. After hitch hiking across the country, I was picked up and taken to a ranch with horses. I now have a father who rides bucking horses. He and his wife decided to raise me as their own. I guess Betty was right that some people would want to adopt someone my age. They don't have pirates here, but, if you can't be a pirate, then a cowboy is the next best thing.

I hope you are doing well with your aunt and uncle. I'm glad we got away from the Campbells and made it to Betty so you could have a good life.

I will try to write again.

Sincerely,

Your Jesse

CHAPTER THIRTY-TWO

As I sat quietly and listened to Jesse's tale, I wiped away tears, chuckled, admired him more, and was so thankful Sawyer had insisted on finding him.

"So, your real name is Jesse," I chuckled.

"Yeah, I was under Betty's spell and the name just slipped. Did the same with Dad, but I've been called J.D. for fifty years now." He looked out across the bay. "I called Greenfield a month later and found out Betty had been arrested. They said shooting Mr. Campbell was justified but they couldn't believe that Mrs. Campbell had caused a threat."

I gasped with a shake of the head, "She would have killed both of us that night if she could."

"And I still have scars on my leg from the buckshot when she shot at me," He nodded, "Betty was ultimately sent to prison for five years."

"I can't imagine that wonderful woman in a cement cell, eating prison food, and behind locked bars."

"Me either, and felt so damn guilty. When Greenfield told me, I almost told him the truth, but I knew Betty wouldn't want me to go to prison for life. If she did, she would have told them the truth. There were a number of people in the prison that had gone through and survived the Campbell's home or one like it. She was very protected in the prison, and she counseled women to help them get ready to be released into a normal life."

"Do you know what happened to her when she was released?"

Jesse smiled slightly, "The Betty Sanders we knew stopped existing that day. When I turned 18, and I knew they couldn't throw me into another foster home or orphanage, I drove back to meet with Officer Greenfield, and he took me to see Betty."

I gasped, "In the prison?"

"Yeah, she only had two weeks left when I got there and when she walked out of prison a free woman, she climbed into my truck, and I drove her back here with me."

"Oh, Jesse!" Tears filled my eyes.

"She had a good life as J.D.'s aunt from back east," He smiled. "Met a widower with five kids and raised them as her own but never birthed any herself. She worked on their farm, helped with Sunday school, and was a well-thought of woman."

"She lived most of her life as your aunt," The thought made me very happy.

"She did."

"And Linda?"

"Well," Jesse smiled. "While Betty was in prison, she and Greenfield worked with a team of foster parents in putting together new rules and requirements for orphanages and foster homes. At that time, there was so much miscommunication of what was right for a child in the system. In the early 70's they thought it was best not to let a foster parent and child bond.

They thought it was easier and better for the child and system if the kids moved from home to home every few weeks."

"That is so wrong."

"And we all know that now, but back then, there were people fighting for what is in place now to protect the children and help them become functioning adults. The system, in the 70's, was overwhelmed with children."

"So, where does Linda come into that?"

"She heads a foundation back east that oversees foster homes and orphanages all across the nation."

"Oh, Jesse," Tears rose again.

"Like I told Greenfield, *"I guess there was a reason for the slight detour on my adventure."* He sighed again. "I wasn't in that orphanage more than a half day, and had met that little girl for just a minute or two..."

"But your paths crossed, and look how many lives changed because of it," I smiled at him. "Look at how my life turned out because of the 48 hours out of 61 years we spent together. Those two days laid the foundation of who I was without my parents."

"A thousand times I have asked myself why I didn't take Kathy to the apple tree with me. I should have seen..."

"You were thirteen," I reminded him. "What would have happened if she hadn't walked into the river? What would have happened if you had left before I arrived? In a way, her passing saved my life and all the future kids that would have gone through that house. So many heart-breaking stories from that home, but there would have been so many more."

"That's what Betty said," He nodded with a sigh.

I sighed and took his hand; they rested over the top of the blue blanket. "I still think of her when she first saw us that morning. Her reaction and the guilt she must have felt."

"Betty had only worked at that office for a month and hadn't placed anyone at the foster home that had died. Trusting her boss, she didn't investigate them herself. She took Kathy's death upon her shoulders and did not fight the five-year sentence. They thought it was for Mrs. Campbell, Betty took it for Kathy."

"I was 21 when I finally found out what happened to her, and I was so shocked and scared for her when I read she went to prison. But after…she was happy?"

He nodded, "She told me she had peace in her heart. Helping all the women in prison, then helping her husband raise his kids. I'm not sure she ever told him of her past, but she was happy with him and adored the kids and grandkids."

"And you Jesse? After what happened? Does anyone else know about you and the Campbells?"

He shook his head, "Just Betty knew, and now you." He sighed and shook his head. "As I grew older, I came to understand what I did and how I should feel. Or, how society thought I should feel. That there should be forgiveness for people like that." He looked me straight in the eye. "I had seen Kathy…the fear in her eyes, throwing up at what he did to her, and the sheer desperation she had felt to walk into the river. I would shoot them again a thousand times to stop what they were doing. It really didn't have anything to do with them accusing me of Kathy's death, it was for all those kids lost in the river and buried in the ground. They ultimately found the bodies of dozens of kids."

I nodded in understanding, "I only thought of getting away from there...never going back to that house." I said honestly. "Before Betty arrived, you said you were going to make sure it didn't happen again and somewhere in my heart, I knew it was you and not Betty that put an end to their terror. But, just know, that no one will ever know."

He nodded with a smile, then turned and looked around the pastures and pine tree covered mountains, "Your parents would be very proud."

Tears filled my eyes, "I truly wanted to live up to the promise I made to you."

"And I wanted to live up to the promise I made to Betty."

"We both succeeded." I nodded. "How long were you on your own?"

"Just under two years."

"During that time, the people that you met, for however briefly, you truly changed their lives."

He chuckled, "Well, I'd like to say it continued that way, but I'm sure my mother, sisters, and 3 ex-wives would disagree."

"Three?" I laughed.

"It took a while for that adventurous kid to grow up," He admitted with a grin. "I got married because that is what I was told was supposed to happen when you grew up. After the third marriage failed, I took the time to figure out who I was. I traveled back to New Zealand for a few years then traveled across Europe before I found Christina."

"How long have you been married?"

"Fifteen years, you?"

"I was married for 38 years to a wonderful man who believed in my dreams. I lost him a few years back."

"Anyone now?"

"A cowboy named Harrison. I'm beginning to feel like he is the one I should finish my life with."

"That could be another twenty-thirty years."

I chuckled, "That would be OK."

"Well, Officer Greenfield is turning 80 in a couple of weeks and Linda is throwing him a birthday party. I would like to invite you and Harrison to fly back with me."

"Oh, Jesse, I would love to meet the man."

"And, I know, he would love to meet the little girl that tackled the dark night and a raging river, and me." He glanced at me. "And I'm pretty sure she could still do it."

"Oh, I could," I chuckled then smiled at him. "But, I really don't want to."

He laughed, "I know how you feel. My wife is up at your clinic. I would like to introduce you."

He helped me stand and held the door open for me, but I stopped in front of the fireplace and looked up at the portrait.

"The first words Officer Lucas said to me were, 'Hello, Honey." I turned to smile at Jesse who was looking at the portrait. "That is Honey, the foundation of my horses here on the ranch."

"He is stunning, and so are the horses in the pasture behind the house."

I chuckled, "The palomino that was watching you come down the drive is Honey's son. His name is Lucas."

Jesse grinned. "You kept your past alive."

"I did," I sighed and looked at the book sitting on the easel in the bookshelf. "Those days were the first days of life without my parents. I never saw anything from my past again except a few photographs. My uncle took those from my parents' house before selling everything else. Not even a stitch of clothing because he thought it would be hard on me. But, what was hard was not having anything from that past. It was as if it never existed…as if my parents never existed." I glanced around the room. "I keep the past alive by naming my animals and ranch after them. It calms me and reassures me that they did exist. What do you have from the past? From before the Campbell's house?"

"Just that old, weathered book," He walked to the book on the easel and lifted it to thumb through the pages. "It's like picking it up from the bookstore shelf." His smile held a bit of history. "The cover is nearly gone from the one I have, and the pages are well worn with a few missing and torn." He turned and looked at me. "It is the only thing I have from my past before arriving at the ranch with Dad. Mom bought a large glass jar and put the book in it and wouldn't let anyone touch it. Somehow, she knew it would be important to me in the future."

"They were good parents?" I asked hopefully.

He chuckled, "They were good. Dad went on the rodeo road riding broncs and driving truck while Mom did her best to wrangle me in." He laughed. "It was the '70's and back then the thing to do was 'moon' everyone. I think everyone in the small town I grew up in eventually saw my ass."

We both laughed and the ease between us increased. It was as if in those two days we were together, a whole past was born.

We made our way to the garage where the 6-wheeler waited.

"Dad tried to make a cowboy out of me, and I have to say the traveling was fun, a bit of that adventurer in me, but I just couldn't stay on those damn horses like he did. I learned to rope but I didn't have a future in that either."

"So, what do you do?"

"I did several jobs through my twenties, then real estate for a while before I started traveling and met my wife. She is a journalist for a travel magazine, so she lives for the adventure, too. She writes, and I photograph what she needs." He chuckled. "Neither one of us could handle being in one place for too long or having that house with a white picket fence."

"Children?"

"She has two, and I have them and grandchildren that I adore. You?"

"A wonderful, beautiful daughter named Sawyer."

He grinned, "From the book."

As he slowly drove us away from the house, I told him how my broken leg led to my telling her of the past and her searching for him.

"She is the reason you received the phone calls."

"I can't wait to meet her. Is she here?"

"Her son is, but she is on the rodeo trail with friends and a cowboy was helping her find you."

"Who was that?"

"Evan Rawlins."

He grinned, "I know Evan. My dad and his were on the rodeo trail together and we saw each other now and again."

As we neared the clinic, I could see a tall woman talking with Harrison and Rafe next to a green SUV. She was smiling brightly as she looked at Jesse.

Harrison assisted me out of the ATV with a warm smile.

"Vic, this is my wife, Christina," Jesse returned her smile then turned to the SUV and opened the back door. "And...I'd like to introduce you to Birdie, my aunt from back east."

My legs shook and Harrison had to grab my arm to keep me from falling as I looked into those eyes from so many years before.

Pride and relief shone in the older woman's eyes as she stood from the vehicle. A shaking cry escaped me as I took her hands in mine.

"Hello, Honey," she whispered and wrapped her arms around me.

Fifty years melted away.

****

Text to Sawyer: Are you able to do a video chat right now?

Text from Sawyer: Yes, we just got to the trailer.

The phone chimed and I pushed the button to see her radiant smile appear. She looked so happy.

"Hi, my mother," she grinned. "What's up? Is Rafe OK?"

"Yes, he is outside saddling Brownie to go on a ride. I wanted to introduce you to someone."

"OK..." She muttered, then her eyes widened as Jesse appeared to my right and Betty to my left.

"Sawyer, I'd like to introduce you to J.D. and Birdie." I smiled.

She stared at both for a moment then her eyes moved to me. There was a silent question.

"Yes," I nodded. "They are who you were looking for."

Her eyes glistened, chin quivered, and hands went to her chest as she took in shaking breaths.

CHAPTER THIRTY-THREE

"Either you take the cast off, or I will."

The nurse smiled at me, "I just said the doctor MIGHT want to keep it on longer."

"And I am getting on a plane in three hours and this cast will not be on it with me."

A small circular saw was set on the table next to me, and the nurse grinned. "You'd be amazed at how many people refuse to keep the cast on any longer."

"No," I chuckled. "I probably wouldn't."

He laughed and slid a long flat bar between the cast and my skin. "That will make sure I don't take your skin with it."

"I appreciate that."

"And where are you going that this cast does not get to see?"

"Arizona for a couple days, then I'm going back East to a birthday party."

"Isn't Arizona hot this time of year?"

"Hmmm, yes, but I lived there most of my life. You just learn to work around the heat."

My phone chimed and as the cast was cut away, a picture of Bubb appeared on my phone. He was lying on a lounge chair with a sunset behind him and he was wearing a dark blue and white Hawaiian shirt and blue shorts with flip flops on his feet. A drink was held up to the camera as a grin shone from under his white, fluffy, signature mustache. His eyes were lit with the true humor of the image.

I laughed and sent him a text.

Text to Bubb: No flip flops in the horse pasture! See you in a couple of weeks.

****

At six o'clock the next morning, Harrison and I walked down the main drive of the Arizona ranch toward the arenas. It was late when we arrived by Uber, so there was no way that anyone at the ranch knew we were there.

"I'm kind of liking this hand-in-hand no crutches in the way," Harrison grinned and squeezed my hand.

"Me, too," I chuckled and leaned into him. The comfort of him was beginning to ease the guilt of him not being Marcus. We were still taking the relationship slowly, and every day it was becoming easier.

I was not surprised to find the brother and sister already in the arena riding Briggs and Dreamer. They were quite surprised to see me open the gate.

"Vic!" Jeff gasped and trotted the horse to me then stepped out of the saddle and wrapped me in his arms.

Ari was quickly wrapped in a three-way hug.

It wasn't exactly a professional employee embrace but these two meant so much more to me. They were my family, too.

"Why didn't you tell us you were coming?" Ari leaned back with eyes darting to my companion.

"Then it wouldn't have been a surprise," I chuckled then introduced them to Harrison as I ran a hand down both horses' noses. "Take a break from the horses for a few minutes so we can have coffee and talk."

They hitched the horses to the post in the shade then joined us at the outside table by the barn.

"Do you remember the first time we met?" I asked the pair.

Jeff chuckled and looked at his sister.

"We just moved into the house next to your old ranch." She said and looked at Harrison. "I was six and Jeff was ten. The first morning we stood in the backyard and watched this horse and rider in an arena. They looked like they were dancing. The second morning, we took our lawn chairs out to the fence and sat and watched her ride. Then the next morning as we sat in the lawn chairs, she and this huge golden stallion rode up to us."

"It was like magic when she let us touch the horse," Jeff exhaled. "We had never been around horses, and we were mesmerized."

I turned to Harrison, "I asked them if they would like to learn how to ride. I offered them riding lessons if they were willing to work at the stalls."

"We asked our parents and they said yes," Ari added with a smile. "Changed our lives forever."

"And, since then, you two have become outstanding trainers and competitors." I added.

"He competes," Ari nudged her head to Jeff. "I would rather train Vic's beautiful horses."

"Well, I wanted you two to be the first to know," I hesitated as both their shoulders rose in anticipation. "I am retiring."

"What?" They both gasped.

"I have done everything I have set out to do in the show ring...actually more than I ever dreamed possible, so I am retiring from competing." It was the first time I had said the words aloud and I felt a sense of ease at the decision. "I will continue, as Rafe says, *doing the coolest thing ever*, by continuing the breeding program at Bijou Bay and I will raise the foals until they are two then send them here to Ari like we have done in the past. At that point, their training and showing fall on you two." They both just stared. "I will begin offering clinics here for anyone that has purchased one of our stallion's offspring, and coach a few competitors of my choosing. Like Camille Madison who will be here next week with the palomino she purchased a few weeks ago."

"I can't believe this," Jeff whispered.

"Well, with that goal in mind, I would very much like you two to accept my offer to become my partner." I continued.

"What?" Ari gasped.

"You will be my partner, co-owners of the horses that come here for training and competition," I smiled. "The paperwork is being put together, and I am making it as fair as possible for all of us. I will own 50 percent and you two, as a company, will own the other 50 percent of the business down here."

"Sawyer is OK with this?" Jeff asked in concern.

"Her interest has never been training and showing but she has taken an interest in the breeding program. She will begin working with Pauline and I next year plus she has decided to take a few classes and become certified. I am also very pleased to say she will begin riding polo again when she can. Her new man-friend has been encouraging her to get back to what she loved."

"You're sure about this?" Ari asked. I could see the excitement building in her, but she had always been the cautious one of the pair.

"Of course," I smiled. "I have decided to move onto the next chapter in my life which includes more time with Harrison, Rafe, Sawyer, and a few friends back east. I'll be traveling more for family than competition, but I do plan on attending your shows." I said to Jeff. "You more than proved yourself in California and there is no one I would trust more than you two with my horses. And, you know how much they mean to me."

They both just nodded. I was sure they were still a bit stunned.

****

A month later, I sat at the table on the back deck of Bijou Bay and pushed the button on the phone.

"Hi, Grandma!" Rafe grinned on the video chat.

"Hello, my handsome grandson. How is your new house?"

"It's ok," He shrugged. "Between school and going to Evan's ranch, we don't spend much time here." He smiled and his eyes twinkled in mischief. "You gone on any walks lately?"

I laughed, "I am not going to break my leg again so you can come stay with me. I will be up there in just a couple of weeks to stay with you while your mother is traveling with Evan. Your mother has already promised you can come up here for Thanksgiving break and I will be there with you the two weeks they are at the National Finals Rodeo in December."

"I guess that will have to do for now," He sighed dramatically. "When I turn eighteen, I want to move into the Trophy House apartment and go to college in Coeur d' Alene."

"Sounds like you have a plan."

He nodded, "Mom said it is a good plan."

"That is a few years into the future, what are you doing today?"

"Homework, which is why I asked you to call."

"And, what do you need from me?"

"Mom said to ask you what a legend is."

"Why would she ask you to ask me and not just have you look in a dictionary?" I scoffed.

"Because..." His mischievous smile returned. "Can you tell me?"

"If you are trying to read a map, and it has symbols on it, there is a list which is called a legend that tells you what the symbols mean."

His brows furrowed as he looked at the monitor in confusion, "No, that's not it."

"A legend is a collection of stories from the past of something great that happened."

His eyes narrowed, "That could be..."

I rolled my eyes in humor, "A legend is someone who has done great things in a particular event and has succeeded in every way possible."

He nodded with a grin, "That's it."

"What are you working on?"

"The teacher wants us to write about our summer and I was writing about you and read in the magazine that Mom has which announced your retirement and the cover reads, "The Legend of Bijou Bay is Retiring." He lifted three pictures to the monitor. "I printed off the picture of you and Honey winning the Super Horse Award, and the one of you riding Lucas to win his last competition before he was retired. And there is this one of Dreamer winning that California event." He looked at the pictures then back to me. "So, each one of them would be a story, plus the story you told me about J.D. and Birdie after your parents died and why you bought your first horse...so, all those stories could be your legend."

"I suppose."

"But then, as the magazine says, you have become a legend in the horse industry because of all your accomplishments in horse breeding and competition."

"Yeah, that's what they wrote."

"So, which is it? Is it your legend, or are you the legend?"

I chuckled and shook my head in humor, "Well, when you decide, you let me know."

He laughed and his eyes danced in humor. "I'll just tell them you're a legend because I'm your grandson."

We both laughed. I deeply missed him and was thankful for modern technology.

****

Lucas lowered his nose to my hip as I slid the halter from him. After a loving stroke of a hand along his side, he trotted back to rejoin his pasture mates. I closed the gate with a satisfied smile. Riding the horse up to the top to the mountain and back had rejuvenated my heart. It was so good to be back to riding.

I turned to walk back up the hill to the barns. As I strode by the spot I had lain on the ground waiting for Bubb to retrieve me, I saw a flicker of white. I stopped and glanced into the grass as the edge of the black asphalt. A long feather lay flittering in the breeze. I lowered to pick it up, then quickly stood and backed away.

"Why do you always pick up feathers?" I asked Marcus on our first date. I was eighteen and we were on a walk at the equestrian park in Scottsdale.

"I like feathers," He picked up the feather then took off his hat and stuck it into the headband. After setting the hat back on his head, he turned to me with a wide grin. "How do I look?"

I smiled and shook my head. "Just as handsome as you did before you put it on your hat."

We both chuckled, and for the first time, he took my hand in his as our walk continued.

I stared at the white feather then lifted my eyes to the sky, "You old goat," I whispered. "I had nearly forgotten that moment."

Months before I had seen a white feather in the same spot as this one. Without thinking, I had bent down to pick it up. When I rose, I stepped backward, caught the toe of my boot on the heel of the other boot, started to fall and dramatically flipped myself in the air to keep from falling on my elbows. Instead, my leg came down hard on the edge of the asphalt that had a four-inch drop before the grass started. My leg hit that one spot and broke both bones.

How was I going to tell anyone that I broke my leg picking up a feather and tripping over my own feet? I had decided then to never tell anyone how I broke my leg. When they asked, I would just say 'I fell'. It wasn't a lie, but it wasn't the ridiculous truth either.

A breeze swept the feather into the air, and it danced away in the wind to disappear into the trees. Now I knew the truth...and still wasn't going to tell anyone.

Inspiration:

Every book starts with an inspiration.

This is not a true story, but it is inspired by a true story.

I have been fortunate to meet the Longfellows; Clyde, Edie, Crystal, Kelly, and Paul. After meeting them, I was told of the story of how Paul came into the family and Jesse's story began.

Although there are a few details from Paul's journey included in Jesse's adventure, this is not an autobiography, it is fiction.

Clyde rode bucking horses into his fifties, and during that time, picked up a teenager hitch hiking to Vegas. Determining the young, underweight boy would not survive in Vegas, Clyde took him home to his wife and two daughters in Idaho. The family took him in as one of their own.

Unfortunately, the story of the Campbell's home was also based on true stories. Although, again, their home and the people are fiction. In my research, I was told of and read horrible stories of foster homes and orphanages in the early 1970's. Too many children did not survive the abuse or spent their lives recovering. In the early seventies, over 200,000 children were in foster care or orphanages with no real control of the running of the homes or the people responsible for the children.

http://history-of-foster-care-nj.org/foster-care-system-history-1960s-1970s/

http://history-of-foster-care-nj.org/milestones-in-foster-care-history-in-nj-the-1970s-formation-of-the-new-jersey-foster-parent-association/

ABOUT THE AUTHOR

I was raised with Shetlands and ponies and have loved horses since I watched a Shetland colt born when I was four.

Growing up, the TV show Bonanza was my favorite. I loved that western life and wanted to be Little Joe and Hoss' little sister. I wanted to live at the Ponderosa. Watching rodeos on television and attending when I could, was the closest I could get to the cowboy way of life.

That changed when I purchased my first 'big horse' when I was twenty-one and living in Alaska. I now have the great-granddaughter of that horse in my pasture.

I am also a photographer specializing in the equine industry; shows, races, jackpots, and rodeos. With my photography, I create my own covers.

The Tagger Herd Series was my first venture into fictional writing and I love the family and horses in the series.

My first 'stand-alone' novel was Hoofbeats in the Wind which ventured into rodeo.

My next book, Coffee With Cowboys delved deeper into the rodeo world and researching for the book was an adventure. I have met wonderful people from fans, stock contractors, and competitors. I thank every one of them that have helped make that book a possibility. It will always be special to me because of the people I met.

Bijou Bay was inspired by Black Rock Ranch and the story of Clyde and Paul.

Writing, researching, photography, my two dogs, Morgan and Tagger, and Kit in the pasture, fill my world and keep me busy.